VIEW FROM A BALCONY

Recent Titles by Louise Brindley from Severn House

VIEW FROM
A BALCONY

Louise Brindley

This first world edition published in Great Britain 2000 by
SEVERN HOUSE PUBLISHERS LTD of
9–15 High Street, Sutton, Surrey SM1 1DF.
This first world edition published in the USA 2000 by
SEVERN HOUSE PUBLISHERS INC of
595 Madison Avenue, New York, N.Y. 10022.

British Library Cataloguing in Publication Data

Brindley, Louise
 View from a balcony
 1. Female friendship - Fiction
 2. Love stories
 I. Title
 823.9'14 [F]

ISBN 0-7278-5479-8

All situations in this publication are fictitious and
any resemblance to living persons is purely coincidental.

Typeset by Hewer Text Ltd.,
Edinburgh, Scotland.
Printed and bound in Great Britain by
MPG Books Ltd, Bodmin, Cornwall.

Remembering the Road
to Samarkand, and a
special friend who came
with me on the journey.

Part One

One

S tepping down from the train, making her way to the station forecourt in search of a taxi, Kate thought at least three things about Scarborough had not changed: the sea fog, the moaning of the foghorn, and the crying of seabirds overhead. But what had happened to the "Brief Encounter" buffet, the wooden ticket hut near the barrier, the newspapers and magazines kiosk on platform Number One and the Nestlé's chocolate machine?

"Where to, Miss?" the taxi driver asked offhandedly, stowing her luggage in the boot of his car.

"The Crown Hotel," she said, glad of the mist, the distant sound of the foghorn, the plaintive clamour of the gulls, as familiar to her as breathing: thankful to be home again, albeit against her better judgement.

Even so, this place, this town had always been at the back of her mind, lovingly remembered, never revisited – until today.

They say we shouldn't look back, much less return to the scene of remembered happiness in search of old familiar landmarks, and people who may no longer exist. But what alternative was possible in her situation? A woman in desperate need of a fresh beginning, the creation of a new life from the ruins of the old.

At least the prestigious Crown Hotel, built in the Victorian era and reminiscent of "Tara" in *Gone With the Wind*, had not changed outwardly in appearance, Kate thought, walking up the front steps to the reception area and signing the register of new arrivals, "Mrs Kate Ford"; her address, from force of habit: "April Cottage, Woodley, Devizes, Wiltshire".

The ironwork felt cold and wet beneath her outspread hands. The sea was invisible but she knew it was there from the relentless ebb and flow

3

of the tide on the shore and the intermittent booming of the foghorn on the lighthouse pier.

Lamplights on the promenade beneath the balcony of her room, diffused by the fog, glimmered softly like pale primroses in a springtime wood.

But this was autumn, not springtime. Now her wood, silent and still, adrift with the fallen leaves of summertime, would have settled down to its long winter sleep.

Rain would soon rot the leaves to compost. The tractor road between the trees, dry and rutted in summer, would become a sea of mud until the frosts of winter stiffened its resolve. Then fitful gleams of wintry sunlight, without warmth, would sparkle momentarily on ice, and there would be icicles, not catkins, on the hazel branches.

Re-entering the warmth of her room, closing the balcony window and drawing the curtains, Kate wondered if it would always be like this, this preoccupation with the past, allowing her no peace of mind.

Even the smallest things possessed the power to unleash a chain of memories best put aside and forgotten. Roses in a florist's window, for instance, reminiscent of her wedding bouquet. Dance tunes of the 50s: "When I Fall in Love", "Tammy", "Witchcraft". Romantic black-and-white movies on late night television; the scent of newly mown grass on summer afternoons. A baby fast asleep in its pushchair – the most poignant reminder of everything she had lost when her husband of twenty years had admitted to having an affair with a younger woman, and asked her to divorce him.

They were in the kitchen at the time, Kate recalled. She cooking spaghetti bolognese, he nursing a glass of Bordeaux. A familiar ritual. Don always drank wine on his return to the cottage after a working day in London as a freelance tabloid journalist – what he termed his "bread and butter" earnings, supporting his output of radio and TV plays, documentaries and short stories for various women's magazines, written in his private sanctum – a refurbished and insulated shed at the far end of the garden.

She had sensed something was wrong. Impossible not to have reached that conclusion with someone she knew almost as intimately as she knew herself. Even so, she had been totally unprepared for the bombshell, the shattering of her life and happiness when he'd told her about the other woman – Lucia Keane, a newspaper colleague, with whom he had fallen deeply in love.

"I'm so sorry," he said. "I never meant this to happen. Never meant to hurt you."

She faced him disbelievingly. "Never meant it to happen? Then why did you let it happen? A man of your age and a girl young enough to be your daughter. What the hell were you thinking of? As for hurting me, you must have known every time you met this – other woman – the risks you were running, what it would do to me if I found out. Or didn't you care? Now *this*!"

"I've said I'm sorry. What more can I say?"

"A great deal more! You can't just turn your back on your responsibilities and walk away from them as if they never existed! I'm your wife, for God's sake! This is your home! Have you so little respect for me to tell me, in the kitchen of all places, that you want a divorce?"

"I know you're angry. Upset. Can't we at least discuss this in a civilised way? I've told you I'm in love with Lucia, that I want my freedom to marry her. I've been entirely honest with you. What's wrong with that?"

The truth had dawned on Kate slowly, inevitably. She said, "Lucia's pregnant, isn't she?" and knew by his face that she had hit the nail on the head.

She had relived this sequence of events time and time again since the break up of her marriage. Now, in desperate need of escape from haunting memories of the past, Kate hurried down a curving Victorian staircase, through the reception lounge and crossed the road towards the railings bordering the steep descent of woods and paths to the Spa Grand Hall and the seashore below.

Silver flecks blurred her vision. Straining her eyes, all she could see was the fog-bound esplanade fronting the hotel. Then, miraculously, there came the smell of seaweed borne inland from the shore. Familiar yet half forgotten, as many things had been forgotten in her transition from child to woman: the bitter-sweetness of a first and only love affair, still linked in her mind to the loss of her parents; leaving home to begin a new life with a comparative stranger – an act of blind faith centred on the belief that the love of two people, herself and Don, would last till the end of time.

Walking alone in the foggy darkness, following the curve of the esplanade by the diffused light of the lamp-standards spaced out like beads on a rosary, she recalled the kindness of her brother Greg and his

5

wife Cynthia's invitation to stay with them indefinitely after the divorce and the sale of April Cottage.

But there were no springtime woods bordering their neatly maintained garden in the Greater Manchester area, and the sprawl of streets and houses, to someone accustomed to space and freedom, had resembled a straitjacket.

She and Greg had always been close to one another, even as children, when they had played together on the sands in summertime, making sand-pies and building castles, soon to be swept away by the incoming tide. He, the older of the two, keeping a watchful eye on his kid sister; holding her by the hand when they paddled together in the rock pools near the Children's Corner.

Recently, deeply aware of her unhappy state of mind, he said gently, "Look, Kate, you're a free agent now. Don treated you shabbily, I know. At least he had the decency to hand over the deeds of the cottage, to grant you a modicum of financial security. Now, isn't it time you stopped fretting over the past and looked to the future?"

"What *future*? I haven't got a future."

"That's nonsense, and you know it! Everyone has a future! I know you're not happy here in Manchester, and I can't blame you for that! I wouldn't be here myself if it weren't for my job and my mortgage repayments!"

He smiled ruefully. "Given half a chance, I'd give up teaching, go back to Scarborough and open a fish and chip shop!"

"I see." Returning his smile, she added, "So that's the future you have mapped out for me, is it? As the proprietress of a 'chish and fip' shop?"

"No, Kate. Far from. All I'm saying is, why not go back to your roots? At least give yourself a fair chance of happiness in a place you love. A new start, a new beginning in life."

She couldn't afford to stay at the Crown indefinitely, Kate realised. Coming here had been in the nature of a "thumb to nose" gesture to bolster her flagging ego. Coming home, she had wanted to splash out on the best that money could buy – a balcony room in the town's oldest and most prestigious hotel, rather than sidle, unnoticed, into a boarding house in the town centre. Well, now she was here, and she couldn't see a damn thing, much less the view from her balcony, for the blasted sea fog blanketing the lights of home.

Regarding the future: she had never had a paid job in her life, so far.

After leaving school, she had been called upon to nurse her mother and keep house for her father. Greg had been at Durham University at the time, coming home at weekends to offer his help and support.

Their mother's illness was something they had never dreamt possible. The sudden death of a beloved person had been their first brush with the harsh reality of life. Worse was to come. Devastated by the death of his wife, their father had taken ill and died a year later. In retrospect, it seemed to Kate that he had simply lost the will to live.

At that rock-bottom stage of her life, when she'd been alone in a rented house far too big for just one person, wandering about the rooms like a lost soul, not knowing what to do for the best, trying to sort out her parents' belongings, to decide what to keep and what to sell when the time came to move out, an old schoolfriend of hers had badgered her into making up a foursome for a trip to the pictures.

Jenny Laird, fun-loving, bubbly and curvaceous, explained the reason for the blind date. Her current boyfriend, a young reporter, sharing digs with a newcomer to the *Evening News*, felt duty-bound to show the chap a good time.

When Kate demurred, "Oh, come on, love," Jenny insisted. "It'll do you good to go out for a change. What I mean is, you needn't see him again if you don't like him. Just sit next to him in the cinema, have a bite to eat and a couple of drinks afterwards. What's wrong with that? His name's Don Ford, by the way."

But she had liked Don Ford a great deal. This was no impecunious cub reporter but a seasoned newspaperman, ambitious, clever and charming. Despite the six year difference in their ages, she'd found him easy to talk to, and sympathetic and understanding when she'd told him briefly about the loss of her parents, not wanting to burden him with her troubles. They were, after all, meant to be having a jolly evening, not a wake.

To her surprise and pleasure, when the evening ended, he had invited her out to a meal the following weekend – "tête-a-tête, next time". Soon they had started seeing a great deal of one another: walking together, hand-in-hand, beneath a harvest moon as summertime drifted into autumn. She falling more deeply in love with him every passing day, every precious hour they spent together; hoping and praying that he too was falling in love.

But how could she be sure? Don had made it clear to her that his stay in Scarborough was of a temporary nature; had stated his intention of moving on when a suitable opportunity occurred – an editor's job, for instance, offering better prospects, a sizeable salary increase. More importantly, the cachet of becoming the man in charge of policy and editorial comment.

Kate's heart had sunk to her shoes when, in the early spring of the following year, Don told her he'd been offered, and had accepted the editorship of *The Wiltshire Herald*. She'd dreaded their forthcoming separation, the absence from her life of the man she loved – until . . .

"I want you to come with me to Wiltshire," Don said, matter-of-factly, planting a kiss on her forehead. "How long will it take you to fix up our wedding? If you want to marry me, that is? Just don't make it a big affair, with a posse of bridesmaids and all that jazz! It's you I want, not the world and his wife!"

And so they had been married, very quietly, early one morning, in St Mary's Church, overlooking the "Old Town" of Scarborough – that maze of streets and alleyways glissading down to the harbour, each of which Kate had known as intimately as the back of her hand during her carefree childhood with her brother Greg by her side. Greg who had given her in marriage to a handsome stranger, against his own better judgement.

On the eve of the wedding, he asked, "Are you sure you're doing the right thing, Kate? How long have you known Don? Six months? Is that really long enough to know your own mind?"

"I love Don, and he loves me."

"I know, and I'm glad you're happy. I just don't want you to get hurt."

"You think Don will hurt me? Why should he? He loves me!"

"He's much older than you are; far more experienced." Greg paused momentarily. "I'm sorry, I shouldn't have said that." He added ruefully, "I'm just saying what Mum and Dad might have said if they were still here. Everything's happened so fast, I guess I haven't come to terms with losing you as well. After all, Wiltshire's a long way from home. I'll miss you, Kate."

Returning to the hotel, Kate wondered if Don would have asked her to marry him had it not been for that editor's job he'd been offered in the early stages of their blossoming love affair.

She preferred to think so, but she couldn't be sure. Losing Don to another woman had planted seeds of doubt in her mind. Raking over the embers of a burnt-out marriage, she asked herself if there had been other affairs of his of which she had known nothing. Had she been too trusting, too complacent, to notice the warning signs? Had her complacency, her preoccupation with housework, cooking and gardening, been to blame for Don's affair with Lucia?

In bed with his mistress, had he told her tales of that boring, predictable wife of his? Her own fault if he had. Kate knew that now. What had she done with her time apart from cleaning house, mowing grass, pulling up weeds, trimming hedges, planning menus and cooking traditional Sunday lunches – prodigious amounts of food which neither of them had really wanted or enjoyed?

Seldom, if ever, had she picked up a book and read it from cover to cover. Never had she evinced the slightest interest in political or social issues. She'd been far too busy making jam and chutney, pickling onions and beetroot, to bother her head about what was happening in the world beyond the four walls of April Cottage; or too busy walking alone in her wood, especially in springtime when the ground beneath the trees was misted over with bluebells, and in autumn when the earth lay thick with fallen leaves, richly patterned in shades of crimson, brown and gold.

Seated at the dressing table, brushing her fair, shoulder-length hair into the semblance of a French pleat, Kate thought that if the future was to hold any meaning at all, she must expand her horizons. Join the human race, find herself a job and a place to live, a furnished flat or a bed-sit.

What kind of job she had no idea. Stacking supermarket shelves or cleaning hotel bedrooms, at a rough guess. Hardly likely that anyone would jump at the chance of employing a middle-aged woman without a hygiene certificate to her name, her only qualification being house-keeping within the parameters of a failed marriage.

Frustrated by her inability to cope with her hair, worn long to please Don, at the first opportunity, Kate decided, she would have it cut short – to please herself.

On the threshold of the dining room, glancing nervously about her at the many occupied tables – busy waiters and waitresses serving the food and wine, feeling intensely lonely and vulnerable, somewhat dowdy in her blue wool dress, more suited to a vicarage tea-party than dinner in a five star hotel, she felt there was no way she could she run the gauntlet of curious glances or walk across the room to a table for one near the window. In which case, the sooner she went back to her room, the better.

A smiling young waiter spared her the humiliation of a full-scale retreat. "A table for one, madam?" he asked pleasantly. Kate nodded. Leading the way, pulling back a chair and handing her the menu, he said, "Would madam care for anything to drink? A carafe of wine, perhaps?"

"No, thanks. Just Perrier water, with ice and a twist of lemon."

Glancing up from the menu, Kate's eyes met those of the man at the next table, also dining alone, informally dressed in a tweed suit, a Paisley scarf tucked into an open-neck shirt, and with a copy of *The Times* propped up against the cruet. He advised her cheerfully to plump for the chicken supreme.

"Thanks, but I'd prefer the grilled plaice," she replied nonchalantly.

Afterwards, in bed, wide awake, Kate heard the faint whirring of the lift, the metallic clang of its gates as they opened and closed on the first floor landing, then a drift of dance music from a function room somewhere inside the hotel – comforting sounds of life going on around her, expelling momentarily her deep-seated sense of isolation.

After falling fast asleep, emotionally and physically exhausted by the events of the day – saying goodbye to Greg and Cindy at Manchester Station, clinging to her brother at the last moment, afraid of the future, Kate awoke in the early hours of the next morning to the sound of silence, apart from the faint murmur of the sea washing in on the shore.

Getting up, swiftly crossing the room, drawing back the curtains, stepping on to the balcony, she saw that the fog had lifted at last.

Looking down, she saw the lights of home shining through the dark. A necklace of lamp lights outlining the sweeping curve of the South Bay. Pinpricks of light twinkling from the "Old Town" of Scarborough, nestled about the harbour, rising in tiers to a vast rocky promontory crowned with the sombre ruins of a floodlit Norman fortress.

Looking up, blinking back tears, she saw, high above her, a black velvet sky littered with a myriad crystal-clear stars shining down on her, and knew, in one blinding moment of revelation, that this homecoming of hers had been no mistake. It was here she truly belonged, and here she would stay, come hell or high water.

Contemplating the stars, Kate uttered a fervent prayer for courage enough to march, unafraid, into the unknown future ahead of her.

Two

There was no sign of the man Kate thought of as "the Loner" at breakfast next morning. He must have eaten earlier and left the hotel. Not that it mattered. "Ships that pass in the night, and speak each other in passing"!

Fallen leaves littered the steeply plunging paths of the Spa gardens. The air was threaded with the scents of autumn: of scythed meadowsweet and those brown-tipped grasses she thought of as "bows and arrows"; the pungent smoke of a bonfire on which council workmen were burning the detritus of summertime.

Pausing awhile, she gazed at well-remembered landmarks: the parish church of St Mary near Castle Hill, standing guard over the Old Town; the lighthouse on the west pier. Nothing had changed much outwardly, Kate thought. But appearances could be deceptive, as she knew to her cost.

Changes were bound to have taken place in the twenty-odd years of her absence. Time moved on relentlessly, sweeping all before it. Gone forever were the happy, carefree days of her youth and childhood lived in anticipation of only the good things in life: school holidays, birthday parties, picnics and Punch and Judy. At Christmas, building snowmen, not sandcastles.

This was a day of latent warmth and sunshine prior to the onset of winter. Soon, children would be lighting bonfires on the beach, burning effigies of Guy Fawkes, letting off fireworks in the cold night air. Then would come Remembrance Sunday, that depressing Cenotaph Ceremony in Whitehall. No warmth, no joy – November . . .

They say we shouldn't look back. It would be tantamount to madness, Kate realised, to revisit St Mary's Church, to dredge up memories best laid aside and forgotten. But what hope for the future unless she came to terms with the past?

The street called Paradise, curving up from Sandside to the parish church was much steeper than she recalled. Gone were the days when she had run up it, not pausing for breath. Inside the church all was silent. No organ music. No echo of a young bride's nervous footsteps on stone flags. No wintry scent of daffodils in the air, just the autumnal smell of chrysanthemums from the altar vases.

Yet how clearly she remembered that cold spring morning long ago. Don turning his head to smile at her as she stood beside him holding her bouquet of red roses. "O, Perfect Love".

All over and done with now – that brief early-morning wedding ceremony, the hastily arranged reception afterwards in the Albion Hotel across the road from the church – salmon sandwiches and sausage rolls, the obligatory speeches, the bridesmaid flirting with every man in sight. Having to keep an eye on the time because the London train was due to leave the station at eleven thirty.

This the first leg of their journey. Arriving at King's Cross, they'd have to cross London to Paddington to catch a connection to the West Country, Don had explained beforehand.

It had been a long, tiring journey. Kate now recalled, as if it were yesterday, her acute feeling of disorientation during that seemingly endless passage through unfamiliar scenery, far from home.

If only Don had suggested breaking their journey – an overnight stay in London, a hotel room somewhere, a decent meal, a continuation of their journey to Wiltshire the following day. Instead of which, she'd been subjected to a mad dash, by tube trains, to Paddington; then, a couple of damp ham sandwiches and a cup of bitter-tasting coffee in a station buffet, before haring along the platform, in Don's wake, to board the mainline train to Exeter. By which time, almost too exhausted to stand up straight, all she had really wanted was a good night's sleep in a comfortable bed. Alone, for preference.

She'd realised afterwards that this had been the culmination of too many emotional upheavals for a girl of her age: the deaths of her parents; falling in love with a man she scarcely knew. Everything happening far too fast – bereavement, grief, uncertainty, the stress of leaving the house that had been her home for as far back as she could remember.

All these things led up to her wedding day nerves and that strange feeling of disorientation on the long journey into an unknown future, wanting nothing more than the benison of hot water, food and an uninterrupted night's sleep – of the kind she had known as a child after a long day on the beach, donkey riding and building sandcastles . . .

Closing the church door quietly behind her, Kate walked down Castle Road to the town centre in search of a hairdressing salon, one of those "Appointments Not Always Necessary" places with assistants at a loose end now the holiday season was over.

"Promise me you'll never cut your hair," Don had said once, long ago. "It's so pretty the way it is." And so she had promised. But promises were made to be broken, weren't they? Especially promises to love and to cherish till death us do part.

When the young male assistant who'd cut her hair suggested having her hair highlighted, Kate told him to go ahead. Anything would be preferable to struggling with that darned French pleat of hers, ending up looking like the archetypal "maiden aunt" in an old Bette Davis movie, mousey and faded.

Seeing her face in the salon mirror as the assistant hooked strands of hair through a kind of bathing cap, lathered on the bleach and applied the strips of foil, Kate thought how drained she looked. Recent events had taken their toll: the divorce trauma, selling April Cottage, leaving behind her all that she and Don had created together during twenty years of marriage.

Would things have been different if their first child had survived the fifth month of her pregnancy? A child they had wanted so much. The bitterest pill to swallow was that the other woman in Don's life was carrying his baby. And that one inescapable truth had meant far more to him than she ever had. Kate saw that quite clearly now, the sexual urge of a dominant male intent on the procreation of his own image, letting his seed fall where it may . . .

"Well, is madam pleased with the result?" the assistant hair-stylist asked eagerly, holding a hand-mirror reflecting the rear view of her shorn head. "Yes," Kate replied, feeling half-naked, yet admiring the highlights and the short, bouffant fringe just clearing her eyebrows. "You've done wonders! Made me feel much younger all of a sudden!"

The thought occurred to her, as she left the salon, that she was not old. She had begun thinking old after her first miscarriage, when a consultant gynaecologist had warned her of the improbability of her ever carrying a child full term. And so she had turned to housekeeping, gardening and cooking as panacea against the pain of regret that she could not give her husband the children he desperately wanted.

After her third miscarriage, she had given up all hope of motherhood. She had, at least, given Don a pin-clean home, glowing, colourful flowerbeds and well-cooked food, none of which he had really wanted or appreciated.

By nature creative and untidy, he had begun spending more and more time in his so-called studio at the end of the garden, and often disappeared for hours at a time to the village pub to play darts and dominoes with the locals, drinking far more than was good for him, returning home when he felt like it, to make love to her – if he felt so inclined.

All over and done with now, Kate thought, walking down Westborough, Scarborough's main thoroughfare. But what had happened to the magnificent Pavilion Hotel opposite the station? What had become of The Londesborough Cinema, where, as a child, she had laughed at the antics of Laurel and Hardy, and thrilled to the love duet "Ah, Sweet Mystery of Life", sung by Jeanette MacDonald and Nelson Eddy, her father in the seat beside her feeding her chocolate drops from a white paper bag.

She and her father had often gone out together to the "first house" of the pictures, Kate recalled, whilst Mum was busy in the kitchen preparing their supper, and her brother Greg was doing his homework.

With infinite pleasure she recalled the thrill of homecoming to that old, draughty Victorian villa in Albemarle Crescent, close to the town centre, and those simple meals of bangers and mash, shepherd's pie or rissoles. They'd never been well-off financially; just rich beyond measure in other, more important ways.

Had her parents lived, she might well have never met Don Ford. In the natural course of events, leaving school, she would have gone out to work like other girls of her generation, as a shop assistant, most likely, in one of the department stores, Marshall and Snelgrove, Tonks or Rowntrees, selling lingerie, lampshades or make-up, paying Mum so much a week from her wages, eventually meeting some nice ordinary young man with whom she'd walk out on Sunday afternoons, subject to her parents' approval. She knew, deep down, that they would not have taken to Don as a prospective son-in-law – a "fly-by-night" newspaper reporter, far too old for a tender, starry-eyed young girl on the threshold of life.

Tired and hungry, Kate had coffee and a sandwich in a snack bar overlooking the main street. Exhausted by memories, the changes wrought by time in this home town of hers, the passing of an old familiar way of life, realising the validity of the words "Nothing in earth or heaven comes as it came before", she knew her future depended on finding herself a place to live, employment of some kind, however menial or uncongenial – not in squandering money recklessly, as she had done so far, on expensive hotel accommodation and an attractive but unnecessary new hairstyle – not in making inroads on her capital from the sale of April Cottage, which was invested in a building society account, but in standing on her own two feet. She must prove to Don and his new wife, Lucia, now living in New York with their offspring, Tobias, that she did not need her ex-husband's maintenance cheques paid quarterly into her Lloyd's bank account.

Above all, she loathed her feeling of dependence on her former husband for the clothes she wore, the shoes on her feet, the food she ate – something she'd endured since that night in the kitchen of April Cottage, three years ago, when after packing his belongings, he had left her alone to return to London – and Lucia.

So what to do about it? Nothing, for the time being at any rate. In need of rest and relaxation, Kate returned slowly to the Crown Hotel to make the most of a soft, warm bed: deep sleep, before her dinnertime appearance in the dining room, sporting her brand new hairstyle. A feeble victory, perhaps. Nevertheless, a much needed boost to her ego, knowing that never again would she have to cope with that blasted French pleat of hers!

The man she thought of as "the Loner" was in the reception lounge when she came downstairs. "Ah, there you are!" he said, stepping forward to greet her. "I thought you might have checked out when I didn't see you at breakfast this morning."

"Really?" She frowned slightly, wondering what business of his it was anyway. "No, I breakfasted early and went out for a walk."

He suggested urbanely, "I thought we might dine together this evening. My name is Alex Arden, by the way. At least I'm properly dressed for the occasion tonight."

He had a direct way of speaking, shrewd, intelligent grey-blue eyes in a lean, suntanned face; greying hair brushed back from a high forehead. An air of authority about him, as if used to getting his own way.

Startled by the invitation, "That's very kind of you," she said, about to add that she would prefer to dine alone. But how could she, without offending the man?

Accepting the inevitable, she said, "My name's Kate. Kate Ford."

When asked which wine she'd prefer to accompany her choice of roast lamb, Kate, feeling gauche and more than a little naive and foolish in the presence of this stranger, admitted that she didn't drink wine. He was obviously a man of the world, a traveller judging by his suntan, now faultlessly attired in a dark-grey suit and tie.

"How wise of you," he commented drily. "So shall we settle for Perrier 'on the rocks' with a twist of lemon?"

Don would have said impatiently, "God dammit, Kate, what have you got against wine anyway? A glass or two would do you good! Loosen those bloody inhibitions of yours once in a while!"

She could almost see him now, standing in the kitchen of April Cottage, nursing a glass of red wine, breaking the news of his love affair with Lucia Keane.

"Kate," Alex asked concernedly, "is anything the matter? Are you feeling unwell?"

Staring at him, unseeing, she answered, "No, just a bit tired, that's all. I'm sorry. This – homecoming, after so long an absence, is not quite what I'd expected. But how could you, a comparative stranger, possibly understand?" She stopped abruptly, knowing she was speaking more to herself than her companion. Obviously, the man hadn't the remotest idea what she was talking about. Aghast, she said quickly, "Please forgive me. I didn't think what I was saying."

"No need to apologise. You spoke of a homecoming, a feeling of disappointment, a long absence from home, myself as a stranger. That's true enough, and it was insensitive of me to presuppose that you would want to have dinner with me when, I imagine, you would have preferred to dine alone. On the other hand, perhaps you need to talk to someone? More specifically, a – stranger. But not here and now. Tomorrow, perhaps, when you've had time to think about it."

Kate nodded. "Thank you. You're very kind – for a stranger!" She smiled suddenly, and the smile lit up her face.

Looking at her across the table, Alex thought what an attractive woman she was, and wondered why she didn't smile more often – why there was an underlying air of sadness about her, as if she had lost her direction in life and scarcely knew where to look for a signpost pointing the way ahead to happiness.

The thought occurred to him that he too was in search of a signpost to, if not happiness, peace of mind – if such a thing was possible for him, knowing that he alone had been to blame for the loss of his wife and their son, Peter. Harm he'd inflicted as surely as if, holding a knife, he had ripped apart the fabric of their lives beyond repair.

Three

N ext day, Alex suggested walking into town across the Spa Bridge. He had some business to attend to which shouldn't take more than a few minutes, then they might have coffee together at the Royal Hotel, if the idea appealed to her.

They met in the reception lounge at ten o'clock. Kate noticed that Alex was carrying a camera, holding the leather strap loosely in one hand, pushing a notebook into his jacket pocket with the other. "To do with my work," he explained, smiling as she came towards him.

"Work? Oh, I thought you were on holiday."

"A combination of the two, in a way. I'm writing a book on Scarborough's development as a seaside resort. At least, I'll start writing when I've found somewhere to live, which is what I am up to this morning. I've arranged to pick up a list of furnished flats to rent. Preferably something spacious and quiet, near the town centre – asking for the moon, I suppose."

"Not at this time of year," Kate said, "now the holiday season's over. I'm on the look out for somewhere myself, as a matter of fact. Not too spacious, just something small and self-contained for the time being, until . . ."

"Until?" he queried when she left the sentence unfinished.

"Until I decide whether or not to stay on here." She smiled. "Shall we go now? It's a lovely morning."

Alex obviously had a warm feeling for the town's unique situation and scenery: the magnificent sweep of the South Bay, the ruined Norman fortress on the windswept promontory dividing the South Bay from the North – a bay of equal size yet more rugged, lacking the tree-clad slopes of its neighbour.

He stopped several times to take photographs from the Spa Bridge linking the South Cliff to the town centre, apologising as he did so, explaining that he wanted to compare shots of present day Scarborough with archive photographs and paintings of the town as it was in its Victorian heyday so as to pinpoint the changes when it came to the nitty gritty of writing and compiling the manuscript.

"There's so much research to be done, it's difficult to decide where to begin," he said impatiently. "You see, what I'm after is a living portrait of the Victorian era, not a dry-as-dust text-book. I want to capture the period precisely: the kind of people who came here, with retinues of servants in tow, to drink the Spa Water, firm in their belief that it would cure everything from gout to chronic indigestion."

"Then perhaps you should think in terms of a novel," Kate suggested. "Unless you've been commissioned to write a text-book, that is?"

"No, I haven't," Alex said thoughtfully. "I haven't received a commission so far. I simply waved the idea of a book about Victorian Scarborough under my agent's nose, and he told me to go ahead with it. Its acceptance, or otherwise, is dependent on the first three chapters and synopsis."

Frowning slightly, regarding the slim figure of his companion – slender, possibly, because she ate scarcely enough to keep a bird alive – he said, "How come you're so knowledgeable on the subject of writing? You're not a writer yourself, by any chance?"

"No, I'm not. But my husband was a writer and freelance journalist by profession."

Kate hadn't meant to discuss her private affairs but, having started, she felt duty bound to offer a fuller explanation. She said hesitantly, "Don was the breadwinner, I was simply his housekeeper, trying my best to keep our marriage on course; failing utterly to do so, as it happened." She paused, looking into the past. "I should have known, should have realised all along that what my husband really wanted was not a – housekeeper – but someone much younger, far more attractive and much cleverer than myself. Well, that's all, really. He found that – someone. Need I say more? Now, I'd really rather not talk about it any more, if you don't mind."

"Fair enough," Alex conceded, thinking that Don Ford must have been a damn fool to part company with a woman of Kate's calibre. More to the point, he told her so.

"Familiarity breeds contempt," she said. "The fact is, I couldn't keep up with him. I never really tried. He was much cleverer than I. Meaningful conversations were held with other people. But I learned a lot about his work: agents, publishers, deadlines and so on. I'd have been a fool not to."

They had reached the end of the bridge, near the amazing bulk of the Grand Hotel, a mammoth red brick building standing as a kind of monument to the Victorian era. Infinitely larger and more imposing than the Crown, but not as old.

Kate said, "Greg – he's my brother – and I once walked inside, as bold as brass, to see how the rich folk lived. I thought we'd be collared and marched out by the scruff of our necks, but no-one took a blind bit of notice of us. I guess they thought we were staying there with our parents." She laughed. "Funny, I'd forgotten that until now."

"And what was it like inside?"

"Enormous. Frightening. Overpowering, smelling a bit 'foody'. I remember thinking that cabbage must be on the menu, and I didn't like cabbage."

They were in a pleasant open square with a central garden, the Grand on one side, a row of tall houses on the other, once privately owned when wealthy folk had servants at their beck and call, now mainly hotels.

Alex said, "Am I right in thinking this square has some connection with the Brontës of Haworth?"

"Oh yes. Anne Brontë died in a boarding house on the site of the Grand Hotel. Charlotte and a friend, Ellen Nussey, were with her at the time. The bridge we've just crossed was well known to them. The perfect place for a stroll and a breath of sea air, I imagine."

"Please, tell me more," Arden said persuasively.

"Well, to spare their father further distress – a third funeral in a short space of time – Charlotte decided that Anne should be laid to rest here in Scarborough. Her grave is in the churchyard near St Mary's, up yonder on the hill overlooking the Old Town."

"You obviously know a great deal about the Brontës," Arden remarked. "May I ask why?"

"It's quite simple, really. I read *Wuthering Heights* when I was fourteen – a birthday present from Greg. Difficult to explain the effect it had on me, a romantically minded, impressionable teenager, but it was mainly a strong feeling of kinship with Emily Brontë. From then on, I haunted the public library to borrow books about them. The more I read, the more fascinated I became."

Kate paused. "Greg and I had planned to visit Haworth one day. But

21

the 'best laid schemes of mice and men . . .'" She smiled sadly. "Greg won a scholarship to Durham University, then our parents died suddenly within a year of one another. I met and married my future husband, Don Ford, within the space of a few months, and went with him to Wiltshire – a long way from home. But I took with me my dog-eared copy of *Wuthering Heights*, and if I were ever called upon to take with me one book to a desert island, that would be it."

They reached the far end of the square and crossed the road to the estate agent's office where Alex had arranged to pick up his list of accommodation. Waiting for him to emerge, Kate glanced in the window. Obviously this was an upper-crust agency. She would need something less pricey and might find what she was looking for in the "Accommodation to Rent" columns of the *Evening News*.

The coffee bar of the Royal Hotel was reasonably quiet. Finding a window table, Alex spread out the information leaflets, unhooked a gold-plated pen from the top pocket of his body-warmer and began ticking the possibilities, crossing out the improbables, drawing Kate into his game of noughts and crosses, letting his coffee go cold in the process, seeking her advice on the possibles, their situations and so on, saying he relied on her knowledge of the town to guide him in the right direction.

"You forget," she said, amused by his boyishness, "it's years since I lived here."

"I know. Even so, areas don't change all that much. Where is Weaponness, for instance?"

"Some distance away from the town centre," she told him, "and terribly 'posh', as I recall."

"Then that's out," he said decisively, crossing it from his list. "What about this? A superior self-contained furnished flat overlooking a pleasant central garden. Two bedrooms, lounge, dining room, bath-room and a large, well-equipped modern kitchen."

"Well, you did say you wanted something spacious," Kate commented drily. "Does it say where?"

He unearthed and popped on a pair of half-moon glasses. "The Crescent," he said, the spectacles perched half-way down his nose.

"The Crescent? But that's spang-bang in the town centre," Kate said eagerly, "directly opposite the old Sitwell house and Londesbor-ough Lodge. You know, the former home of Lord and Lady Londesborough where Edward the Seventh contracted some loathsome fever or other on account of the drains, and very nearly died as a result?"

Arden shuddered slightly. "No, I didn't know, and I rather wish you hadn't told me."

"Now I remember. It was typhoid fever. But I shouldn't worry too much if I were you. I expect the drains have been fixed by now!"

Alex laughed at her teasing. "So you think this flat might be worth a visit?"

"Yes, I do. I mean, viewing costs nothing, and you'll know right away if it's right or wrong for you. When you've finished your coffee, why not go back to the estate agent's for a key to the flat?"

"OK, I'll do just that. On one condition – that you'll come with me."

"But surely you can make up your own mind? You don't need me."

"Of course I do, to point out the defects, if any; to give me the benefit of a woman's advice regarding the fixtures and fittings. Besides which, you came out with me at my invitation, and I'm not about to part company with you yet."

Kate sighed deeply. "All right, if you insist," she agreed reluctantly, wondering what she was letting herself in for, reminding herself that she had no part to play in Alex Arden's life, that it was her own future, not his, that really concerned her. Despite his charm, his quirky sense of humour and his mature good looks, she realised full well the necessity of standing firm and strong on her own two feet, within her own depth, not his.

They hadn't far to walk to the Crescent and there had been no problem about handing over the keys of the flat since, as Alex explained, he and the estate agent had met socially on several occasions, and the man knew he was unlikely to make off with the family silver.

"Is that the Sitwell house over there?" he asked.

"No, that's Londesborough Lodge. The Sitwell house is further along, behind that high brick wall." Kate felt on familiar territory here. Scarcely anything had changed at all. It was just as she remembered it.

The flat was certainly spacious. On the top floor of a tall house midway along the terrace, its front windows overlooked the garden and the honey-coloured façade of Londesborough Lodge.

Alex spent some time at the drawing room window, enjoying the view, before turning his attention to the rest of the flat. "Well, Kate, what do you think of it?" he asked when they had made a tour of inspection. "I sense an air of disapproval. Am I right? Come on, speak up. Tell me what you've got against it."

"It's too fussy," she said frankly, looking distastefully at the ornaments arrayed on the marble mantelpiece, the many side-tables adorned with bobble-fringed lampshades, the deep, obviously comfortable and expensive settee and armchairs grouped around the fireplace. "You couldn't write here, not in this room at any rate. The only sizeable table is in the dining room, and that's far too highly polished. I'm sorry, Alex, but what you need is something more functional, much plainer. Somewhere you could work without worrying about the furniture. A place with a good old-fashioned kitchen table, for instance, to spread out your notes and photographs, your typewriter and so forth."

"You are quite right, of course," he admitted. "I got carried away with the view. The practicalities escaped me. Now you can see why I needed your advice."

Kate wondered in what surroundings he usually did his writing? Don had always professed himself unable to write anywhere except his studio or his London office. There had been a spare room in the cottage which he'd refused to use because of "household distractions". She had known he meant her.

Alex said, "I'd better return the key to the agent, then we'll find somewhere to have lunch. Or am I taking too much for granted?"

When Alex had returned the key, explaining that the flat was not quite what he'd had in mind, after passing the Royal Hotel, they walked along St Nicholas Street, Kate glancing about her at the buildings, noticing the changes wrought by the passage of time, regretting the loss of Marshall and Snelgrove's department store in particular. The façade was still intact, but the shop itself had been carved up into separate units occupied by a variety of traders including a furniture retailer's, and a catering firm advertising "Coffee, Snacks, Hot Soup, and Fish and Chips"!

Alex said gently, "The old order changeth, you know, Kate?"

"I know," she said, "but that doesn't make it easier to bear."

"Perhaps you are looking at the past through rose-tinted glasses?" he suggested.

"You could be right," she confessed, "but isn't that the charm of youth? The ability to see the world through rose-tinted glasses?"

"I wouldn't really know," he said quietly. "The fact is, I was sent to boarding school, aged ten, by parents who couldn't wait to get rid of me." He smiled grimly. "They made no secret of the fact that I stood in the way of their full enjoyment of life. Their trips abroad, and so on. So no rose-tinted glasses for a little lad scared almost witless by the harsh school discipline he was faced with, with no one to turn to for comfort and support.

"You, at least, had a happy, fulfilled childhood with your parents and your brother, Greg. I envy you that, Kate. I really do!"

Kate said simply, "I'm so sorry, Alex. I had no idea."

"It really doesn't matter any more, does it? What matters is not the past but the future?"

Kate asked, on a sudden impulse, "Tell me, Alex, have you ever been married?"

He screwed up his eyes against the sunlight of the bright October day. "Once, long ago," he confessed wearily. "But, taking a leaf from your own book, I'd rather not discuss the matter further, if you don't mind! Just tell me, where do we go from here?"

They were standing at a crossroads: St Thomas Street straight ahead, Westborough on the left, Newborough on the right, St Nicholas Street behind them.

"Let's try Newborough, shall we?" Kate said, tucking her hand into the crook of his elbow, guiding him gently, as she might have done a little boy for whom she felt suddenly responsible.

"I thought we might walk down to the Foreshore," she said, self-consciously removing her hand, thinking, How ridiculous – a little boy indeed! "There's a fish restaurant near the harbour. At least there used to be."

Walking downhill towards the Old Town in the lee of Castle Hill, suddenly the old fortress seemed to dominate the skyline, appearing almost benign and friendly, gilded with October sunlight.

The thoroughfare was lined with modern shopfronts – shops geared mainly to the sale of goods likely to appeal to summer visitors, thin on the ground now that the holiday season was over.

Passing the old George Hotel, Kate paused to look at a gift shop window packed with mementos of Scarborough, with soft toys, baubles, bangles and beads, her eye caught by a series of hand-written adverts offering second-hand bargains for sale – prams, bicycles, washing-machines, cookers, job lots of furniture and other unwanted items – among which she spied a card: "Accommodation to Let.

Maisonette, fully furnished, two beds, bathroom, kitchen, sitting room. Sea views. Attic studio. Reasonable rent. Enquire Within."

Standing beside her, Alex read the card through his half-moon glasses. "Wherein lies the snag?" he asked. "There must be one."

"Only one way to find out," Kate reminded him. "Shall we go in and ask?"

"Lead on, Macduff," he laughed, "though it's probably chatty, with mouse droppings on the kitchen floor."

"O ye of little faith," she said light-heartedly, entering the shop.

They were directed to a private entrance round the corner from the shop. A long flight of stairs led up to a sitting room, kitchen, bathroom and bedrooms. More stairs, narrow and somewhat rickety, led to an attic studio.

"Ye gods," Alex breathed ecstatically, approaching a wide dormer window overlooking the South Bay. "Now that's what I call a view! This is *it*, Kate! Absolutely perfect! Just what I had in mind! What do *you* think?"

"I agree with you. It *is* perfect. And no mouse droppings on the kitchen floor. Oh, Alex, I'm so pleased for you. Now you'll be able to get on with your book uninterrupted!"

"I have you to thank. If it hadn't been for you . . ." He paused, then added, "You will have dinner with me tonight, won't you, by way of a celebration?"

"Dinner?" she said, tongue-in-cheek. "We haven't even had lunch yet."

Four

A lex's housing problem settled, it was time for Kate to give some thought to her own, to which end she approached various agencies and looked at several flats before deciding, the following day, on a sitting room and kitchen combined, with an en-suite bedroom, overlooking the Valley Bridge and the steep, wooded gardens below.

The sitting room, reasonably well furnished, light and airy by reason of a Victorian bay window and high ceiling, was divided from the kitchen by a kind of bar-counter, behind which stood a sink unit, cupboards and work surfaces, a small electric cooker, mini refrigerator, electric kettle and a stand containing various pots and pans. More than adequate, Kate reckoned, for the requirements of a single person who wouldn't be doing much cooking anyway.

She had hoped for a separate bathroom with a proper bath, not a shower unit. But this was the best accommodation she had seen so far, and she loved the view from the sitting room window: the feeling of space imparted by the bridge into town, and a sense of life going on around her from the constant flow of traffic and pedestrians crossing the bridge; the many criss-crossing paths leading down through a thickly wooded area of autumn-tinted trees to Valley Road – a wide thoroughfare running from east to west like an artery pumping life-blood to the town centre, the Spa and the seafront of Scarborough.

To her surprise and disappointment, Alex Arden had left the Crown Hotel without bothering to say goodbye to her. From a distance, she had caught sight of him stowing his luggage into the boot of a silver-grey Mercedes. She hadn't even known he owned a car. Scarcely surprising since she knew next to nothing about the man apart from his penchant for *The Times* newspaper, his literary ambitions, that he had once been married. Above all, that he had made use of her.

Well, she had been made use of before today, and in all probability she would be again, Kate surmised, as she waited for the removal of her own luggage, by taxi, two days later. Men, she thought bitterly, Who needed them anyway?

She felt lonely at first in her strange new surroundings. This was a sizeable house with broad landings and passages, carved up into various flats and bed-sits, but she didn't see a soul as she went upstairs to her third floor apartment to start unpacking. Well, what had she expected? A brass band, balloons, a "Welcome Home" sign?

Then, opening the door, she saw a letter on the carpet. Greg and Cindy had written to wish her luck in her new home: the letter was enclosed in a greetings card embellished with white heather and a silver horseshoe. Close to tears, she propped up the card on the mantelpiece. Then came a knock at the door, and an elderly woman handed her a bunch of flowers in Cellophane, tied with a red ribbon bow.

"These came for you, dear," the woman said, "and I've brought you a few teabags and a jug of milk in case you felt like a cuppa."

"Oh, how kind of you. Won't you come in?"

"No, dear. I don't want to intrude. But if there's anything else you need, my room's downstairs. Room six. Don't be afraid to ask. My name's Fanny, by the way. I'm what you might call the caretaker. Leastways, I clean the stairs and the front entrance. Keeps me out of mischief."

"I'm Kate Ford. And thank you so much for taking care of my flowers; for the teabags and milk. I'll put the kettle on right away."

"That's right, dear. I always says there's nowt like a good hot cuppa to make you feel at home."

That brief encounter with Fanny had made all the difference to Kate. Fanny, the card, the letter and the flowers Greg had sent her, cheered her enormously. And the flowers were lovely, a dozen long-stemmed red roses. Greg would have ordered them himself, Kate knew, by-passing the seasonal, common-or-garden chrysanthemums in favour of something special. "For Someone Special", was written on the card tucked into the bouquet.

Later, when she had unpacked and stowed away her belongings, she went up the road to the Ramshill Road shops to buy eggs, bread, butter, milk and cornflakes, planning a simple supper of scrambled eggs on toast – a far cry from the more exotic fare of the Crown Hotel, especially the "celebration" meal she'd eaten with Alex Arden a few nights ago.

She wondered how he was getting on in his new environment. Chances were, feeling hungry, he would eat at the nearest restaurant. Hardly likely that he would be bothered to cook for himself, a man accustomed to the good things in life. Unlikely they would meet again, except by chance. Bumping into each other in the street, perhaps?

Twilight was falling when she returned home. This was the time of day she loved best: street lamps springing into bloom against the encroaching darkness of night, the sky a greenish blue, translucent as a robin's eggshell, a slip of a moon, a scattering of stars.

Crossing to the window, Kate saw that the Valley Bridge was aglow with the head and tail lights of homegoing traffic, resembling rubies and diamonds strung on a slender gold chain. In the distance, the concentrated glow of the town centre lamps and neon shop signs lit up the sky as twilight faded and night swallowed up the remains of the day.

Going through to her bedroom, Kate undressed, showered, then put on her old favourite dressing gown, warm and comfortable with knitted cuffs and a stand up collar. Returning to the living room, she switched on her radio to the opening strains of Debussy's *Clair de Lune*.

The last thing she wanted was to watch television. The set squatted opposite an armchair drawn up near the hearth of what must have been an open fireplace when this house had been a private dwelling, with servants to clean the grates, riddle the ashes and bring up scuttles of coal from the cellars.

The fireplace was now boarded up, and the hearth contained an electric fire with a simulated coal effect. Suddenly Kate recalled April Cottage: open fireplaces and log fires, gazing into the heart of the flames, firelight dancing on walls and ceilings. All over and done with now.

Preparing her supper of scrambled eggs, she wondered suddenly what the hell she was doing here. A stranger in a strange place, virtually alone in the world apart from Greg and Cindy, and Fanny on the floor below.

Come Monday, she thought, she must try to find herself employment of some kind, however menial, to give herself some purpose in life, a sense of direction connected to precise time-keeping and getting up early to wash, dress and breakfast.

But what if nobody wanted her? How could she possibly spend her days confined within this circumscribed living space of hers, however comfortable and well furnished, or wandering the streets of Scarbor-

ough like a lost soul, tormented by memories of past happiness? She
simply couldn't, and she knew it! On the other hand, how could she
possibly return to the Greater Manchester area to spend her days in a
mental and physical straitjacket?

Kate knew that Greg would welcome her return with open arms. She
also knew that his wife, Cindy, was and always had been jealous of their
brother and sister relationship, which made her feel like an outsider
when their shared memories of the past came uppermost in conversation. And in no way would she, Kate, wish to drive a wedge of
dissention between husband and wife, however innocently. She knew,
for instance, that Greg would not have told Cindy about the bouquet of
red roses he'd sent her, "For Someone Special!", for the simple reason
that her dispassionate sister-in-law, brought up within the compass of a
large family – seven siblings all told, had no way of understanding how
close just two siblings, one brother and his sister, had grown towards
one another in the halcyon days of their youth and childhood.

Switching on the electric fire and a red-shaded table lamp beside the
armchair, she ate her supper seated on a high stool at the room-dividing
counter, deriving comfort from the lights of home beyond the window,
the flame effect of the fire, the glow of the red-shaded lamp; listening to
piano music, Listz, Chopin, Rachmaninoff – a calming influence on her
unsettled state of mind, wondering what she could do to make the flat
more homely.

Tomorrow, perhaps, she would rearrange the furniture? Clean the
cooker, sink and work surfaces, buy a Sunday paper from the news-
agent's in Ramshill Road and, if the little supermarket was open,
purchase washing-up liquid, other cleaning materials, plus cheese,
macaroni – not spaghetti! She would never willingly eat spaghetti
again for as long as she lived.

Kate missed her garden – the joy and physical exercise involved in
weeding, planting and hoeing, imbuing her life with a sense of purpose
when Don was away from home, as she missed what she would always
think of as "her" wood where, often, when she stood quite still, wild
creatures – baby rabbits, robins, squirrels – came close to her, betraying
no fear at her presence in their midst.

She had never told Don about the wood, and so it had become her
secret sanctuary at times of stress, especially after the loss of her first
child, a son, almost perfectly formed, yet lacking a heartbeat. But that
had not prevented her giving him a name – Roland. Her other two

unborn babies she had named April and Jonathan, in her heart of hearts.

How strange that she had felt unable to share, with Don, those secret components of her life, just as he had felt unable to confess to his adultery with that "other woman" until Lucia's pregnancy had forced the issue into the open.

Then had come the bitter realisation that their marriage possessed little more substance than a sandcastle built within reach of the incoming tide, albeit a brave little sandcastle initially, with a deeply dug moat and little paper flags flying from the sand-pie parapets.

"Never mind, Sis," Greg used to say, drying her tears of disappointment, "we'll build a better castle tomorrow, just you wait and see!"

Now, that tomorrow was here! Her marriage was over and done with. She was no longer a starry-eyed girl but a middle-aged woman vaguely attempting to create a new life from the ruins of the old, with little or no guarantee of success unless she built the future ahead of her, not on sand, but solid rocks far beyond the reach of the incoming tide!

As she got ready for an early night, exhausted by the exigencies of the long day behind her, the doorbell connecting her flat to the world outside suddenly rang shrilly and repeatedly until, clad in her dressing gown and slippers, she hurried downstairs to answer the summons.

Alex Arden, the last person on earth she had expected to see, was on the doorstep.

"What on earth are you doing here, at this time of night?" Kate demanded fiercely. "In any case, how did you find me?"

"With considerable difficulty," he said urbanely. "In reply to your first question, I really need to talk to you, Kate. In any case, why 'at this time of night'? It's scarcely ten o'clock yet!"

"Can't it wait till morning?"

"Very well, then, if you insist. Shall we say ten o'clock, at my flat? No need to breakfast beforehand. I'll have coffee and croissants awaiting your arrival!" And then he was gone, swallowed up by the darkness of the October night, leaving behind him, on the doorstep, a bouquet of pink carnations and a bottle of Perrier water, which must have been there all the time, if she had taken the trouble to notice.

Kate scarcely slept at all that night in her stange new bed, wondering what on earth Alex wanted to talk to her about. At the same time she was faced with the realisation that she had been inordinately pleased to see him again despite her acid words spoken in the heat of the moment, and had been disappointed that she was looking far from her best in her dressing gown and slippers, her face devoid of make-up, her hair still damp from the shower.

His flowers she had arranged to their best advantage in a water-jug that she'd discovered in one of the kitchen cupboards and placed on her bedroom chest of drawers.

Up and doing early next morning, she moved a small settee nearer to the fireplace, the chair closer to the window – as a kind of "seat in the circle". Next to it, she placed a small round table, handy for library books, reading glasses and so on, for when she got around to joining the library, which she fully intended in due course, to catch up on all the books she had always meant to read. An exciting prospect. Never too late to learn, she thought, removing several gimcrack ornaments from the mantelpiece and stowing them away in a kitchen cupboard.

A woman of simple taste, a homemaker by nature, she deplored the "busy" wallpaper and carpet. Nothing to be done about the latter, but a couple of coats of emulsion paint would soon put paid to the jazzily patterned paper and create a more restful background, provided she could borrow a step-ladder. She must ask Fanny about that later. Not today. Sunday was probably the old lady's day of rest.

Thankfully, the paintwork would need nothing more than a good wash with hot soapy water, and the plain moss-green velour curtains did not clash too violently with the green and brown carpet or the dralon-covered settee and armchair. This, after all, was temporary accommodation, so no use spending a small fortune on redecoration until she knew for certain whether or not she would remain here for any length of time: the future dependent on finding work of some kind to obviate the necessity of delving into capital or the meek acceptance of Don's quarterly hand-outs.

At half-past eight, ready for action, Kate went to the small super-market – open for business as she had suspected it would be – to purchase her cleaning materials, plus various items of tinned and frozen foods to store in her kitchen cupboards and the deep-freeze compartment of her work-top refrigerator, feeling guilty as she did so.

Never, in her April Cottage days, would she have even dreamt of buying convenience food! Frozen chips and fish-fingers, of all things! Ready-made stew and dumplings! Had she gone raving mad all of a sudden? But did it really matter what she ate nowadays as long as it proved sufficient to keep body and soul together? Why cling to worn out shibboleths and customs no longer valid in her present circumstances?

At a quarter to ten she set off to walk to Newborough for her meeting with Alex Arden, pondering the reason why he had proffered this strange invitation to have breakfast with him? Not lunch or dinner, but *breakfast*, of all things!

Reasonably she assumed it was because she had refused to talk to him the night before. But how could she possibly have invited him up to her flat in a state of dishabille? Standing on the doorstep, she had felt that she was being watched, had noticed the slight twitching of a net curtain at a ground floor window by someone anxious to get a better view of the grey Mercedes parked in the road outside the iron gate.

"Sorry about last night," Arden said laconically, by way of a greeting. "I didn't mean to embarrass you. I should have realised you'd be under surveillance by nosey-parkering neighbours." He chuckled. "I couldn't help noticing the twitching of the front room curtains.

"Make yourself comfortable," he continued, leading the way upstairs to the living room, "while I make the coffee and warm up the croissants."

Sitting down, Kate noticed that the table had been set with cutlery, plates, butter and a pot of marmalade. "Thanks for the flowers," she called out to him, wondering why he had put them on the doorstep instead of handing them to her. Better not to ask, she decided. Possibly he had felt it inappropriate to appear as a Greek bearing gifts after his hurried departure from the Crown Hotel without bothering to say goodbye to her. She had not forgotten or entirely forgiven his lack of sensitivity on that occasion.

"Mugs all right?" he asked, appearing from the kitchen.

"Fine. But if you mean you haven't any cups, why bother to ask?"

"The thing I like best about you, Kate," he said, setting down the tray, "is the way you speak your mind straight out. No prevarication, no archness or pretence, and let the barbs fall where they may."

"In which case, why am I here? You said you wanted to talk to me. What about?"

"Frankly, I need help with my research," he said bluntly, taking a leaf from her book. "We made a good team, I thought, and you are familiar with the town and its history, which would help me enormously. It could be quite fun, don't you think?"

33

Kate paused momentarily. "I'm sorry, Alex," she said. "The answer has to be no."

"No?" Arden frowned, surprised by her negative response. "But why not? I've said I'm sorry about last night. Surely we can discuss the matter further?"

"There's nothing to discuss. The fact is, I'm planning to find myself a job. I need to earn a living. If I were a lady of leisure, money no object, I'd enjoy helping you. As things stand, I can't afford the luxury of a 'fun' pursuit."

"I see." Alex poured more coffee from the percolator. "What kind of work are you looking for ?"

"Anything that's available. I'm not qualified for anything in particular. Housework, maybe. I'm quite used to that. Cooking, perhaps."

"Can you type?"

"No."

"Not to worry. That isn't important. You could easily learn. It's just a question of mastering the keyboard."

'I bet that's what Chopin was told by his music teacher!"

Arden laughed. "How about sewing?"

"What kind of sewing? Embroidery? Dressmaking?"

"Plain sewing. Curtains."

"Yes, I've made curtains." She frowned. "What is all this?"

"Well, it comes under the heading of an interview." Alex smiled, obviously enjoying being mysterious – a facet of his quirky sense of humour.

"An interview for *what*?" Kate demanded, losing patience.

"The job I'm about to offer you as my personal assistant cum cook-housekeeper and seamstress. I'll need new curtains throughout," he said matter-of-factly. "Plain curtains. I really can't live with all this chintz."

Kate looked at him in amazement. 'Is this some kind of joke?"

"Not at all. You need a job, I need help. It's a matter of supply and demand. Hours flexible, to suit both parties, excellent rates of pay, plus overtime as applicable. Well, what do you say?"

"I don't know what to say." It hadn't sunk in that she had been offered a job at all, much less one that she could cope with and would, in all probability, enjoy very much. It seemed too good to be true.

"Damn it," Alex said, "those croissants are still in the oven. I'd better rescue them before they're burnt black."

Kate guessed he had made that an excuse to give her time to think things over, and was grateful for the respite. But what, after all, had she got to lose? She could cook, clean and sew curtains standing on her head: second nature to a housewife of twenty years. It was the research aspect of the job that intrigued her most of all.

When Alex returned with the croissants, he said lightly, "Guess what? I forgot to switch on the oven!"

Kate said, "When would you want me to start?"

Five

A lex had been teasing her about making curtains, Kate discovered. He would take the measurements, then she could choose the materials at a shop specialising in the ready-made variety.

"Good lord, girl," he said, "you didn't really imagine I'd expect you to slave over a hot sewing-machine, did you?"

Frankly, Kate hadn't known what to expect in her capacity as general factotum to a quixotic character like Alex. The *un*expected most likely!

She'd felt embarrassed at first by the rates of pay he'd suggested over the croissants and coffee that Sunday morning. "I'm sorry, but I couldn't possibly accept that amount," she'd said quickly, decisively.

"Why? Isn't it enough?"

"Not enough? It's far too much!"

"Allow me to be the judge of that," he'd countered swiftly. "You'll earn every penny, believe me! Wait till you're on your knees in the kitchen with a scrubbing brush and a bucket of hot water!"

Knowing he was joking about that at any rate, she'd said, "I still think you are being over generous, and I'm not looking for – charity."

"The thought never entered my mind. Plainly and simply, I need someone to take care of me. Above all, to help me with my research. Someone of taste and discernment with a brain in her head and a depth of feeling for the place she still thinks of as home. You, Kate, are that 'someone'. Need I say more?"

The weather had changed abruptly. Wind and rain had put paid to the Indian Summer days which seemed almost dreamlike now that November was here.

Kate realised Alex would need new curtains, lined to keep out the draughts of cold air rattling the windows, particularly those of his attic studio which, to her surprise, now contained a business-like desk, swivel chair, several metal filing cabinets, bookshelves, wall-to-wall carpet, a divan bed, and two long, Dimplex heaters turned on at full blast.

"You've certainly been busy," Kate commented, wandering from room to room on her first day at work, noticing various other additions to her employer's living space: leather armchairs to supplement the sitting room furniture; a brand new electric fire in the hearth; thick rugs on the floor. In the kitchen, new pots and pans, cups and saucers and electrical equipment. In the bathroom, a heated towel-rail and a newly installed shower-unit. "You must have spent a small fortune."

"Money has never been a particular problem of mine," he said edgily, "thanks to my parents who left me well provided for when they had the misfortune to die together in a car crash on the Route Nationale." He paused momentarily, then continued, "They were on their way to Arles, at the time, to witness a bull-fight, so I'm told. My father was at the steering wheel of the car – most probably drunk, knowing him! At any rate, he pulled out to overtake the car ahead of him and smashed headlong into an oncoming lorry."

"I'm so sorry," Kate said. "How dreadful for you."

"Not as dreadful, I imagine," Alex replied bitterly, "as witnessing the death of a magnificent animal in a blood-soaked arena. Now, let's change the subject, shall we?"

"Yes, of course." At that stage, Kate put forward her idea of planning menus on a monthly basis; mealtimes and so on.

"Oh, to hell with all that," Alex interrupted wearily. "Feed me baked beans on toast! Pig-swill, for all I care! My main concern, right now, is getting to grips with the history of Scarborough's development as a seaside resort. If only I knew where to begin."

"Then why not begin at the beginning, with Scarborough's first ever custom-built hotel?" Kate suggested quietly.

"You mean – the Grand?" Arden asked.

Kate shook her head. "Oh no, not the Grand – the Crown. The Grand came later. The Crown came first," she told him, remembering her underlying reasons for wanting to stay there in a balcony room overlooking the South Bay: because of its uniqueness and because generations of Victorian families, long dead and gone, had stayed there way back in the mid-1800s, those inhabitants of a world distanced far from the present-day world of the 1970s, devoid of the horse and carriage, bustles and parasols.

At least she, Kate, had achieved a long-cherished ambition to keep company with the ghosts of all those people who had once stood on the balcony before her.

Next day, she and Arden went to the library to research the history of the Crown Hotel from bound volumes of the *Scarborough Gazette and Herald* dating back to the last century. They turned the brittle pages with great care, making notes, exclaiming excitedly when one or the other came across nuggets of information relevant to their quest. Like digging for buried treasure and finding it, Kate thought.

Glancing at Alex, she recalled the bitterness in his voice when he had spoken about his parents, and realised that, despite his veneer of charm, she still knew nothing about him or his past life apart from his lonely childhood and his, presumably, failed marriage. Not even his writing background, how many and what kind of books he had published, or where he came from. Nor was she likely to find out unless he imparted the information of his own volition.

But wasn't she in the same boat? A woman with her own secrets to keep, fearful of intrusion into her personal life? Or had she already revealed too much in confessing that Don had left her for another woman? Why had Alex's marriage failed, she wondered. Had his wife been having an affair? Or had *he*?

"Have you noticed, Kate," Alex said suddenly, "the many references to one John Fairgray Sharpin, the first tenant manager of the Crown Hotel? According to this, the Crown was built by a consortium of businessmen smart enough to realise that the old coaching inns and hostelries, beloved of Charles Dickens, would soon become redundant when the railways came into being."

"Yes, I had noticed. They must have had their heads screwed on the right way."

"What puzzles me is their choice of a manager," Arden continued. "A man in his early twenties, a Yorkshireman by birth, a wine merchant by profession, ambitious enough to open his own business in London – but it failed miserably by all accounts. Rather odd, wouldn't you say?"

"That depends on what he had to offer. Youth, flair, enthusiasm, imagination. Presumably his job as a warehouseman failed to satisfy his creative instincts. I came across a reference to him as a man of vision. I have it down here somewhere."

She riffled through her notepad. "Yes, here it is. 'A Man of Vision, small in stature yet possessed of an abundant energy and engaging in manner. By means of clever advertisement in certain prestigious London newspapers, extolling the excellent amenities of The Crown Hotel, the unparalled splendour of its position overlooking the South Bay and its close proximity to the Spa, notable for the health-giving properties of its mineral water, Mr John Fairgray Sharpin has successfully lured to our shores the *crème de la crème* of high ranking members of the aristocracy, Churchmen, Members of Parliament and many other distinguished personages.' "

Kate laughed. "Well, there you have it! Nothing succeeds like success! J.F.S. – as he was affectionately referred to by his peers on the Town Council when he became Britain's youngest ever mayor – must have been quite a man! A force to be reckoned with! Can't help wishing I'd been alive at the time to shake hands with him."

"Perhaps you were, "Arden said unexpectedly, "if, like me, you believe in reincarnation?"

"I don't, as it happens," Kate said levelly, suppressing a shudder, as if a goose had walked over her grave. "I think that one appearance on this merry-go-round we call life is more than enough for anyone to endure. I'm not into retrogression or whatever it's called. The here and now is quite enough for me to come to terms with." She paused a moment, then, "I've had enough of research for one day," she said lightly. "In any case, it's almost lunch time."

They spent the afternoon in the attic studio, collating the notes they had made earlier, making comparisons, putting various dates in order, beginning with the opening of the Crown Hotel in the year 1844, to create a precise framework of known facts vital to a history of Scarborough's emergence as a famous seaside resort. Yet Kate was far more intrigued by the personality of John Fairgray Sharpin.

Leaving Alex to type his notes, Kate went down to the kitchen to begin the shepherd's pie she'd planned for supper, having told Alex that she wanted to leave early that evening to decorate her flat. Peeling potatoes, she thought about those old copies of the *Scarborough Gazette* that she had looked at that morning; her joy of discovery as if the past had suddenly come alive, especially reading those lists of visitors to the Crown Hotel in its Victorian heyday. Among them earls and countesses, lords and ladies, high ranking politicians, generals, rear admirals and churchmen.

There had also been detailed descriptions of the food served at various banquets and dinner parties, balls and other functions: salmon mousse, quails' eggs in aspic, game, poultry, roast meats, rich desserts. Little wonder, she thought, that they needed the restorative properties of Spa mineral water to offset the dire effects of so much rich food; gargantuan breakfasts and five course luncheons into the bargain. The miracle was that women of that era did not burst out of their whaleboned stays in the face of such gluttony at table.

But what of the retinues of common-or-garden folk, the ladies' maids, footmen and coachmen in attendance on their lords and masters? Scarcely likely they would have stuffed themselves to repletion in the servants' dining hall. Possibly they had been too tired to care about anything but sleep once they had finished work.

The working conditions of the lower classes of that era touched Kate deeply. She hoped that the book Alex was about to write would not focus entirely on the leisure pursuits of the rich and famous. The more she thought about it, the more she wished that he would try his hand at a novel. She had a strong feeling, however, that he would go for the softer option of a non-fiction book.

At twenty to seven, she called up to him that supper was ready, anxious to get the meal over with as soon as possible. She was running late this evening, but there was still no sign of him and time was ticking away.

At this rate, it would be half seven at least by the time the meal was eaten. This really was too bad of him, she thought angrily, keeping her waiting unnecessarily when she had other things to do. Oh, drat the man! What was keeping him! Then she'd have the washing up to see to, the pots to put away – which meant she wouldn't be home till eight, at the earliest.

When Alex eventually put in an appearance, "I was just about to leave," Kate said, bringing the food to the table.

"But we haven't eaten yet!" Alex raised his eyebrows. "Is anything the matter?"

"Since you ask, I'm finding my working hours a bit too flexible for my liking."

"You mean I'm taking up too much of your time?" he lay down his cutlery. "But I thought you understood there'd be no hard and fast rules. I assumed that ours would be a working relationship based on friendship. Apparently I was wrong."

Kate said coldly, "You're missing the point. What you seem to forget is that I have affairs of my own to attend to."

"Such as?"

"My flat, if you must know! The sitting room's in a state of chaos. The curtains down, carpet turned back, paint rollers everywhere, not to mention the stepladder I borrowed from my downstair's neighbour. I *did* tell you! Apparently you weren't listening!"

"You mean you are decorating? Doing it yourself? But that's crazy! Why didn't you tell me? I'd have hired a firm to do it for you!"

"The reason *why* I didn't tell you! I happen to prefer doing some things myself, to retain a modicum of independence. And it would help if you came down to meals on time!"

"I see. So I'm being punished for keeping you waiting a few minutes? For keeping you from your blasted paint tins and rollers? Most women would want to go home to get on with their knitting; read a good book. But no, not you!"

"I'm not 'most women'," Kate retorted. "In any case, it wasn't a few minutes, but twenty!"

Arden sighed deeply, impatiently. "But nothing was spoiling, was it? After all, a shepherd's pie!"

"That's beside the point. For all you knew, it might have been a – cheese soufflé!"

"In which case, you'd probably have stormed upstairs and dragged me down by the hair!"

"Don't put ideas into my head!"

"All right, Kate," Alex conceded. "You win! So let's take it from here, shall we? Unless you're thinking of handing in your notice. *Are* you?"

"I'm not sure," she retorted, angry with herself for being angry, remembering the many occasions Don had gone missing at mealtimes, leaving the food she'd cooked for him untasted; disappearing in the direction of the village pub, staying there till well past closing time.

Intuitively, Arden said, "You'll have to let go of the past sooner or later, you know that, don't you?"

"I don't know what you mean," she snapped back at him defensively.

"Of course you do! You pride yourself on your honesty, so why not face up to the fact that, unlike Lazarus, the past can't be resurrected? However hard you try, it's gone, over and done with. Now, sit down and eat your supper, then I'll drive you home and give you a hand with the decorating."

41

"Oh for heaven's sake, Alex," she said wearily, "at least try to be practical. You know damn well what I'm up against. The twitching of the net curtains, remember?"

"So what is it you're afraid of?" he said bluntly. "Shocking the neighbours? Or are you too proud to accept help when it's offered? Independence is one thing, letting false pride ruin your life's a different matter entirely.

"Think about it, Kate! True independence means not giving a toss what other people think of you, and I should know. Why, do you imagine, do I behave so badly at times? I'll tell you why. Because, that way, I can't be categorised as a good guy or a bad. It's the best form of self defence I know. You should try it yourself sometimes.

"Look at it this way. In my experience, the bitchy women of this world fare somewhat better than the haloed variety. The meek don't always inherit the earth, you know?"

"And have *you* inherited the earth?" Kate asked coolly.

Arden laughed softly. "No, far from. But I've enjoyed building up my defence system against the holier-than-thou brethren of this particular planet!"

"I see." Kate smiled, heartened by the devil-may-care cheek of the man. "Very well, then, I accept your offer of help. So let's get started on the decorating, shall we?"

Six

This was a facet of Arden's character Kate had never suspected or would have believed existed had she not seen him on the stepladder wielding the paint-roller with the panache of a professional decorator.

What a surprising person he was, and how quickly he was getting on with it, she thought, on her knees washing the skirting boards.

Later, she made coffee, which they drank near the uncurtained window. "You certainly have a lovely view from here," he remarked, coffee mug in hand. "We Londoners have street lights in abundance, no views worth mentioning. Lots of parks and open spaces, of course, but nothing comparable to the feeling of space and freedom I've discovered here in Scarborough."

He spoke softly, as if to himself. Kate remained silent, unwilling to break his train of thought, hopeful of further disclosures of his background. None was forthcoming.

At least she knew now that he lived in London, possibly within striking distance of some park or other. But which? Regent's, St James's, Green Park? Impossible to decide which, though she'd bet her bottom dollar on St James's.

Not that she knew London all that well. She had simply gone there occasionally with Don, in the early days of their marriage when, as a freelance theatre critic, he'd attended various matinée performances, leaving her to her own devices.

He'd been faintly amused that she had spent those afternoons sightseeing from the upstairs of double-decker buses. It was amazing how much she'd gleaned about that teeming city from those lumbering red vehicles. Changing buses frequently, she had revelled in the sight of famous landmarks: St Paul's Cathedral, Marble Arch, the Houses of Parliament, Westminster Abbey, the Albert Hall, the Tower of London.

A young bride, proud of her clever, successful husband, she had never stopped to wonder why she was not included in those theatre visits of his.

The reason why not seemed abundantly clear to her now. As long ago as that, there must have been other women in his life of whom she had been blissfully unaware. What a naive fool he must have thought her, a starry-eyed teenager content to lumber round London on double-decker buses whilst he was palm-paddling his latest female conquest.

When they had finished their coffee, Alex moved the ladder to begin painting the fireplace wall. "With luck," he said, "I'll have this finished in an hour or so. Then, tomorrow morning, when the paint's dry, I'll hang the curtains and re-lay the carpet."

"Thanks, Alex," Kate said, "I can't thank you enough."

"No thanks necessary," he assured her. "Anything to help a damsel in distress – to make up for the shepherd's pie hiatus. I'm really sorry about that."

He meant what he said; knew he behaved badly at times. His many faults and failings, of which he was acutely aware, included a degree of arrogance, shortness of temper, fondness of having his own way, inability to suffer fools gladly, an inclination to take down a peg or two the sycophants and the "pompous bastards" who crossed his path now and then.

But never, by word or deed would he willingly hurt or offend Kate Ford, whose friendship and plain speaking he valued as pearls beyond price. This woman was no fool, no sycophant, and he knew it.

They were talking and laughing when suddenly, without warning, the door was flung open and an elderly man, obviously angry, clad in pyjamas, a dressing gown and slippers, barged into the room.

"Fine goings on, I must say," he thundered. "But make no mistake, I shall write a letter of complaint to the landlord first thing in the morning!"

Rounding fiercely on Kate, who obviously hadn't a clue who he was, "I've warned him time and time again of the inadvisability of letting his flats to unsuitable tenants: flighty women such as yourself who bring in their 'fancy' men without a by-your-leave."

Perched atop the ladder, paint-roller in hand, Alex said – equably for him, "Tell me, sir, do you make a habit of bursting into other people's flats – without a by-your-leave – clad in your night attire? If so, I may well write a letter of complaint to your landlord warning him against the advisability of letting his flats to evil-minded octagenarians such as yourself."

Dismounting from the ladder without undue haste, facing the old man and towering above him, Alex continued levelly, "Tell me, sir, have you a solicitor? I mean a really *good* solicitor?"

"Huh?" The old man's mouth sagged open, revealing his toothless gums. "I don't know what you mean. What would I want with a – solicitor?"

"I thought that would have been perfectly obvious to a clever fellow like you," Alex said coolly. "Or perhaps the services of a barrister would be a safer bet in a trial for slander when your case comes to Court.

"You see, old son, I shall make it my business to sue the pants off you for referring to Mrs Ford as a 'flighty' woman, myself as her 'fancy' man."

He added mischievously, "Needless to say, I shall look forward enormously to your definition of a 'fancy' man from the witness box; a 'flighty' woman, come to that.

"Do remember, my dear sir, that when your case comes to Court, you will have to swear, on oath, that upon bursting into Mrs Ford's flat, clad in your night apparel, you found myself atop a ladder, paint-roller in hand; Mrs Ford on her hands and knees washing the skirting boards. Scarcely a romantic situation, wouldn't you say?"

"Oh, very well then," the old man mumbled, "have it your own way."

"I fully intend to," Alex said grimly. "The trouble with nasty-minded people like you, they poison the atmosphere with the sheer filth of their warped imaginations.

"Now, I suggest that you get the hell out of here before I evict you forcibly with . . ." Arden's lips twitched upwards in a smile. "Well, that's up to you. I'll give you to the count of ten. Ten, nine, eight, seven, six, five . . ."

At the count of five, the old man hurried down to his own apartment as if the devil was after him.

Kate looked stricken. Alex said, "Try not to let it upset you too much. After all he's just a silly old man with a bit of a power complex in need of a lesson in manners. Don't worry, he'll think twice about bothering you again after the scare I gave him."

45

He paused, then asked, "You didn't take seriously all that stuff and nonsense I spouted?"

Kate shook her head. "No, it's just that I felt – safe – before. I don't now. Not any longer."

Arden knew what she meant, and no matter how hard he might try to persuade her otherwise, the damage had been done. Her privacy had been invaded.

He said, "Let's not wait till tomorrow, shall we? The sooner the decorating is done, the curtains hung and the carpet replaced, the better."

"But that could take till the early hours," Kate demurred, dreading a second confrontation with her downstair's neighbour.

"No matter how long it takes, I want you to wake up in the morning to find everything done and dusted. I'll take the empty paint tins away and dispose of them for you."

"Thanks, Alex." She felt like crying, he was being so kind to her, revealing the softer side of his nature, a deep concern for her welfare at odds with his usual brusqueness of manner erected as a barrier against the world. How had he put it? "A defence system". Yes, that was it. He was certainly not on the defensive now.

It would be wonderful to have the flat put to rights. Then, perhaps, she would begin to feel secure again, to put the incident of the old man into its proper perspective. What price the idea of standing on her own two feet if she fell at the first hurdle? What, after all, had she expected? That independence, peace of mind and contentment would be handed to her on a plate?

If so, she'd better think again! Life was not like that, and she knew it. There would always be problems to face, niggling worries, sleepless nights, haunting memories both happy and sad to contend with. And burning questions to be answered: "Where did I go wrong? When did Don stop loving me? What if our children had lived?" Except that there were no answers, simply the feeling that her life had stopped abruptly three years ago, leaving her stranded in a limbo-land somewhere between a ghost-ridden past and a future she had scarcely, as yet, come to terms with.

Kate returned the ladder to Fanny, who kept it in the cellar for general household use.

"I heard tell old Joe Updike had a go at you the other night," she said. "Huh, the trouble with him and his missis, they've been here that long they think the place belongs to them! The last woman moved out because of him and his complaints. The television was on too loud or she had too many callers coming and going at all hours.

"He's going ga-ga if you ask me! I called him Hitler to his face when he complained about the vacuum cleaner – said it was too loud. Well, I told him straight it weren't my fault if it was, an' what did he want me to do? Get down on my knees with a dustpan an' brush?"

"Oh, surely not in this day and age?" Kate broke in.

"He has it in for me 'cos I live here rent free. But dammit all, I only have the one room with a bit of a kitchen in one corner. No bathroom or loo. I have to go along the landing to the communal bathroom when I want to have a bath or spend a penny.

"I know what's bugging him! He thinks I should live in the cellar, not in a room next door to him an' that miserable wife of his. You know the kind? Enjoys ill health! Truth to tell, I wouldn't mind living in the cellar. At least I'd get a bit of peace and quiet down there!"

She laughed suddenly. "Hark at me! Grumbling my head off! Must be catching! But I'm not really complaining, just letting off steam! I think myself lucky to have a job at my age. I've been a cleaner all my life, like my mother before me. I worked at the Crown Hotel in my younger days. When I retired, they had a party in my honour an' presented me with a cut glass vase an' a lovely bouquet of flowers."

"How lovely for you," Kate enthused. "Then what happened?"

"The manager made a speech, an' I had my photograph in the paper. Eh, I were fair taken aback! Well, to cut a long story short, I got this job on the strength of that photo of me in the *Evening News*. Now, here I am and here I intend to stay, an' it'll take more than the likes of Joe Updike to get the better of me."

She concluded cannily, "An' you shouldn't let him get the better of you neither!"

Kate felt like kissing Fanny at that moment, a proud, invincible, gutsy old lady facing life squarely on her own terms, with not a sign of self-pity in her make-up.

Shakily, close to tears, she said, "Thanks, Fanny, I'll try not to!"

Unexpectedly, Fanny continued, "I've never been one to pry into other folks' business, but I couldn't help noticing how lonely you were the day you came here to live, an' I thought what a pity it was. I wondered if you'd lost your husband recently?"

Kate nodded. Strangely enough, she didn't mind the older woman's question or giving her a straightforward answer. "My husband left me for another woman some time ago. We'd been married a little over twenty years when he asked me to divorce him.

"I was born in Scarborough. When my parents died, I got married and went to the West Country to live. After the divorce, I sold my home and stayed with my brother and his wife in Manchester until I decided what to do next. So here I am, back where I started."

"But surely you have friends hereabouts?" Fanny said sympathetically. "People you knew before you left home?"

"No one close, I'm afraid, except a girl I went to school with. We wrote to each other for a while, then lost touch. You know how it is? She may not live here now for all I know."

"Aye well . . . But you'll make new friends, I'm sure, a bonny lass like you!"

"Lass?" Kate smiled. "Hardly that: I'm into my forties now."

Fanny pulled a face. "Huh, that's nowt to worry about. I'm into my seventies an' still going strong. Mind you, I never was what you might call good-looking, an' I never married. I wouldn't have said no, mark you, if anyone had asked me, only no one did. I was born Frances May Kiddy, an' that's the name that'll go on my headstone, I reckon."

Bidding Fanny a fond farewell, Kate hurried down Newborough in the teeth of a bitingly cold November wind. Kiddy, she thought. What an unusual surname. One that she had never come across before.

In boisterous, expansive mood, when Kate appeared on his doorstep, fully booted and spurred, awaiting her arrival, Alex announced cheerfully that they were about to go walkabout.

Teeth chattering, "Where to?" Kate asked suspiciously, longing for a cup of hot coffee to warm the cockles of her heart before setting off on a journey into the wild grey yonder.

"You'll find out soon enough! Just follow me," Alex adjured her, striding along King Street towards St Nicholas Cliff, then down the "Zig-Zag" near the Grand Hotel to the seafront. From thence to the Valley Gardens.

"Now, Kate, tell me what you see around you." Alex had stopped walking to survey the scenery, an air of excitement about him. "Take your time."

"What, on a day like this?" Kate grumbled, wondering what she was supposed to be looking at. "Oh, very well then, if you insist."

Breath whirling away like smoke she said, "I see lots of trees; trunks and branches, no leaves. Paths and shrubberies, the spandrels of the Valley Bridge, a few empty beer cans and cigarette packets . . ."

"No need to be facetious!"

"I'm not. You asked me to describe the scene, and that's what I'm doing!"

"All right. Get on with it!"

"Well, obviously there's the old duckpond over yonder, and a bit of a scummy pool under the bridge, with a rusted metal tripod as a centrepiece." She broke off suddenly, recalling her younger days when the scummy pool was afloat with waterlily pads, and a small fountain from the then gleaming tripod splashed water into the now derelict pond.

The equally neglected duckpond, edged with Victorian wooden railings in a criss-cross pattern, Kate remembered as a shining expanse of water alive with a flotilla of ducks swimming from their nesting places on the small island in the centre of the lake to gobble up the bread that she and Greg had thrown to them.

"I'm sorry, Alex," she said, "I'm not enjoying this very much."

"So I gathered. But never mind about that. Tell me what else you can see from where we're standing."

Gazing about her, she said, "The gardens of Londesborough Lodge on the right hand side of the road, far better maintained than the scrubby area opposite, I dare say, since the Lodge and its grounds are now the property of the local Borough Council."

"Anything else?" Arden peristed.

"Well, yes. Plantation Hill leading down past the old Sitwell house, with its arched gas-lamp brackets still in situ . . . How odd. I thought they'd have been relegated to the scrap heap ages ago."

Arden smiled mysteriously. "Thanks, Kate," he said. "Now I'd like you to imagine yourself walking down Plantation Hill wearing a long skirt, ankle boots and a wide-brimmed hat, to witness the opening ceremony of 'The People's Park'. The brainchild of your hero, John Fairgray Sharpin!"

"Really?" Kate's eyes shone. "I had no idea. You mean that he . . . ?"

"Was responsible for the duckpond?" Alex said, latching on to her train of thought. "Apparently so, plus the landscaping of the area as a pleasure ground for the working-class folk of Scarborough, who came here in their hundreds to watch the procession of carriages from the Town Hall."

He added dreamily, "The month was May. There was magic abroad in the air." Then, more matter of factly, he said, "I brought you here to gauge your reaction to the idea of starting my book with a chapter describing the events of that night, and the role played by Sharpin in Scarborough's development as a first-class seaside resort. Well, what do you think?"

"As a novel, you mean?" Kate asked hopefully.

"No, of course not," Alex said impatiently. "I'm not into writing romantic fiction. I thought you knew that! There are women writers enough engaged in churning out that kind of nonsense, in my opinion! Now, isn't it about time for some hot, strong coffee? Don't know about you, but I'm frozen stiff with all this standing about on a day like this!"

Of all the impossible men, Kate thought as, turning abruptly, he strode ahead of her up the Zig-Zag and along King Street to his flat.

Seven

"The month was May. There was magic abroad in the air. Darkness had fallen. Lamplights glimmered like fireflies, seeming to move and dance in the gentle breeze blowing inland from the sea."

Kate smiled reflectively. "The People's Park" had fired her imagination to the extent of wanting to write about it in her own way. Nothing whatever to do with Alex's more prosaic approach to the subject.

What had it really been like that night, she wondered, when throngs of working class Scarborians had trooped down Plantation Hill to the valley below to witness the opening of their very own pleasure ground?

Giving rein to her imagination, she visualised the scene in her mind's eye: colourful Chinese lanterns strung between the branches of the trees; sounds of music and laughter, the quacking of ducks from the newly established duckpond; children's swings and roundabouts; the bunting-bedecked platform awaiting the arrival of Town Hall dignitaries and their ladies, in open landaus, to add a certain weight and solemnity to the occasion.

Not that the onlookers would have cared tuppence about top-hatted, grey-bearded town councillors and their lady wives, in direct contrast to the "Man of the Moment" – the young, dark-haired, charismatic Mayor of Scarborough, John Fairgray Sharpin.

And when the carriage procession had returned from whence it came, what then? Kate wondered. What did people in celebratory mood usually do? Eat, drink and make merry, she imagined, as they had done since time immemorial. The Victorian women, despite their clothing – long skirts, ankle boots, high-necked blouses, tightly-laced corsets and layers of petticoats, their menfolk in their sombre suits, starched collars, and waistcoats and the married couples with children in tow would have made the most of that golden opportunity to revel in the many sideshows, beer tents and hot-food stalls.

She envisaged savoury ducks, pease-pudding, sausages and hot mutton pies; wide-eyed children staring up at a Punch and Judy show; hoop-la stalls, coconut shies; young couples walking hand-in-hand beneath lantern-lit branches.

People would have come from all areas of the town: off-duty chambermaids, porters and stable-lads from the Crown Hotel, more than likely; ganzied fishermen from the Old Town – keeping an open eye for pretty young lasses in muslin dresses and tip-tilted boaters, they on the look-out for handsome young men.

Kate imagined the kissing and canoodling that went on in the rustic shelters along the way on that warm, heady May night long ago, the scent of lilacs and May blossom borne on a breeze blowing in from the sea, the murmur of the tide washing in on the shore, the tinkling of water from the fountain into the lily pool beneath the bridge. Except, of course, there wouldn't have been a bridge spanning the valley in those days.

Her heart lifted suddenly at the possibility of writing her own version of Victorian Scarborough via a series of random jottings written purely for her own pleasure, so imparting a new sense of purpose to her finding out all she could about that particular era, if only to prove to herself that she possessed a mind of her own above and beyond her failed capacities as a wife and mother in what she now thought of as her "Don days".

Next morning, not hearing the usual clatter of typewriter keys when she arrived at Alex's, Kate went upstairs to his office and found him, in tetchy mood, kneeling on the floor surrounded by photographs, note-books and newspaper clippings.

"Well, don't just stand there," he said abruptly, "go down and make some coffee! I've been up since the crack of dawn trying to make sense of this lot!"

"Why? What's the problem?" she enquired mildly.

"The problem is," he said sarcastically, "that I need some hot, strong coffee right now, not in the middle of next week!"

"You're wrong, Alex!" Kate said uncompromisingly, "Apart from a shave, a shower and a haircut, what you really need is a skivvy, not a so-called housekeeper. In which case, the sooner you find yourself a skivvy, the better!"

This said, shored up by her new-found purpose in life and sick and tired of the male gender in general, Kate marched downstairs to the side door.

Deeply shaken, Alex called after her, "Hey, hang on just a second! You can't simply walk out on me like this!"

"Oh, can't I?" she called back to him. "Just watch me!"

"At least tell me where you're going!" Alex demanded hoarsely from the upper landing.

"To the library, if you must know," Kate conceded, coming to terms with the realisation that her life would be much poorer without Alex Arden, yet unwilling to allow him dominion over her life lest she ended up a cipher once more, as she had done with Don.

"Very well, I'll see you there in an hour," Alex said urbanely, pulling up his defences, unwilling to admit to himself, or Kate, how much he had come to rely on her friendship. He added, "You really must stop taking umbrage the way you do."

"Perhaps I shall," she said coolly, "when you stop behaving like a bear with a sore head!"

At the library, using her recently acquired membership card, Kate chose several books pertaining to the Victorian era which she stowed in her shopping bag, after which she applied for, and received, permission to enter the inner sanctum of the Scarborough Room – an accolade accorded only to members of the public engaged in bona fide research connected with the history of Scarborough.

She was there, turning pages of the *Gazette and Herald* when Arden entered the room. "Feeling better now, are you?" he asked brusquely.

She glanced up at him. "More to the point, Alex, are *you*?"

"You know, Kate," he said, tongue-in-cheek, "I can't help thinking that had you treated your ex-husband as badly as you treat me, you might well still be married to him; based on the premise that a man would be more inclined to leave a boring woman; seldom, if ever, a troublesome one!"

Faced with the strong tide of feeling surging between them, yet unwilling to admit its existence, Kate suggested, off-handedly, "Well, shall we stop wasting time and get on with our research before you find out how troublesome I could be if I tried harder?"

The nature of the "tide" was not entirely clear to her. It seemed as changeable as the sea itself, a strange combination of admiration and irritation, liking and disliking, to do with the complex character of the man himself, coloured by her own refusal to accept male domination ever again.

She had come a long way since her "Don days", with every step along the road to recovery a hard-fought battle against despair and loneliness. And the battle was not yet won, nor would it be until she had learned how to stand, firm and proud, on her own two feet.

But could any human being become so insular as not to need companionship? Even the emotionally-challenged companionship of a man like Alex Arden?

Their morning's research concluded for the time being, he said, over lunch – hot soup and toasted sandwiches in the Royal Hotel snack bar – against a background of whirling snowflakes seen through the window, "By the way, Kate, I'll be spending Christmas in London. How about you?"

"*Christmas?*" Kate frowned slightly. "I don't know. I haven't really thought about it yet."

"But, my dear girl, it's only three week's away from now!" He paused, "Surely you'll be spending it with your brother, in Manchester?"

"Greg won't be in Manchester at Christmas," Kate said. "He and his wife, Cindy, usually spend Christmas with her family, in Bradford."

"So what's to prevent you spending Christmas in Bradford?" Alex persisted.

"First and foremost, I haven't been invited," Kate said defensively. "More importantly, even if I had been, I'd have turned down the invitation!"

"May I ask why?"

Kate countered his question with one of her own: "Tell me, Alex, how would you react to a houseful of spoilt children, running amok?"

"I get the picture," he said wryly. "In which case, how would you react to spending Christmas with me?"

"In London, you mean?" Kate asked warily.

"A strong possibility, since that's where my home is. Of course, I could hire a caravan north of the Watford Gap and commute daily, if you'd prefer."

Kate laughed. His quirky sense of humour was the thing she liked most about Alex. "Ask a silly question, you'll get a silly answer!" she said.

"Then how about a sensible answer? Think about it, Kate. I have business matters to attend to before Christmas, and you'd be a great help on the domestic front: opening the house, so to speak, doing the shopping and so on."

"I see. So this would be in the nature of a working holiday for me?" Kate asked, wanting to get things clear in her mind.

Arden frowned. "Only in the sense that you'd be shopping and cooking anyway even if you stayed here in Scarborough and, frankly, I'd rather you spent Christmas with me than alone in your flat."

What he said made sense. Even so, Kate needed to know exactly what she'd be letting herself in for. "Would we be alone in the house?"

"Yes, of course. Why? Is that a problem?"

"No. I simply thought you might be expecting – house guests over the Christmas weekend."

"No way," Alex assured her briefly. "I've had enough of house-parties, dinner parties, luncheon and cocktail parties to last me a lifetime!"

Glancing across at him, noticing and understanding, by the sudden air of weariness about him, that he too was ghost-ridden by past events – memories of a lost love, almost too hard to bear at times, she said quietly, "Very well, then, I accept your invitation."

Alex had elected to travel south, by rail, on the nineteenth of December, a much easier and more direct means of transport than road travel, he explained, hence his decision to garage the Mercedes pro tem, until their return from London ten days later.

In a whirl, Kate had sent presents to Greg and Cindy, and made up a hamper of treats – chocolates, biscuits, various tinned foods, glacé fruits and a Christmas pudding – for Fanny, before treating herself to various items of clothing – a couple of new sweaters, a hostess gown, high-heeled sandals, plus a cotton nightgown and matching peignoir, just in case she bumped into Alex on her way to the bathroom.

Alex arrived at the station ahead of her. The eight o'clock train was standing at Platform One. It was a bitterly cold morning. A hailstone-threaded north-east wind scurried along the platforms.

"Ah, there you are," Alex commented drily, "I'd begun to think you'd changed your mind at the last minute."

"Why? I'm not late, am I?" Kate asked anxiously, unaccountably nervous all of a sudden, wondering what she had let herself in for, feeling a bit like "Alice in Wonderland" about to disappear down a rabbit hole.

"This train's fairly crowded," Alex said, taking her by the elbow and urging her along to the front of the train. "Not to worry, I've booked

First Class seats from York to King's Cross so we should be able to get some decent coffee *en route*."

After heaving their cases into a luggage rack, he continued when they were seated, "We'll lunch at King's Cross then take a taxi to St John's Wood. I daresay the house will feel chilly to begin with, and the beds will need airing, but once the central heating and the electric blankets have been switched on, it will soon begin to thaw out, and so shall we!"

So Alex owned a house in St John's Wood? Not just a flat, but a whole house? Possibly a very large house, Kate reflected nervously, with an enormous kitchen and a cooker big enough to roast an ox, let alone a turkey. Well, so be it. Too late to turn back now!

The house, in a tree-lined avenue, was a three-storey building of Victorian vintage, with steps to the brass-letterboxed front door, a spacious vestibule set with richly patterned floor tiles, and with a half-glass inner door beyond which lay a wide hall and a broad mahogany staircase.

Picking up a scattering of mail which he stuffed carelessly into his valise, Alex led the way across the hall to the kitchen quarters where he fiddled briefly with the controls of the central heating system, while Kate, glancing about her new domain, felt somewhat nervous at the sight of an Aga cooker, stainless steel sinks and draining-boards and a towering refrigerator capable of holding and keeping fresh their Christmas food supply – when it had been purchased.

Daylight was fading. Alex was right about the house being chilly. Kate said, "Now might be a good time to do some shopping, don't you think? We'll need food for the morning, something for supper later on tonight."

"I'd thought of dining out. There's a decent restaurant in the shopping area," he said, having set the central heating controls to his satisfaction.

"No, Alex. I'd much rather settle in first, get my bearings, do the shopping, serve the supper, then have an early night." The last thing she wanted was to dine out in public before she'd had a bath or shower, and there wouldn't be any hot water for ages yet. Besides, she hadn't seen her room or switched on the electric blankets, and the Aga needed lighting and stoking in readiness for tomorrow, she pointed out to him.

"Of course, you are perfectly right," he admitted. "I had a man-servant in the old days, who took care of such matters for me after . . . well, no matter. Suffice to say that he knew his job like the back of his hand – an ex-army batman experienced in caring for officers and gentlemen. A veritable Jeeves to my ineffectual Bertie Wooster, if you like."

"What happened to him?" Kate asked.

"Oh, that? I pensioned him off when it became abundantly clear that the job was becoming too much for him," Alex said carelessly. "Found him a ground-floor room in a retirement home not far from here, where I knew he'd be well looked after for the rest of his days." He added, "Which reminds me, I must call round to see him before Christmas; take him a bottle of Scotch!"

In need of exercise and fresh air, Kate insisted on walking to the shopping centre, but before they left the Aga had been lit and fed coke from the fuel store, the electric blankets had been switched on, and the house had begun to feel marginally warmer than it had done before. It was a strange house, Kate thought: certainly spacious, even rambling, but lacking an atmosphere of homeliness – a so-called "woman's touch" – as if every reminder of the woman, once the mistress of the house, had been deliberately got rid of.

Finding a supermarket, Kate set about loading her shopping trolley with what she regarded as the necessities of life, as she had done so often in her "Don days". No shopping list necessary: she knew exactly what she wanted.

It hadn't quite dawned on her yet that she was actually here, in London, the world's most exciting city. Strange to think that, within striking distance of this common-or-garden supermarket lay the bright lights of Piccadilly, the Haymarket, Shaftesbury Avenue, the Strand, and Trafalgar Square. With luck, she'd be given the chance to explore the City to her heart's content whilst Alex was engaged in attending to the business matters he'd mentioned earlier. This time, not from the front seat of a double-decker bus, but on her own two feet.

At the supermarket checkout, Alex added to the contents of her trolley a bottle of malt whisky, smoked salmon, several boxes of chocolates, a roll of wrapping paper, and a large Christmas pudding.

"Not to worry, Kate," he said lightly, footing the bill, "I'll ring for a taxi!"

The house felt slightly warmer on their return. The central heating was obviously doing its stuff, and so was the Aga. Besides which, Alex had switched on the drawing room electric fire at full blast before they'd set out on their shopping expedition. Even so, the room still felt cold to Kate's way of thinking, robbed of a woman's touch – flowers and family photographs, chintz-covered armchairs and settees. Or perhaps the ex-Mrs Alex Arden had not cared much for chintz; had preferred leather settees and armchairs?

In the kitchen, unpacking the groceries, Kate placed bacon, sausages, milk, vegetables, a cold roast chicken and the smoked salmon in the refrigerator; tins of salmon, tuna, soup, baked beans and corned beef in the store cupboards above the laminated work surfaces. In the cupboards beneath the sink units, bottles of washing-up liquid, household bleach, and so on, necessities of life which most men assumed grew on trees.

Her bedroom at least had not been stripped bare of womanly touches: cretonne-skirted dressing table, triple mirror, matching bedside tables with pink-shaded lamps. But hardly likely that Alex would have bothered about guest rooms occupied by weekend visitors. There was Chanel soap and bubble-bath in the en-suite bathroom, fluffy pink towels and a basket containing small items such as hairpins, a spare toothbrush, shower-cap and body lotion.

Kate wondered if Alex occupied what had once been the marital bedroom, or if he had elected to sleep elsewhere when his wife went away?

The water was not yet hot enough for a bath, she discovered, running the washbasin tap. Washing her hands and face, she changed her outdoor clothes for a lightweight tweed skirt and one of her new sweaters, applied a modicum of make-up, combed her hair and went downstairs to get the supper ready.

Alex appeared in the kitchen to find her preparing salad, washing lettuce, slicing tomatoes, red and green peppers, de-stringing celery and grating carrots.

"I'll carve the bird," he said, "and we'll eat in the drawing room, near the fire."

"It's not exactly heart-warming food, is it?" Kate said.

"No, but there's plenty of it, and we can at least boil the kettle for some hot coffee – to soften the blow."

He was being kind, and she was grateful for small mercies. One never knew with Alex if one was in for a kick or a kiss, metaphorically speaking. In bad humour, he'd have probably said that she was to blame for turning down his dinner invitation at that "decent restaurant" he'd mentioned earlier.

"Quite honestly," she said, "I'm not in the mood for salad. I'll settle for a chicken sandwich and a cup of coffee, then have an early night, if you don't mind."

"Me too," he said unexpectedly. "You see, I'll need to make an early start in the morning. I've arranged several important appointments with my bank manager, estate agent, and literary agent. And, well, quite frankly, I feel that I'm giving you a raw deal, leaving you on your own all day – a stranger in a strange place."

"If that's bothering you, forget it," Kate reassured him. "I have plans of my own in mind!"

"Really?" He frowned slightly. "Such as?"

"Oh, visiting the National Gallery; looking up at Nelson's Column; standing on Westminster Bridge. You know the kind of thing I mean?"

"All by yourself?" Alex's frown deepened at the thought of Kate alone in London.

"Yes, of course. Why not? I've been 'all by myself' for some time now. I'm beginning to get used to it, to value my independence. One day, in the not too dim and distant future, I may even take a trip abroad, to Paris, for instance, to see the Eiffel Tower, Notre Dame – the Mona Lisa!"

They ate their chicken sandwiches and drank coffee in front of the drawing room fire. "Well, what do you think of the house?" Alex asked abruptly.

Sensing a mood change from the affable to the impossible, Kate replied cagily, "I don't really know; I haven't seen all of it yet."

"In which case, if you've finished eating, perhaps you'd care for a guided tour?" Arden suggested sourly. He added flamboyantly, "Might as well get used to catering to the curious since I've decided to sell it! And you *are* one of the curious, aren't you, Kate? So come with me, allow me to introduce you to my fine spacious dining room, the scene of more bloody awful dinner parties than I care to remember!

"My ex-wife had a penchant for parties, you see? Any excuse would do for the killing of the fatted calf! Note the mahogany dining table and twelve chairs, the marble-topped Georgian side table, the silver candelabrum. Impressive, don't you agree?"

"Please don't, Alex," Kate pleaded, suddenly afraid of his loss of control. As if years of built-up tension had focused suddenly on the storm centre of his life so that he could no longer hold back his intensity of hatred towards a woman who, presumably, he had once loved enough to ask her to marry him.

"And this, Kate, is my study," Alex said, opening the door of a small, book-lined room with a central desk, typewriter, and piles of A4 paper. "At least it was in the dim and distant past when I knew how to write. A forgotten art nowadays, I'm afraid!"

It was there, in that room, glancing at the titles of the books on display, that Kate, adding two and two together, realised that the author Sandy Alexis, whose output of travel books had been published to great acclaim twenty years ago, and Alex Arden were one and the same person.

"Why didn't you tell me?" she asked.

"Because Sandy Alexis no longer exists," he said briefly. "He died and was buried; forgotten a long time ago."

Eight

E arly next morning, Kate came downstairs and went into the drawing room to clear the remains of last night's supper. Crossing to the rear window, she drew back the curtains. There were French doors leading to a paved terrace, a long garden beyond: frost-rimed grass, stark trees, high brick walls, neglected shrubberies.

The house felt warmer. Crossing the hall to the kitchen, she refuelled the Aga, deriving a modicum of comfort from the performance of a task as familiar to her as breathing. Even so, the atmosphere of the house weighed heavily on her, and the sleepless night she'd spent worrying about Alex's state of mind had undermined her hard-won self-confidence, her pleasurable anticipation of the days ahead. Her so-called holiday.

She was washing up the coffee cups and plates from the night before when Alex entered the kitchen.

He said, without preamble, "I owe you an apology for my bad behaviour last night. Please, forgive me!"

Facing him, she knew that he hadn't slept either. His face looked grey; eyes haunted. The eyes of a man forced to look into the depths of his own soul; to hate and despise what he had found there.

"What is there to forgive?" she said.

"Bringing you here in the first place," he said tautly. "I should have known better! I knew, you see, what would happen the minute I entered this damned house again! And I was right! They were all here, awaiting my return, those bloody awful memories of mine!"

"Sit down, Alex! I'll make some coffee. I know what you're going through, believe me!"

"That's just it, Kate," he said despairingly, "you couldn't begin to know, how could you, the way I felt when my wife told me the child I adored as my own son, Peter, was not mine at all, but the result of a one night stand during one of those damnable weekend house parties of hers, with a man whom I had regarded as my best friend!"

He continued hoarsely, "When Leonora finally told me the truth, not kindly but cruelly, relishing every detail of the telling, I lost control of myself completely! Told her to get out of the house; to go to the devil for all I cared. Her and her bastard son included!"

He covered his face with his hands. "If I had only known! I loved that child so much, you see? Had I kept control of my emotions, not acted so hastily, begged Leonora to leave Peter with me, things might well have worked out quite differently in the end."

Sitting opposite him at the kitchen table, Kate asked quietly, "So exactly what did happen?"

Uncovering his face, staring into the past, Alex said haltingly, "Leonora's car was parked in the road in front of the house. She got into it, dragging Peter by the hand. I made no attempt to stop her! I was so bloody angry, so bloody-minded, that I just wanted rid of her as quickly as possible. *Her*, not Peter! After all, an innocent child I had brought up and loved dearly as my own flesh and blood, until . . ."

"Go on, please," Kate begged him. "I'm listening."

Alex said tonelessly, as if drained of emotion, "I watched the car drive away. Leonora at the wheel, the boy beside her, his face wet with tears, not knowing what was happening, calling out to me, "Dadda, Dadda," over and over again until the car was out of sight.

"At midnight, the police arrived on the doorstep to break the news that my wife's car had been involved in a fatal accident at a busy roundabout on the outskirts of Oxford; that both she and her passenger, a child aged seven years or so, had died instantaneously when their vehicle had struck the bonnet of a ten-ton lorry travelling in the opposite direction."

Reliving the horror of that night, he said, "I nearly went crazy with grief over Peter. I should have kept him with me at any cost. Should have held my temper in check. I couldn't see beyond Leo's betrayal at the time; that Peter was no part of me. It was hearing him calling my name, the look of misery on his face that brought me to my senses. But it was too late then. I'd lost him, the only person I've ever really loved."

His face crumpled suddenly. Tears were close to the surface. Shoulders hunched forward, mouth trembling, he was fighting hard for self-control.

Understanding Alex's suffering, knowing that whatever she said would sound trite or inadequate under the circumstances, Kate made some toast and coffee.

"I don't want anything to eat," he said wearily.

"Fair enough. But at least drink your coffee," she said levelly. "What time is your first appointment, by the way?"

"Ten o'clock. And, thanks, Kate."

"For what?"

"Not smothering me with sympathy. I don't deserve it."

"I've learned that we don't always get what we deserve, in this life," Kate said wistfully, looking back into her own past. "In any case, sympathy isn't always the answer. A helping hand, a bit of common-sense advice is far more useful in the long run."

"Really?" Alex attempted a smile. "So what piece of common-sense advice are you about to offer me?"

"First and foremost, stop dwelling on the past and look to the future! Your advice to me, as I recall. What's done is done, and can't be undone. How did Omar Khayyám put it? 'The moving finger writes; and, having writ, moves on: nor all thy piety nor wit. . .' I'm sorry, I've forgotten the rest of the quotation."

" 'Shall lure it back to cancel half a line, nor all thy tears wash out a word of it,' " Alex reminded her.

"Well yes," Kate conceded, deeply aware of her dislike of the house, longing to get away from it as quickly as possible, sensing something unnerving about it. A vengeful watcher in the shadows, perhaps?

"Meaning what, exactly?"

"That you should cram all your business appointments into one day, if possible; that you – I mean we – should then catch the first available train home!"

"Back to Scarborough, you mean?"

"Where else?" Kate asked.

"But I thought you had your own plans in mind?" Alex demurred. "Shopping, sight-seeing and so on?"

"Oh, forget all that," Kate adjured him. "Frankly, I'd far rather spend Christmas alone in my own flat than stay here in this dreadful, ghost-ridden house a moment longer than necessary."

"Ghost-ridden?" Alex asked sharply. "You mean you've seen something that – frightened you?"

"No, not at all! Something far more subtle than that! A sense of –

brooding evil in the atmosphere, impossible to explain or to quantify. As if our presence here is unwelcome."

Arden shuddered. "I know. I've been aware of it myself. And I think you are right, that we should go back. I'll do as you suggest, make my business appointments as brief as possible. My bank manager had suggested lunching together. I'll make my apologies."

Drinking the last of his coffee, he stood up. "I could ring the estate agent I have in mind; ask him to look over the house this afternoon. That can't be avoided, I'm afraid. I'll explain it's a matter of some urgency; say I'm leaving London sooner than expected. At the same time, I'll arrange the removal of the furniture for auction."

"All of it?" Kate asked.

"Every stick of it," he said brusquely. "I hope never to set eyes on it ever again."

"But what about your books?" Kate spoke anxiously, not wanting him to act in haste, repent at leisure.

"You mean Sandy Alexis's books? The works of a dead and forgotten author? No, Kate, they can go on a bonfire for all I care!"

"They'll do no such thing," she protested vehemently. "*I* want them."

"*You?*" Alex frowned. "But why the hell should you?"

"For my brother," she said, "because they meant so much to him. Quite simply, you were a kind of 'folk hero' of his twenty years ago, along with T.E. Lawrence and 'Grey Owl'."

"Two other 'phonies' as I recall," Alex said sarcastically. "But if you want them, take them, they're yours!"

"You misunderstand," Kate said proudly, "I want to buy them, not have them given to me as a – load of rubbish! Because they are *not* rubbish, and you know it!"

"Very well, Kate, have it your way!" Alex glanced at his watch. "Before I go, what are your plans for the day?"

"I'm staying here," she said decisively. "Only right and proper, don't you agree? After all, I am your 'housekeeper', and it would seem a pity not to cook you a decent meal in the Aga – before it finally goes out."

When Alex had gone, alone in the house, Kate wandered from room to room – a fine, spacious house, worth a great deal of money, she surmised, albeit an unhappy house in view of the dreadful happenings that had taken place there.

And yet she was not sorry that she had come here. Doing so had given her a deeper insight into his past life, his difficult to understand personality; rapid mood changes, outbursts of temper, yet his underlying decency of spirit – witness his kindness towards his old retainer, for whom he had bought a litre of malt whisky as a Christmas present to take to him in the retirement home Alex had chosen for him, footing the bills for his upkeep himself, more than likely, Kate assumed. Correctly, as it later transpired . . .

She kept well out of the way that afternoon, in the kitchen, when Alex and the estate agent were together discussing matters pertaining to the sale of the property, busying herself in preparations for the evening meal.

When the man had gone, Alex said urgently, "Look, Kate, I really must visit my old friend Gabriel Owens before supper; take him his Christmas present. You do understand, don't you, that I couldn't possibly leave London tomorrow without saying goodbye to him?"

"Of course I do," she assured him. "In fact, I'd like to come with you, if you don't mind."

"Mind? Of course I don't mind. Why should I?"

And so they went together to visit Gabriel Owens, a still-handsome man despite his years; obviously frail now, yet possessed of a lively intelligence, who obviously adored his former employer.

"My dear Mr Alex," he said shakily, attempting to rise from his wheelchair, "how good it is to see you again! You've made Christmas for me, you really have!"

"Stop trying to show off, Gaby," Alex said huskily, kissing the old man's forehead. "Sit down and shut up! Just because there's an attractive woman in the room! This, by the way, is my – friend – Kate Ford."

Stepping forward to shake hands with Gaby, Kate explained, light heartedly, "Actually, I'm Mr Arden's current housekeeper."

Gaby's eyes twinkled. "Well, you're far better looking than the old 'un, that's for sure!"

He was obviously over the moon with the bottle of whisky Alex placed in his lap on the point of their departure. Tears filled his eyes when they bade him goodbye. He said proudly, choking back his emotion, "I'll never forget your kindness to me, Mr Alex. The peace of mind you've given me, in my old age!"

Tucking the old man's rug about his knees, hiding his own emotion, albeit unsuccessfully, Alex said brusquely, "The trouble with you, Gaby, you chose the wrong career! You should have been a parson, not a bloody batman!"

Bending down to clasp the old man's hands in hers, Kate murmured, "I'm so pleased to have met you, Mr Owens. Well, goodbye for now, and God bless!"

Retaining her hands in his, digging his nails into her palms, Gaby murmured fervently, sotto voce, "Please, promise me you'll stay with him, take care of him, for my sake, and his! You see, he really does need someone to take care of him!"

Kate murmured softly, in reply, "Very well, Gaby. At least I'll try."

She and Alex dined royally on their return from the old people's home, on smoked salmon and the chicken casserole she had prepared earlier. At least they might have done so had either of them felt hungry.

Kate asked warily, "Did you see your literary agent, this morning?"

"No, I cancelled the appointment. There was really no point since I haven't even got to grips with my book about Scarborough." He paused briefly, then continued, "Remember when you came upstairs that day to find me on my hands and knees trying to sort out my notes and photographs?"

"Shall I ever forget?" Kate murmured, tongue in cheek. "The day I walked out on you; told you that what you needed was a skivvy, not a housekeeper?"

"I was angry, that day," Alex said despondently, "because I knew that I was a spent force so far as writing's concerned! I'd been up since the crack of dawn, attempting an opening chapter which any sixth form schoolboy might have tackled far more successfully than I, a so-called professional writer, could ever hoped to have done, given the prevailing circumstances. Lack of self-confidence, for one thing, in my ability to string together two sentences, plus a synopsis which I knew damn well that my agent, let alone a hard-nosed publisher, would reject out of hand. And rightly so. Very kindly, of course. Nevertheless the bitterest pill of all to swallow!"

"But aren't you jumping the gun a little?" Kate queried intently. "Isn't it possible that, given time, you may well regain your old prowess as a writer?"

"No, I don't think so," Alex said briefly. "Too much water has passed under the bridge since my 'glory days' as Sandy Alexis, when, travelling the world in search of adventure, from the Gobi Desert to the rain forests of the Amazon, I somehow assumed the mantle of an explorer. I was nothing of the kind. A dilettante with a penchant for words would be nearer the mark.

"I made no discoveries of importance. I simply indulged a passion for travel, losing myself in far flung places, made observations, kept diaries which I extended and enlarged upon when I returned to so-called civilisation. This was simply a means of filling the empty spaces of my life – a rejected human being with money to burn. The success of my books went to my head like strong wine. For the first time in my life, I was in demand: feted, famous.

"Then I made the greatest mistake of my life. I married Leonora."

"Were you in love with her?" Kate asked quietly.

Alex shrugged. "I thought I was. She was very beautiful, incredibly sexy. Not clever, but smart, quick-witted. I soon discovered that she was also incredibly selfish: wanting the good things of life, clothes, money, jewellery. Not that I blamed her for wanting what most women want – beautiful women, that is. Above all, Leo wanted admiration, to be the centre of attention, and she was, believe me, on a seemingly endless merry-go-round of parties, dinner dances, cocktail and champagne parties, house parties. You name it."

He brushed a hand across his eyes wearily, a gesture Kate found infinitely touching, revealing as it did the little boy lost, lurking beneath a manly façade.

He said slowly, painfully, "I desperately wanted a child. Leo told me, in no uncertain terms, that a baby was the last thing on earth she intended to be lumbered with."

He continued awkwardly, "Nothing would induce her to . . ." He stopped speaking abruptly, not knowing how to express that his marriage to Leonora had been a precautionary tale from beginning to end.

"Throw caution to the wind, you mean?" Kate suggested mildly. "Then it must have come as quite a shock when she told you she was pregnant? I imagine she gulled you into thinking that, on at least one occasion, she *had* thrown caution to the wind?"

"Well, yes. Or so I believed at the time," Alex conceded, deeply grateful of Kate's understanding, her way of coming to the nub and kernel of a problem and finding a solution, as she had done in suggesting spending Christmas in Scarborough, not in this prison-house of his, with all its unhappy memories of a past best forgotten if the future was to hold any meaning at all for a man robbed of all that he had once held dear to him. His wife, his son, Peter, his writing career. Above all, Peter, the only person he had ever really loved . . . until now!

Nine

They arrived back in Scarborough to steadily falling snow; twinkling fairy lights strung between the branches of trees in Westborough; crowds of people thronging the main shopping centre in search of last minute presents; red neon signs and brightly lit shop windows dispelling the gloom of a wintry December afternoon.

Emerging from the station, Alex hailed a taxi, handed the driver their luggage to stow in the boot of his car, and gave his Newborough address as their destination.

Making no comment as the taxi sped into the traffic, Kate realised that Alex had taken for granted their spending Christmas together under his roof. Not that she minded. They could scarcely have taken separate taxis to different destinations.

This way, at least she would be able to fulfil her promise to Gaby Owens to "take care" of Alex to the best of her ability: to make certain he had enough to eat and drink over the Christmas period; a warm, comfortable bed to sleep in; holly and mistletoe; a Christmas tree in the sitting room; soft lights and sweet music; roast turkey plus the usual trimmings for Christmas Day lunch.

She would enjoy to the full all the shopping, cooking and planning involved, relevant not only to Alex's comfort and well-being, but hers also, as a woman in need of the fulfilment denied her so often during her "Don days" – when she had discovered, to her dismay, that Don regarded Christmas as a pagan, not a Christian festival. And yet they had been married in St Mary's Church.

But *why*? she had often wondered since then. Why the pretence of a solemn, Church of England wedding ceremony which the bridegroom, an agnostic, must have viewed, all along, as a sham, a kind of sick joke, even as he had uttered his vows of fidelity to one woman alone for the rest of his life?

Deep down, Kate knew exactly why. Because Don had wanted her

68

physically – a desirable young girl on the threshold of life – and marrying her had seemed the only way of gaining entry to her bed. Morality had been much stronger in those days. Girls of her generation had been taught to "save" themselves for their wedding night. The war had undermined morality to some extent, Kate realised, and it was easy to understand why. Young men on embarkation leave not knowing when – or even if – they would return home when the war was over. Young girls desperate to give the ultimate proof of their love before it was too late. Living for the moment with no thought of the future. There, but for the Grace of God . . .

Of course she had wanted, desperately at times, to give Don the ultimate proof of her love, before marriage. Head over heels in love with him, she had come dangerously close to forgetting her upbringing and her mother's strongly held views on morality. Not that she had ever preached sermons on the subject. A gentle person, she had stated simply her beliefs in what she'd termed "decency", the "honourable estate of matrimony", based on the happiness of her own marriage to a decent, forebearing man who had obviously not sought sexual favours from her until their honeymoon at a small hotel in Blackpool.

Would things have been different, Kate wondered, had she succumbed to Don's passionate desire to possess her during the days and nights of the courtship? More than likely, had he done so, their wedding might well have never taken place at all! Too late to wish, now that it hadn't!

That way, at least she'd have been spared the final humiliation of betrayal, the untold grief of three miscarriages, the wasted years of caring for a man who, obviously, hadn't cared a damn about her in the long run!

"Well don't just stand there dreaming, Kate!" she heard Alex saying forcefully. "Hadn't we better go shopping? Don't know about you, but I'm so hungry I could eat a horse!"

"Yes, of course," Kate said mildly, returning to the present, thankful to be home once more, well distanced from that ghost-ridden house in St John's Wood. "I'm ready when you are."

She had never enjoyed a shopping spree so much before. In expansive mood, he'd marched into the St Helen's Square Market Hall, a stone's throw away from his flat, to fill their shopping bags to capacity with fresh fruit and vegetables before turning his attention to a butcher's stall, when Kate had pointed out to him the inadvisability of ordering a twenty pound turkey which they'd never get through in a month of Sundays.

"Very well, then, you do the ordering," he said, "while I take a look at those Christmas trees over yonder!"

Amused by Alex's enthusiasm, at the same time Kate couldn't help thinking that he seemed a shade too excited, febrile almost, verging on impatience, as if he wanted Christmas organised, over and done with as soon as possible. On the other hand, it was good to think that his enthusiasm derived from the release from spending Christmas in London. And if he had taken for granted that they would spend Christmas together in his flat, so be it. Just as long as his present state of euphoria lasted long enough to ensure a happy and peaceful holiday together. So why the uneasy feeling that it might not?

Deep down, Kate had to admit to herself that she liked Alex's flat far better than hers. Well, his was not really a flat at all, but a house with a private entrance, no busy-body neighbours to twitch back net curtains or notice their comings and goings.

Privacy meant a great deal to her. A throwback to April Cottage, Kate imagined, set in a half acre of ground, far removed from the staring eyes of curious neighbours. The reason why she had never really cottoned on to Greg and Cindy's modern bungalow on a housing estate in the Greater Manchester area, the garden of which was overlooked by the owners of similar bungalows, within a mile-wide radius of neatly-mown lawns, bird-baths, fishponds, rose-beds, and herbaceous borders.

Now, on Christmas Eve, listening to the Service of Nine Lessons and Carols broadcast from King's College, Cambridge, making preparations for Christmas Day, baking mincepies and sausage rolls, Kate had seldom felt happier in her life then she did then, thinking that she had, perhaps, come home at last. She was finally acknowledging the strong tide of feeling running between herself and Alex Arden. If not love, then damn close to it, she realised. He was, after all, a man who had occupied the greater part of her life since their first meeting, without whom her life would scarcely be worth the living, or so she believed, pushing to the back of her mind that she had once felt the same way about Don, wondering if she had a penchant for charismatic men who treated her badly at times.

These past few days, at least, Alex had been utterly charming towards her; helping her to set up the Christmas tree in the sitting room and decorate it with coloured fairy lights; poking and prying about the kitchen when she was busily occupied in preparing and cooking their supper, obviously with something important on his mind by the way he looked at her, thoughtfully, intently, then dismissively, as if what he had intended saying to her would be far better left unsaid.

After Christmas Day lunch, he suggested taking a walk to Castle Hill to blow away the cobwebs from his mind. The bitter wind blowing in from the sea would certainly do that, Kate thought, as they battled their way to the headland overlooking the Marine Drive, a broad road at the base of the cliffs, linking the north and south bays, almost devoid of traffic and pedestrians on this cold December afternoon.

Families would be indoors on a day like this, gathered round the fire, children playing with their new toys, although a few intrepid individuals were on the north beach, walking their dogs – one individual, a tall man with grey hair and wearing a Burberry, apparently shell-gathering. Alex, on the other hand, appeared to be wool-gathering.

"You're very quiet," Kate commented. "Is anything the matter?"

"Yes, as it happens," he said, as if relieved that she had asked him. "I've been meaning to tell you."

"Tell me – what?"

"The fact is, I entered negotiation some weeks ago with the owner of my flat, with a view to buying the property outright, the gift shop included. This entered my mind when I decided to sell my London house. I didn't want to find myself homeless."

"Well, that's fine, isn't it?" Kate asked uncertainly, puzzled by his apparent lack of enthusiasm. "Unless the deal fell through?"

"No, it didn't. The owner was happy to accept my offer. He was on the verge of retirement anyway, and my offer was generous, to say the least."

"I see," Kate said bemusedly. "But what about the shop?"

"No problem," Alex assured her. "The manageress has agreed to keep it on as a going concern."

Then why her gut feeling that something was wrong? Kate wondered. Why her instinctive, sneaking suspicion that he was holding something back?

She said, shivering in the teeth of the cold north-east wind, "I've had enough fresh air for the time being. I'd rather like to go home now, if you don't mind."

Unexpectedly, Alex said, "I'm glad you regard it as such, Kate. Gull House as your home, I mean!"

She hadn't a clue what he meant – unless? Her heart lifted suddenly to the possibility that he had in mind a proposal of marriage. If not a marriage made in heaven, at least a deep and lasting relationship based on their need of one another.

There would be certain pitfalls along the way, Kate realised; heated exchanges of opinion; endless rows, soon over and done with. But above all, an underlying understanding of one another's past lives, which had shaped their present destinies beyond their power of control.

Unlike Don, Alex was not a womaniser, thank God. A little too rich for her liking, perhaps, whilst she was clinging on, for dear life, to her nest-egg from the sale of April Cottage. Even so, taking all these things into consideration, if Alex asked her to marry him, Kate knew she'd say yes. Why? Because she had fallen deeply in love with him. As simple as that!

Kate made tea on their return home from their wind-scoured walk to Castle Hill and back, rejoicing inwardly that Alex had possessed the foresight to purchase the property he now regarded as home. Hers also, one day, God willing. "Gull House" – she liked the name enormously.

"Could you be happy living here?" he said. "Leaving your own flat?" As if he had somehow read her mind.

"Moving in with you, you mean?" She had to be sure of her ground.

He frowned slightly, "That's not exactly what I had in mind."

"Then – what? I'm sorry, I don't understand."

"I asked you a question. You haven't given me an answer. Please, Kate, I need an answer. It's very important."

"An answer to what exactly?" She hadn't the remotest idea what he was driving at. An air of unreality had crept into the conversation.

"It's simple enough, surely? I asked if you'd be happy living here; giving up your own flat."

"That's two questions," she reminded him. "When I asked if you wanted me to move in with you, you said that wasn't exactly what you had in mind. So tell me, Alex, what have you in mind? I'm no good at guessing games."

A sudden thought occurred, a possible solution of the mystery, utterly ludicrous, and yet . . . She said disbelievingly, "Don't tell me you want a live-in housekeeper? Someone at your beck and call all the hours that God sends? If so, the answer is no! I'd rather keep my independence!"

"You misunderstand entirely," he said quietly. "What I'm in need of is not a housekeeper but a reliable tenant to look after the property. Please hear me out, Kate, before you climb aboard your independence bandwagon. What I'm offering you is rent-free tenancy of this house, plus expenses to cover the costs of maintenance – repairs, heating, and so on, plus an increase of your present salary to ensure your peace of mind during my – absence." He paused briefly. "Think about it, Kate. It's an offer worth your consideration, at least I hope so."

Kate looked at him disbelievingly. "During your absence?" she uttered bleakly. "You mean you are going away?"

"I have to," he said wearily.

"But where to? For how long?" She felt that her world had shattered suddenly like broken glass, as it had done so often before; when her parents had died, when she had failed so miserably to give birth to those dream children of hers. Above all, when Don had walked out of her life, leaving her alone in April Cottage to piece together the shattered fragments of her life as best she could. Now, she could scarcely bear the thought of losing Alex; of picking up the pieces of her life all over again.

"I can't answer your questions, I'm afraid," he said tautly, "for the simple reason that I don't know where I'm going or how long I'll be gone. That depends on how long it takes to find what I'm looking for, and where."

"And what *are* you looking for?" Kate asked him in a low voice, hoarse with emotion, in desperate need of reassurance that he regarded her as something more than an – employee. Or perhaps she was wrong in believing – hoping – that they had some kind of a future together?

"Peace of mind," he told her, speaking gently, knowing he had hurt her, at the same time realising how much more he would hurt her by staying on here in his present mood: an overwhelming restlessness of spirit, impossible to deny or to come to terms with until he'd had time and space enough to distance himself from the past, to try, at least, to make sense of his life.

How simple it would be to take the soft option, to tell Kate that he had fallen in love with her; ask her to marry him, and take it from there. And then what? He knew only too well. He would make her life a misery. Inevitably so, resultant upon his introspective concern with the past, those events: hatred of his parents, the faithlessness of his wife Leonora, the death of her son, Peter; the loss of his writing ability, which had changed him, beyond recognition, from the man he once was, to the man he was now – a sour, tetchy individual, incapable of either happiness or peace of mind, until he taken a journey into nowhere; a voyage of discovery, perchance, not into the past, but the future.

He had in mind, albeit vaguely, Afghanistan, Turkestan, Mongolia – wide open spaces far away from the pressures of modern day living: back-packing, carrying with him merely a razor, toothbrush, a couple of spare shirts and cashmere sweaters; wearing boots and an anorak; sleeping under the stars . . .

"Very well, then," Kate said coldly, "I'll think about it. But if I accept your offer, it will be with certain reservations. First and foremost that I may not still be here, if and when you decide to come back to Scarborough again. In which case, should I leave the property empty, or sub-let it to another 'reliable' tenant, such as myself?"

"Please, Kate," Alex implored her, "don't make things more difficult for me than they already are!"

"I'm sorry," she said, realising the futility of argument. "It's entirely up to you to make the necessary arrangements, to come and go as you please. It's your life when all is said and done. I just hope you'll find what you're looking for."

They had been sitting near the fire, by lamplight and the twinkling lights of the Christmas tree, in a shadowy corner of the room. When she'd brought in the food from the kitchen, the sandwiches, the cakes she'd made, the tea-things, placing then on the low coffee table drawn up between them near the hearth, she had experienced a thrill of pleasure in Alex's company. Getting up to clear the table, she wondered how she would feel, alone in the house, when he had gone away? Would the loneliness prove unbearable as it had done at April Cottage when Don had left her?

Alex's presence had filled the house, as it had filled her life. The place would seem empty without him. She might well feel nervous all alone in a house of this size. Besides which, how would she fill in the empty days ahead of her with no one apart from herself to cook for?

But beggars could not be choosers. This way, at least she'd be spared the necessity of seeking alternative employment, she would have a safe roof over her head for the foreseeable future. Alex, she knew, could be trusted to secure, legally, the financial details of her future welfare, as only a rich man, with money to burn, possessed the power to do.

And yet, Kate considered wistfully, after carrying the tea things through to the kitchen, her hands deep in the washing-up water, had Alex been as poor as the proverbial church mouse, and had he asked her to marry him, without a penny to his name, she would not have hesitated to say yes to his proposal. Loving him so much, how could she possibly have said no?

When later, he followed her into the kitchen to ask what she had planned for supper, she said crisply, proudly, "Sorry, Alex, I've decided to go home, to spend the rest of the holiday alone."

Ten

S he needed space, time to think things through coolly and calmly.
Above all, realistically.

She and Alex had been through a great deal lately. Their ill-fated trip
to London, the atmosphere of the house in St John's Wood, discovery
of the secrets of his past life, had heightened, intensified her feelings
towards him. But was she really in love with him, or merely seeking
security, as she had been when she married Don?

She could see it all clearly now, her desperate need of love and
security after the deaths of her parents, so that she had not even
stopped to consider what she might be letting herself in for, rushing into
marriage the way she had done.

Greg had tried to warn her, to no avail. She hadn't wanted to listen,
so certain of her love for Don that she had brushed aside her brother's
misgivings as airily as a cobweb on a window pane.

Alone in her flat, looking out at the lights of the Valley Bridge, being
brutally honest with herself, Kate recognised and accepted the similarities between the past and the present. Alex, like Don, had entered her
life when she stood in need of help and support. Both were charismatic
and clever, charming yet selfish.

Alex had been born rich. Don had become rich eventually by reason
of his relentless, driving ambition to climb to the top of his chosen
profession as a writer. Alex, on the other hand, had become a famous
writer more by accident than design.

As for herself, Kate realised, all Don had really wanted from her was
sex and children. Alex apparently wanted a dogsbody. A custodian.
Obviously he harboured no deeper feelings for her. She was simply a
handy person to have around to provide his creature comforts. A
difficult man to understand or get close to.

Thankfully, she had betrayed no sign of her feelings towards him.
And what did those feelings really amount to? Had she mistaken

sympathy, physical attraction, his powerful presence in her life for love? Had she imagined that tide of feeling, running between them so strongly at times? Had she fooled herself into believing that they might find happiness together?

Common sense told her the sooner she relinquished hope of a future with Alex, the better. Reaching a decision about the future must be based on doing what was best for herself and no one else.

Two choices were open to her. She could stay on here in this flat, start looking for another job and put all thoughts of Alex out of her mind. Or, she could accept his offer of continuing employment as the custodian of his house, as such retaining her links with him, however tenuous they may be; living in hope that he would, one day, return to Scarborough.

Kate sat in her chair near the window till the early hours of next morning. When she finally got up, rather stiffly, at three a.m., switched off the lights and went to bed, she had reached her decision.

Alex had spent a miserable time since Kate's departure. Even so, he had recognised her need of solitude to think over the proposals he had put to her in his usual clumsy fashion, God dammit!

Somehow, he had never been able to express his feelings for her in words: clearly, simply and succinctly, as he had so often wished to do. Why not? he wondered.

Deep down, he knew the answer. Because he was afraid of commitment, of possible rejection by another woman, apart from his mother and – Leonora.

The desolation of his past life still clung to him as a shroud. Never had his mother shown the slightest degree of affection towards him. She had simply appeared to him as a glamorous, butterfly creature flitting in and out of his childhood on her way to some function or other, passing his nursery on her way downstairs without bothering to kiss him goodnight.

He had grown up taking wealth for granted – the opulence of the family home in Hampstead, richly furnished, with servants at their beck and call. Their riches were derived from various sources; tea plantations in Ceylon, timber mills in Canada, cattle ranches in Texas – handed down from father to son, from son to grandson and so on, originating with a long dead and gone forebear of his who had created the wealth of the Arden family in the first place. Alex's great, great grandfather, Adam Arden.

The plantations, mills and ranches had been sold off to other companies in the course of time; assets ploughed into other ventures closer to home. Alex's grandfather had established a chain of food-stores in major cities the length and breadth of Britain, had invested money in country properties going for a song, which he had upgraded and turned into luxury hotels.

With visionary foresight, he had also bought into a publishing concern, a race-track, several famous hotels and theatres in the centre of London, and a film company situated in Elstree, on the outskirts.

It grieved Alex to think that, after the death of his grandfather, his own father had chosen to squander the family wealth in high living: countless holidays abroad, to the Caribbean, the Seychelles, Turkey, Morocco, Sardinia, Corfu, Paris, Rome, Nice; drinking far more than was good for him, not giving a damn that his only child had been condemned to life in a boarding school he'd loathed and detested. Later to a public school, equally hateful.

And yet, after the death of his father and mother in that fatal car crash on the Route Nationale, there had been more than enough money left in the family coffers to assure his own lifestyle for the foreseeable future, his grandfather's solicitor had assured him, anxious, at the same time, to impress on him his responsibilities as the heir of the Arden family fortune.

But young Alex, at that stage of his life, could not have cared less about responsibilities. All he had wanted was freedom. And so he had gone off into the wild blue yonder, leaving business matters in the hands of those who understood them far better than he ever would; appointing the solicitor, Mr Daker, a man of the highest integrity, to act on his behalf, instructing him to sell the Hampstead property and its contents, which he loathed and wished never to set eyes on again.

All that seemed a very long time ago. Now, history was about to repeat itself. His urge to travel was as strong as it had been then, and for the same reasons: a need of self discovery, of escape from the complexities of life. Curiously, the sale of another property, the house in St John's Wood, was involved in this, his second bid for freedom.

Missing Kate intensely, he thought suddenly of his promise to let her have those old books of his she wanted to give to her brother, and remembered, ruefully, that she had likened himself to T.E. Lawrence – Lawrence of Arabia. If only . . .

Even so, perhaps there were similarities inasmuch as Lawrence had also sought escape from his own persona. He had based *The Seven Pillars of Wisdom* on his experiences of the First World War when, as a British Intelligence officer, he had dramatically led the Arabs against the Turks to capture the seemingly impregnable fortress of Akabar for his own compatriots, his own country, to his everlasting fame and glory. And yet Lawrence, turning his back on fame and fortune, had ended his days as a low-ranking member of not the army but the RAF, a partial recluse living alone in a tiny cottage, "Clouds Hill", frugally furnished, close to his RAF camp in Dorset, and had died tragically in a road accident when the motorbike he was riding had swerved suddenly to avoid two boy cyclists and hit a tree. A fine, brave human being.

That, thought Alex, was where the similarity ended. There had been nothing in the least brave or fine about Alex's own life, so far. Nothing uplifting or transcendental. The best he could hope for was that his future would be more settled, more rewarding than his past.

Meanwhile, so much depended on Kate's decision regarding her own future, somehow linked inexplicably with his. So why was she taking so long to reach that decision? Why didn't she come to him to put him out of his misery?

The sudden realisation that she might well not come to him at all added to his misery. After all, why should she? She probably hated his guts! He hadn't been very kind to her at times, and she was so deserving of kindness, a lovely, intelligent, caring human being, albeit with a mind of her own, a mile wide streak of independence inside her. She'd taught him lessons in good manners more than once during their brief relationship, he recalled, willing her to come to him, knowing that his life, his future, would be unbearable without her.

Moreover, he was worried about her physical requirements. She had left abruptly, taking nothing with her apart from an overnight case. She had no food. What was she living on? Fresh air?

He spent Boxing Day restlessly pacing the house, pausing now and then to make lists of all that needed doing in readiness for his departure early in the new year.

There were urgent letters to be written to his trustees – descendants of old Mr Daker, who had died some time ago, informing them of his intention to go abroad for some considerable time, his destination as yet undecided.

Unable to settle, to think clearly, he wished that Kate was here to bring light and common sense to bear on his present state of confusion.

How could he possibly proceed further until he knew her answer to his proposals concerning the tenancy of the house?

Only one way to find out! Putting on his outdoor things, he hurried downstairs. Opening the door, he jerked back a little in surprise. Kate was there on the doorstep. He said abruptly, "I was just on my way to your flat. Well, don't just stand there! Come in!" What he really wanted to say was: "Thank God you've come. I've missed you!" But of course, he didn't say what he meant. Old habits died hard. He sounded tetchy, irritable.

"I'm not stopping long," Kate said, beginning to wish she hadn't come at all.

"Don't be ridiculous. Of course you're stopping. There's enough food in the fridge to feed an army!" Alex led the way upstairs.

"Food's the last thing on my mind at the moment," Kate retorted.

"Then for goodness sake sit down and tell me what is!"

"Very well. I've decided to accept your offer."

"You have? Thank God for that!" His relief was evident. He actually smiled at her. "So why the nonsense about not stopping? We have a great deal to discuss."

"Not now, Alex. In any case, what *is* there to discuss? All I need to know is when you'll be leaving. Meanwhile, I intend staying on in my own flat. A period of unpaid leave, if you like, time in which to make my own arrangements, to visit my family in Manchester, if you've no objection? Frankly, I'm tired, in need of a change and a rest before taking on the responsibilities of my new role as your – agent – for want of a better word."

"*Agent?*" He looked shocked. "Dammit, Kate, that's the last thing I had in mind!"

"I'm sorry, Alex," she said calmly, "but that's exactly what you have in mind. Someone to act on your behalf when you're away. You spoke of expenses to cover the costs of maintenance, repairs, heating and so on. All well and good, but it will be up to me to decide what to do, who to send for if, say, the roof springs a leak or the brickwork needs repointing, with insurance claim forms to fill in."

"And *you* said there's nothing to discuss," he reminded her tartly.

"There isn't, for the simple reason that it is up to you to leave me explicit instructions how to act in an emergency beforehand, some higher authority I can turn to for help if faced with something totally unexpected. A break in, a burglary, for example, connected with the gift shop next door."

"My God, Kate, you really have been doing your homework, haven't you?" Alex said sarcastically.

"Yes, I have." She smiled briefly, "Now, it's high time you did yours, don't you agree?" Thinking, at one and the same time, how much she would miss this cut and thrust between them when they were far apart from one another.

When Kate had gone, taking with her her heavier suitcase in the boot of a taxi, Alex set about doing his "homework" as she had suggested. The trouble was, he couldn't concentrate on the task in hand. Her image, the very thought of her, kept on getting in the way.

Speaking her mind, as usual, she had brought to his attention the heavy burden of responsibility her tenancy would entail if things went badly wrong with the property; the necessity of covering every eventuality – Acts of God, fire, flooding, theft – the mood he was in, possibly the collapse of the whole bloody building from old age, he shouldn't wonder, beginning to wish he'd never bought the damned house in the first place.

Even so, he marvelled at her perspicacity, her grasp of fundamentals, her sense of self-preservation, akin to his own. At their first meeting, he had seen her as a nervous, lonely, lost individual. And perhaps she had been, then. No longer. Had his own selfishness somehow rubbed off on her? he wondered. Had she finally reached the hard-won conclusion that she was nobody's fool, but a clear-sighted, straight-thinking individual, capable of standing alone on her own two feet?

Alex might well have changed his mind on that score, had he realised Kate's true state of mind concerning her future, her desperate need of the only person in the world she could turn to for help, comfort and advice. Her brother, Greg!

"Of course, Kate," he'd said on the phone, "you know you're more than welcome to stay with Cindy and me any time, for as long as you like!" He'd added anxiously, "You sound a bit fraught. There's nothing wrong, is there?"

"Nothing that seeing you again won't put right," she'd assured him, trying her best to sound light-hearted. "I'm just a bit tired, that's all; in need of spiritual refreshment. In any case, it will only be a flying visit. A long weekend, if that's all right?"

Greg said, "Cut the cackle, Sis! This is *me* you're talking to, remember? Don't tell me, let me guess! Another sandcastle built within reach of the incoming tide?"

"Something like that," Kate confessed. "Some folk never learn sense, do they?"

"I take it, then, that your latest 'sandcastle' has to do with what's his name? Alex Arden? Your rich employer?" Greg asked gently.

"Yes, it has," Kate admitted, "but I'd rather talk about it in person, not on the telephone, if you don't mind."

"Fair enough, love," Greg conceded thoughtfully, "so just tell me the date and time of your arrival. I'll meet your train, and we'll take it from there, shall we?"

Meeting her at the station, he took her to a nearby pub for a brandy and soda, saying she looked in need of a warmer. In any case, they could talk better in a quiet corner of the bar parlour than a crowded station buffet.

Dear Greg, she thought, always on her side, doing what was best for her, still taking care of her as he had done when they were children. Not making a fuss, that was not his style. He was not nor ever had been particularly handsome. He had no outstanding physical features. His hair, thinning a little now, was brown in colour, his eyes a light hazel, twinkling eyes betraying a sense of humour and much more besides – an innate wisdom and kindness of heart. She said, "Oh Greg, I've missed you so much," and wondered, not for the first time, if he and Cindy were happy together? Difficult to explain, but he didn't look – cared for. His shirt collar needed ironing, and his loosely fitting tweed jacket had seen better days.

"I've missed you too, Kate," he said quietly. "Now, tell me what's wrong."

It was harder than she'd expected to put her feelings into words. When Greg asked her gently if she was in love with Arden, "I don't honestly know," she confessed. "I thought so, now I'm not so sure. In any case, he's not in love with me, and a one-sided love affair just isn't possible." Kate smiled ruefully.

"And yet you're willing to take on the responsibilities of his house?" Greg queried.

"For purely selfish motives," she said. "I need a job, and this is the only offer I've had, so far."

"Doing what, exactly? I'm sorry, love, but won't you feel lonely and bored without something positive to do each day? A sense of purpose in life?"

He continued thoughtfully, "You've always been such an active person: cooking, cleaning, gardening, caring for others. Remember how you looked after Mum and Dad, running that big, old house of ours single-handed? Then, forgive me for saying so, I know all the hard work entailed in turning April Cottage into a home. I've kept all your letters. Remember, you used to write to me daily in diary form then post the letters to me when they were almost too fat to fit into the envelopes?"

"Yes, of course I remember," she said mistily.

"I still read through them now and again," Greg admitted fondly. "They were so brilliantly funny at times! You up a ladder, a paint pot in one hand, a brush in the other; that bird trapped in a chimney! You'd just nicely finished your painting when down came the bird along with a downfall of soot which stuck to the wet paint as if it had been glued onto it! So what did you do?"

"After spending the best part of an hour cornering the damn thing and hustling it into the garden to rejoin its wife and babies, I can't honestly remember," Kate said, frowning.

"Then I'll tell you exactly what you did. You sat cross-legged on the floor not knowing whether to laugh or cry. The compromise you reached was laughing till you cried."

"Did I really do that?" Kate asked wistfully.

"Much more. Next day you climbed back up your ladder to begin painting the room all over again!"

"I must have had a lot more energy then than I have now," she commented drily, "and a better sense of humour."

"We both had more energy in those days," Greg reminded her, "but there's nothing wrong with your sense of humour—"

"Yours either," she interrupted.

"Thanks, love." He paused momentarily. "What I'm trying to say is this. Don't make the same mistake you made over Don in letting Alex Arden rule your life, the way Don did. Remember that you are a person in your own right with a life of your own to live. All right?"

"Yes. Fine. Message received and understood," Kate assured him. Glancing at her watch, she added, "Won't Cindy be wondering where we've got to?"

"No. She's having her hair permed this afternoon. She left me instructions to give you sandwiches for lunch; said she'd be home around five to start cooking supper. Sorry, 'dinner' as she prefers to call it now she's rubbing shoulders with our rich new next door neighbours." Greg laughed. "The husband's in 'oil' by the way!"

"So are sardines," Kate said wickedly as she and her brother drained their glasses of brandy and left the pub, arm in arm, to find Greg's car, a battered Volkswagen, parked somewhere near the station, though he appeared to have forgotten exactly where.

"Not to worry, Sis," he said gaily, "it'll still be around somewhere or t'other. I mean to say, who, in their right senses, would want to pinch a clapped out Beetle? The bane of Cindy's life, by the way! She's always on at me to buy a better car, and I dare say she'll have her own way in the end. She usually does!"

At that moment, Kate knew beyond a shadow of doubt, that all was not well between her brother and his wife.

At the bungalow, Greg made "ham" sandwiches, as per Cindy's instructions, from a sliced white loaf of bread and a packet of moist luncheon meat.

Coming through to the kitchen from her bedroom where she had dumped her belongings, Kate could have wept at the sight of Greg cutting the crusts from the sandwiches.

"Here, let me help you," she said quickly. "You make the coffee – meanwhile, I'll slip the sandwiches under the grill to toast." At least toasting would dry out the limp luncheon meat to some extent, Kate thought, wondering, as she did so, what her lazy sister-in-law had planned for their so-called dinner? Something in oil? Sardines on toast, perhaps?

No wonder Greg's clothes were fairly hanging off him, Kate thought angrily, for the simple reason that he wasn't getting enough to eat! But what, if anything, could she do about it? Nothing, her common sense warned her. She was merely Greg's sister. Cindy, on the other hand, was his wife, the woman he had vowed to love and to cherish till death us do part, and in no way was she prepared to come between husband and wife, no matter how tempting the desire to do just that, to tell Cindy, in no uncertain terms, exactly what she thought of a woman too idle to iron her husband's shirt collars!

It was a fraught weekend, all told. When it was over and done with, Kate returned to Scarborough, to her own flat, to find a letter from Alex on her sitting room carpet, pushed under the door, most likely by her friend Fanny.

The letter read briefly:

Dear Kate,

This to inform you that all the legal details of your tenancy of "Gull House" have been dealt with, hopefully to your entire satisfaction. Also that, my travel arrangements having been concluded after various delays, I shall be leaving Scarborough on 14 January, prior to which date I suggest a meeting between us to conclusively iron out the final details to our mutual satisfaction.

Yours sincerely,

Alex

P. S. There'll be documents to sign, requiring both signatures, yours and mine.

So that's it, is it? Kate thought sadly, crumpling up the letter in the palm of her hand, the end of an affair that had never even begun. But ah, how dearly she wished that it had.

Part Two

Eleven

S he had lived through all this before, Kate thought. The circumstances were different but the feelings of loneliness and loss were every bit as acute now as they had been when Don walked out of her life.

She moved into Gull House the day before Alex's departure, thinking he'd need help with his last minute arrangements, plus a good breakfast inside him before catching the early morning train to King's Cross.

Knowing Alex, he'd probably say he wasn't hungry, but she would cook bacon and eggs anyway. Whether or not he ate it was up to him entirely. She couldn't force him to eat. A law unto himself, Alex would do exactly as he pleased. Men usually did, within her limited experience of the male gender.

As she had anticipated, the house was in an uproar upon her arrival: stacks of unwashed pots in the kitchen sink, dust everywhere, his bedroom a tip, clothes strewn on the floor, the Christmas tree still in situ in the living room, pine needles thick on the carpet, an unopened crate blocking the landing.

"As you can see, I'm in a bit of muddle," was his opening gambit as she followed him upstairs. "The crate, by the way, contains the books you wanted."

"Thanks," she said briefly, edging past it, wishing she possessed the leg power to kick the damn thing downstairs. Alex also, come to think of it!

Bitterly disappointed by his lack of enthusiasm at her appearance on his doorstep, marching into the kitchen, donning an apron and rolling back her sleeves, Kate made a start on the mess in the sink. A "bit of a muddle", she thought mutinously, a "disaster area" would be nearer the mark!

Every work surface was littered with biscuit tins, crumbs, bread and cheese boards, empty milk and wine bottles, stained glasses and coffee cups. Mice, if there were any, would be having a field day.

Next she tackled the sitting room. Alex came in to find her struggling to remove the Christmas tree in its bucket of soil.

"I'll do that," he said. "Where do you want it?"

"The yard might be a good idea. I thought you'd have got rid of it by this time."

"I've had other things on my mind. I've sold the car, by the way."

"No point in keeping it, I suppose. When you've seen to the tree, there are some bags of rubbish in the kitchen to go down to the dustbins; left over food from the refrigerator, empty wine bottles and so on." Her anger was apparent. "When I've finished clearing up after you, I'll go shopping."

"Well, I did warn you that things were in a bit of a mess. Your fault for walking out the way you did on Christmas Day," he reminded her.

"Funny, I thought you'd end up blaming me. But then, no good keeping a dog and doing the barking yourself, is there?" Her anger evaporated suddenly. "I'm sorry, I shouldn't have said that. After all, clearing up after you is what I'm being paid for, and I'll clean the house from top to bottom after you're gone!"

"That's up to you entirely. I want you to feel at home. Oh, remind me to give you a spare set of keys." He picked up the tree which promptly parted company with the container. Soil showered on to the carpet. That's all she needed, Kate thought, feeling the way she had done at April Cottage when that bird came down the chimney along with a mound of soot, not knowing whether to laugh or cry. Suddenly, she laughed.

Might as well make the best of a bad job, she told herself. There'd be all the time in the world to clear up when Alex had gone. No use ruining the little time they had left together being angry or upset.

When Alex returned from his trips to the yard via the kitchen fire-escape, she asked him, as she made coffee, if he'd decided where he was heading for? His ultimate destination on his long trip abroad. Not wanting to pry, but needing some idea, for her own peace of mind.

Feeling more relaxed since her recent outburst of laughter which had lightened the atmosphere between them, he told her that he intended to fly from Heathrow to Saudi Arabia, from there to Tibet. He couldn't be more precise than that. He had no fixed itinerary in mind. He would play it by ear, as his mood dictated. The whole point and purpose of the excursion, when all was said and done.

They spent a pleasant if somewhat silent evening together. Kate had made a chicken and mushroom pie for supper after tidying his room, making his bed and bundling his discarded clothing into the washing-machine.

There seemed little left to say to one another. Both were physically and mentally tired: Kate from all the running about she had done that day and dreading the thought of tomorrow; Alex from the sheer volume of planning involved in his bid for freedom, which had irritated him past bearing at times these past few days. Going away entailed masses of red tape: inoculation jabs at his doctor's surgery; prolonged interviews at a local travel agency to ascertain that his passport and other documents were in order; sessions at his bank with regard to his traveller's cheques – far beyond their usual remit, amounting to not hundreds but several thousand pounds. Funds sufficient to underwrite the various expeditions he had in mind.

Importantly, at the back of his mind lay the dread of saying goodbye to Kate, the woman he loved, but lacked the courage to tell that he loved her. To what purpose, since she was so obviously not in love with him? And yet he could have sworn, in London, in the St John's Wood house, especially when he had shown her his study and those old books of his, that she had fallen in love with him, as he had with her.

Apparently he was wrong as he had been so often before during his chequered lifetime.

And yet, early next morning, on the point of departure, having stowed his luggage in the boot of the awaiting taxi, seeing Kate standing forlornly on the doorstep of Gull House, on a sudden impulse, he turned back to cradle her briefly in his arms, to murmur gently, "God bless you, Kate, and thanks for your friendship, which has meant more to me than you'll ever know."

Then suddenly he was gone. The taxi sped away, and Kate's loneliness began.

Fanny was deeply upset when Kate told her she was leaving her flat. "If this has owt to do with old Joe Updike," she said, "I'll give him a good helping of 'tongue pie'!"

"No, it hasn't." When Kate explained the situation, Fanny said wistfully, "Will you come to see me once in a while?"

"Of course I will." Kate held the old woman's hand. "And you must come to see me whenever you feel like it. Promise?"

"Aye, I'd like that." Fanny smiled reminiscently. "Gull House, you say? I know it well. I used to play there as a kid with a schoolfriend of mine. Eh, the things we got up to in that there attic! Mekkin' tents out of bedclothes and an old clothes' horse! Having dolls' tea-parties an' suchlike!" She sighed deeply. "Happy days, they were! My friend's name was Clara Marshall. Her mother was a widow-woman who took in lodgers to make ends meet.

"Eh, how that poor woman worked to keep the cart on the wheels! Forever washing, cooking an' cleaning, she was, an' it weren't exactly an easy house ter foller, them stairs being so steep. But the house was all in one piece in them days, before what used to be the kitchen and the front room were knocked into one to make room for that gift shop!"

Fascinated, Kate longed to hear more. Talking to Fanny, listening to her reminiscences of Gull House which the old lady had known well, long before she was born or thought of, seemed akin to the pages of a history book being turned by the gnarled fingers of a woman who knew the Scarborough of long-ago as intimately as she knew the age-spots on the back of her hands. A vaguely formed yet thrilling idea had stirred in Kate's mind. Bidding Fanny goodbye, she walked back to Gull House to explore the possibilities of Alex Arden's typewriter.

The woman in charge of the York Place Business Agency, tall, spinsterish, grey haired, with horn-rimmed glasses, seemed nonplussed at first when Kate told her that she had no interest in learning short-hand or bookkeeping, that all she wanted was to learn touch-typing.

It seemed odd at first looking not at the keys but at a chart on the desk beside her, but Kate had every intention of getting up speed on Alex's typewriter, not prodding with two fingers when it came to writing the book she had in mind: a novel set against the background of Victorian Scarborough. The novel she had urged Alex to write, to no avail.

Researching her book would provide a new interest and impetus to her life, Kate realised, and learning the art of touch typing would add to her store of practical knowledge.

Furthermore, since Alex's departure, she had spent her evenings reading books, borrowed from the Vernon Road Library, on the lives of eminent Victorians – Elizabeth Barrett and her husband, Robert Browning, Charles Dickens, Lord Melbourne and the old Queen herself – with a view to soaking herself in the Victorian era, to reach a closer understanding of the shibboleths of that age, reading between the lines to discover that human beings had been every bit as fragile and vulnerable then as they were now.

Around midnight, switching off the sitting room lights and the electric fire in the hearth, after making certain that the house was securely locked and fastened for the night in fulfilment of her role as the custodian of Alex's property, Kate would go up to her room to make ready for bed, often to lie wide awake till the early hours of next morning, wondering where he was, imagining great tracts of wastelands beneath burning sun or starlight, eventually turning on her side to fall fast asleep from sheer mental exhaustion, and awakening, after a few hours of uneasy sleep, to review, over a cup of coffee and a slice of toast, the new day ahead of her.

On Mondays, Wednesdays and Fridays came her thrice weekly visits to Miss Murgatroyd to master the art of touch typing. Above all else she must keep busy, to which end she had begun decorating the kitchen and her own bedroom. At April Cottage she'd spent the long lonely days following Don's departure outdoors in the garden or in the greenhouse. Later, perhaps, here at Gull House when the weather was warmer, she would colourwash the yard's high brick walls and make a kind of patio with terracotta pots and hanging baskets of flowers.

Whether or not she would prove capable of writing a novel, Kate had no idea. To begin with, she would need several strong central characters and a gripping storyline. No use thinking she could cobble together a plot as full of holes as a threadbare blanket. Food for thought, and food for thought was something she desperately needed right now to keep her mind occupied with thoughts other than those centred on Alex.

Soon after his departure, she had opened and unpacked the crate on the landing and carried the books it contained upstairs to his study, where she arranged them carefully on the bookshelves he'd had built to house his collection of reference literature pertaining to the Victorian era in particular; the coming of the railways; Continental spa's and watering places; social habits and customs of that era, alongside a leather-bound volume of *The Seven Pillars of Wisdom*; paperback copies of the poems of Wilfred Owen, W.H. Auden, John Betjeman and Rupert Brooke – none of which she had felt inclined to peruse. To have done so would have seemed an intrusion of his privacy. Not the books so much as his personal choice of poetry.

The titles of his own books appealed to her strongly. Among them: *In Search of a Dream, My Brothers, the Bedouin,* and *Wide Rivers Run Deep.* These she would, perhaps, read in the fullness of time, but not now. Not yet.

Come next summer, she would invite Greg and Cindy to stay with her, Kate decided, when she would give her brother the books as a surprise birthday present, by which time, hopefully, her patio garden would have come to fruition, the tubs, hanging baskets and the terracotta Provençal pots burgeoning with lavender, night-scented stocks, colourful snapdragons, begonias and gloxinia.

Looking forward with hope, she reckoned, was far better than looking back in despair. Better by far to fill each waking moment with either sheer physical hard work or its mental counterpart, than to squander time feeling sorry for herself, as she had done when Don had left her.

But Don, after all, had been her lawfully wedded husband, whose defection had entailed the intervention of lawyers in the subsequent, unsavoury divorce proceedings. Alex, on the other hand, was nothing more than her employer, free to come and go as he wished. No promises made, therefore none to be broken. That he had chosen to leave her, albeit well provided for, Kate realised, was his prerogative entirely. Therefore, no legal lash-ups. No messy divorce proceedings. Equally, no – love. Just friendship.

In the Scarborough Room, Kate spread out a copy of the *Gazette and Herald* on the long oak table, her notebook and pen beside it, and knelt on a chair to inspect more closely the typescript, resembling a geologist examining a rock face in the hope of finding a vein of gold running through it.

Half an hour passed by. Nothing. No reference to the Crown Hotel. Her mind began to wander. Her thoughts strayed from the printed pages to Alex Arden. She wondered where he was right now, missing his tall, familiar presence in the room, his owlish appearance when he perched his glasses halfway down his nose, his habit of ruffling his hair with his hands when deeply preoccupied with the task confronting him, his occasional deep grunts of satisfaction when he came across nuggets of information relevant to his quest.

Then, suddenly, idly turning a page, Kate's eyes opened wide in surprise! She could have whooped for joy! There it was, in black and white, the name Albert Kiddy, of Newborough, Scarborough, winner of the May Day Horse Procession's First Prize of a blue riband and rosette in respect of the immaculately groomed and decorated team of dray horses, owned by his employers, Theakston Breweries, under his command.

The newspaper report continued in the fulsome fashion of the mid 1800s, not that Kate bothered to read on. All that really interested her was the name Albert Kiddy, almost certainly a forebear of Fanny's? Her great grandfather, most likely! Only one way to find out!

Next day, over a cup of afternoon tea in Fanny's bed-sitting room, "Oh aye, Albert were my great grandad right enough," the old woman said proudly. "I've got some cuttings and photographs in an old trunk of mine in the cellar. I keep it down there 'cos there ain't room for it up here. I could look them out for you, if you're interested."

"Yes, I am, very interested," Kate said. "I'd like to know more about your family tree."

"You would?" Fanny seemed doubtful. "But they were just ordinary working-class folk. Nowt posh, like me. Winning that there ribbon an' rosette was the highlight of great granda's life. Mind you, he was well thought of by the brewery, an' they gave him a grand send-off when he retired. A bit of a do, beer and sandwiches laid on, sherry wine for the ladies, a framed test – testawhat's it – an' a nice sum of money. Fifty guineas, an' that were a small fortune in them days."

Fanny continued mistily, "He kept that framed 'testament' of his over the mantlepiece till the day he died, which weren't very long after his retirement. Not that I remember owt about it. I wasn't born or thought of then. But he made good use of that money, the poor old fellah, setting up his son, John, my grandad, in his own cabinet maker's workshop in St Sepulchre Street."

"Look, Fanny," Kate suggested quietly yet eagerly, "why not come to Gull House for tea on Sunday afternoon? Bring your cuttings and photographs with you? I'll have a good old bake-up beforehand: make lots of cakes and scones. We'll have time for a proper chinwag, and I'd love to hear more about the house as you remember it from your schooldays."

"Oh yes. Thanks, my dear, I'd really like that," Fanny said gratefully. She added mischievously, "Just one thing, if you're thinking of mekkin' sandwiches, I'd rather you didn't. Truth to tell, I'm sick an' tired of sandwiches. I'd far rather have a slice or two of cooked ham on a plate any day of the week."

Kate smiled sympathetically. Looking round Fanny's bed-sitter with its limited cooking facilities, she well understood the old lady's need of a good substantial meal inside her apart from soup, sandwiches, biscuits and boiled eggs.

"Leave it to me," she said briskly, bidding Fanny farewell. "Till Sunday, then? I'll look forward to it enormously."

"So shall I," Fanny said fervently.

Fanny had mentioned cooked ham, but Kate wanted to give her guest something hot and sustaining, so, apart from cakes and scones, she made a substantial meat and potato pie, to the old lady's obvious delight when Kate produced it, piping hot, from the oven, along with a jug of gravy and a tureen of vegetables.

"Eh," Fanny said wonderingly, "I thought we was having afternoon tea, not a bust-up dinner! Not that I'm complaining, mind you! I haven't had a meat and tater pie since – I can't remember when. But what a lot of trouble you've been to!"

"No trouble at all, I assure you," Kate laughed, serving her guest a sizeable chunk of the pie. "I've missed having someone to cook for other than myself."

Kate had elected to serve the meal in the kitchen, where they would feel more at home. When they had finished eating, she would show Fanny the rest of the house. Later, they would sit near the front room fire where, hopefully, Fanny would reveal the contents of the carrier bag she had brought with her.

But first she must tell the old lady exactly why she had expressed so much interest in her family background: her intention of writing a novel with, possibly, Albert Kiddy as one of the key characters. To do otherwise was unthinkable. For all she knew, Fanny may well stubbornly refuse to give her consent to a fictionalised version of her family history. Not that Kate imagined for one moment that even if the book was written, it would stand a chance of publication. Even so, she must give Fanny the right of refusal on so delicate an issue.

To her surprise and delight, Fanny embraced the idea wholeheartedly: obviously pleased and proud that her great grandfather would receive the recognition he deserved – apart from his blue ribbon, rosette, "testament" and the lump sum of fifty guineas he'd received on his retirement from Theakston's Brewery.

Soon the low table drawn up to the sitting room fire was littered with the contents of Fanny's carrier bag, including the tattered remains of Albert's blue riband and rosette, and daguerrotype photographs of him as an old man, taken alongside an elderly woman whose right hand rested on his shoulder; plus an upright, serious-faced young man with fair hair whose head appeared to be held in a vice, and a slender young woman, dark-haired and wearing a white dress and a broad-brimmed hat.

"That's my great grandad and great grandma," Fanny said eagerly. "The young man's my grandad. Leastways he was. He'd dead now, of course, an' so is his sister, Lucy – the one wearing the hat. My word, the trouble that lass caused them you wouldn't believe."

"Really? How come?" Kate asked.

Fanny sighed. "Well, they do say there's one in every family, and she was it! A born troublemaker. Course, tales might have got a bit exaggerated in the telling. But she *was* a bonny lass, no doubt about that, as you can see for yourself. Trouble was, she knew it, and wouldn't settle her mind to anything.

"Her an' her brother were as different as chalk and cheese. When John left school, he started work as an apprentice joiner. No messing. He knew exactly what he wanted to be. Not so Miss Lucy! Oh no, not her! She wanted to be 'different' –" Fanny chuckled – "an' seemingly she got her wish in the long run."

Kate listened intently as Fanny got into her stride, running on like a stream in full spate, recounting the family history from hearsay, leaving gaps now and then, not unusual for a woman of her age.

"Ended up the wife of a rich man twice her age, by all accounts," Fanny went on, "who treated her like dirt an' made her life a misery with his 'extra-martial' relationships an' so on, till she finally ran away with a handsome young sea-captain, half *her* age, an' was never seen or heard of again, as if she had disappeared from the face of the earth. I've often wondered what became of her, poor lass. Perhaps they were shipwrecked on a desert island? Who knows?

"Summat I know for certain, leaving school, Lucy started work as a chambermaid at the Crown Hotel. It happened this way. My great grandad Albert knew the owner quite well by way of his drayman's job, delivering beer to the hotel vaults at regular intervals, an' he asked the man if he could find employment for his young daughter, as a waitress or whatever . . ."

Kate's eyes glowed. At last, her metaphysical hero, John Fairgray Sharpin, had entered the arena as a vital, living person in the Kiddy family's history, not merely as a name printed on the pages of a dusty newspaper in the Scarborough Room of the local library.

"What was the man like?" she asked breathlessly.

"Eh?" Fanny looked puzzled. "Oh, the owner of the Crown Hotel, you mean? Why, I can't say for sure. All I know is that old Albert was as pleased as Punch when he gave young Lucy a job as a chambermaid. Not that she stuck it for long, the daft cat! Next thing they knew, she'd run off with a cellarman old enough to be her father, and married into the bargain. What I mean to say is, the man was married to someone else, not Lucy. The father of four, no less. Well, you can imagine the schemozzle that caused! Then my great grandad went in search of them.

"Not that they took much finding! They'd landed up working in a posh hotel in Brighton, posing as a married couple. The bloke had been daft enough to leave a letter from the Brighton hotel in a wastepaper basket in his room."

"Then what happened?" Kate asked intently, deeply interested in the machinations of poor Lucy Kiddy, the undoubted heroine of her embryo novel.

"Well, Lucy was hauled home in disgrace. But had she learned her lesson? No fear! Six months later she was involved in a love affair with a young fisherman she'd met in The People's Park, or whatever it was called – a kind of fairground in the Valley, so far as I can make out, with all kinds of wickedness taking place there! A bad influence on the town as a whole, in my opinion."

"I'm certain it was never meant to be anything more than a source of happiness and relaxation for the ordinary folk of Scarborough," Kate said quietly, in defence of her long dead and buried hero, John Fairgray Sharpin. A man for all reasons . . . Then, smilingly, she suggested making another pot of tea to revive Fanny's flow of energy and good humour.

The tea made and more cakes consumed, Fanny said she'd best be getting back home. Putting on her outdoor things, she thanked Kate profusely for giving her such a grand time. Kate reminded her that she'd left her carrier bag in the sitting room. "I hadn't forgotten," Fanny said. "I thought you'd like to take a closer look at the stuff I brought with me." She chuckled. "That way I'll be bound to see you again soon, shan't I?"

When the old lady had gone, in a taxi Kate had ordered and paid for, and taking with her the remains of the meat and tater pie and a bag of left-over cakes and scones, protesting there was really no need but ta just the same, Kate went back to the sitting room to gather together the scattered photographs, various scraps of paper and the rest of the nostalgic reminders of the Kiddy family, which she returned carefully to the carrier bag and took upstairs to the attic studio.

Gripped with a strange feeling of excitement, she would be unwise to even attempt looking at the contents of the carrier tonight. Akin to a greedy child at a birthday party eating for eating's sake. What she needed right now was time to digest the mass of information she'd received so far.

Fanny's visit had been fun, but exhausting. When Kate had showed her round the house after their main meal, the old lady had recounted endless stories of her childhood days, fascinating but bewildering – a bit like listening to a switched on tape-recorder without a pause button, Kate had thought at the time.

Then had come her more interesting, slower-paced revelations of her family history, which Kate had found utterly absorbing, especially those snippets linked to Albert Kiddy's relationship with John Fairgray Sharpin, when suddenly the past had come alive for her, so that beyond and above Fanny's monologue she had imagined that meeting between Albert and Sharpin, when the drayman had asked the charismatic tenant manager of the prestigious Crown Hotel if he could provide employment for his daughter, Lucy.

Kate knew instinctively that Sharpin would have treated Albert as his equal, not patronisingly or high-handedly, but as a fellow human being. Possibly Albert had confided in him that Lucy was – in present day parlance – a bit of a problem child, with a will of her own and strong aversion to work in any shape or form whatsoever.

Nevertheless, Sharpin had taken the wayward Lucy under his wing, for friendship's sake, knowing full well the calibre of the man making the request: a decent, upstanding honourable man deserving of all the practical help that was within his power to provide.

And so young Lucy Kiddy had gone to work at the Crown Hotel as a chambermaid, against her will, more than likely. And what would it have been like for her, Kate wondered, an impressionable, discontented teenager, brushing shoulders with elegantly dressed women on their way downstairs to the dining room, whilst she was on her way upstairs to turn down their beds for the night?

Little wonder that poor Lucy had hopped it to Brighton with that cellarman, Kate conjectured as she made ready for bed. In desperate need of love and attention – romance with a capital R – she would have easily fallen under the spell of a man much older than herself: walking hand-in-hand with him beneath a moonlit sky; turning up her flower-like face to be kissed by him; listening to his lies, believing every word he uttered . . .

And she, Kate, should know. For hadn't the self same thing happened to herself at roughly the same age as Lucy Kiddy?

On the verge of sleep, there should be a law against moonlight, she thought hazily.

Twelve

"April, April, Laugh thy girlish laughter. Then, the moment after, Weep thy girlish tears".

The words of an old poem, learned at school, entered Kate's mind as she stood at the sitting-room window staring out at the pouring rain. Moments before, the sun had been shining, and it would be again once this rain shower had passed.

April! Almost four months since Alex had left Gull House, and she had heard not a word from him, had received not so much as a postcard. But perhaps they didn't sell postcards in the Arabian Desert? And it was likely there were no post-boxes handy!

All very well to view the situation with a wry sense of humour, to imagine a camel train hitting some twentieth-century oasis complete with postcard stands and pillar boxes; possibly even a bedouin super-market selling pickled sheep's eyes and bottled beer? Utter and absolute rubbish, of course, and she knew it!

Deep down, she was seriously worried by Alex's lack of communication during the seemingly endless days since his departure into the wild blue yonder. But what, if anything, could she do to relieve her anxiety? The answer came pat, simply and clearly. Nothing! Nothing at all! All she could possibly do was to get on with her life in her own way, as best she could, to live in hope of some kind of message from him in the not too distant future.

She had at least learned how to touch type, and had begun writing, albeit tentatively, the first chapter of her novel. (Sod's Law, she thought ruefully. Now she could type faster than she could think!) At least the York Place Business Agency was doing a roaring trade in A4 paper and correction fluid.

The thought occurred that she was jumping in at the deep end in starting a novel without a clearly defined outline of the plot and the characters involved. And so, curbing her enthusiasm and getting down to the nitty-gritty, she had painstakingly set about typing lists of information relevant to her brain child, beginning with her notes on the history of Scarborough in particular; the Victorian era in general.

Next on the agenda came a series of thumbnail sketches of the characters involved: their appearance, mannerisms, backgrounds, social habits, and so on.

Fanny's "bag of tricks" had yielded several surprises in the shape of old letters and documents, school exercise books in John and Lucy's handwriting, household accounts kept by Mavis Kiddy, Albert's wife; John's indentures of apprenticeship to one Martin Gooch, a Master Cabinet Maker of Dumple Street; bits and bobs of jewellery, a coral necklace and a tiny gold ring such as a child might have worn. Lucy, most likely.

Kate's nucleus of main characters included Albert, Mavis, John and Lucy Kiddy and John Sharpin, very clear and real to her. But there were many others not so clearly delineated in her mind's eye: Lucy's elderly husband, for instance, the cellarman she'd run off with to Brighton; the sea captain with whom she had presumably ended her days, the young fisherman she'd met and fallen in love with in the People's Park.

Kate knew exactly where and when she would begin her novel – on that May evening long ago when the Kiddy family had trooped down to the Valley to witness the opening of the pleasure ground. How the story would end was far more difficult to decide. Readers of romantic fiction wanted a happy ending. Perhaps she'd settle for Lucy and her sea captain standing at the prow of his ship, gazing at the far horizon, contemplating their happy future together?

At least, doing the spadework beforehand, Kate found the intended novel had begun to assume shape and form. Whether or not she possessed the ability to breathe life into her characters, to write convincingly about the Victorian era, remained to be seen.

Meanwhile, life went on, and she had other things to see to: planning her patio garden, for instance; cooking, cleaning and shopping. More urgently, worrying about the shop below when the manageress, a Mrs Dorothy Paulson, handed in her notice unexpectedly due to family problems beyond her power of control: a sick husband on one hand, a cantankerous mother on the other, living under the same roof and fighting like cat and dog.

"I'm sorry, Mrs Ford," Dorothy said weepily, "but I'm needed at home right now! My husband has Parkinson's Disease, and my mother's in the early stages of senile dementia. So you see how it is? But I do really need the money!"

Kate thought quickly. Presumably Mrs Paulson had known the pitfalls ahead of her when she'd taken on the responsibilities of a manageress. "I'm sorry this has happened," she said, "but perhaps we can reach a compromise?"

"What sort of a compromise?" Mrs Paulson dabbed at her eyes with a hanky.

"Perhaps you could work part time?" Kate suggested, feeling sorry for the woman. "That way you'd still have some money coming in, and it would be a great help if you could stay on long enough to show someone else the ropes."

"You mean a replacement manageress?"

"No, an assistant saleswoman's more what I have in mind. I'm sure we could come to some satisfactory arrangement. Above all, I'd appreciate your doing the buying as usual, knowing the reps, the amount of stock to order, and so forth."

Mrs Paulson managed a smile, "Yes, I think I could manage that all right. Thank you, Mrs Ford."

"Call me Kate."

"And you can call me Dot, or Dotty."

"Thanks – Dot! Well, let's mull things over for a while, shall we? You work out how much time you can spare, meanwhile I'll advertise for an assistant, and we'll take it from there."

"Have you thought of working here yourself?" Dot asked. "That way there'd be no need to advertise."

"No, I'm sorry." The sooner that notion was knocked on the head, the better, Kate thought. She had quite enough on her plate as it was. Besides, the shop was not strictly her province. Dot's wages were paid by Alex's London-based firm of solicitors, who also settled the stock bills and various other accounts – light, heating, insurance, etc., on a monthly basis – at Kate's insistence before Alex set forth on his voyage of discovery. Kate thought she had made it perfectly clear to him that she wanted nothing whatever to do with the shop. And she had meant what said she'd said.

Frankly, she'd considered him mad to even contemplate keeping on the gift shop in the first place, although his reasons for so doing had made sense inasmuch as one day, perhaps, he might wish to restore

Gull House to its original state: an impossibility if ownership of the downstairs premises changed hands.

"Fair enough," she'd conceded, "just as long as you don't expect me to become involved in the running of it."

"You have my word."

Now, here she was up to her eyes in it! But not for longer than she could help. No fear! But then, business matters were one thing, human problems a different matter entirely. No way could she have failed to respond other than sympathetically to Dot Paulson's anguish over her domestic dilemma, to try her best to come up with a reasonable answer to a decent woman's *cri de cœur*.

In thoughtful, nostalgic frame of mind, Kate walked up to Westborough where she paused for a while, shoring up her courage before turning into Albemarle Crescent to re-visit the house she had loved so much in her childhood years – uncertain that she could bear to look at it without bursting into tears.

An impossibility, she realised, tears flooding her eyes as, looking up at the windows, she imagined her mother's face smiling down at herself and Greg as they had set off, buckets, spades and shrimping nets in hand, to spend carefree hours on the beach.

Things were different then from now, life lived at a slower pace. Children came on holiday with their parents for a week or a fortnight, staying in one place, usually in some small boarding house well known to them to which they returned year after year – the Albemarle Crescent house, for instance, where Kate's mother had taken in boarders during the summer months to help pay the rates, as had most other housewives in Scarborough with rooms to spare.

Standing on the pavement, she could see, in her mind's eye, the Saturday morning crop of new arrivals from the railway station, decent, ordinary couples with well-behaved children in tow: the husband, neatly dressed in a suit, collar and tie, his wife wearing a skirt, blouse and hand-knitted cardigan, the little girls in summer dresses, the boys in short flannel trousers. The father would be carrying the cases, his wife various brown paper carrier-bags with string handles; the children, buckets and spades.

How hard Mum had worked to give those people a good, carefree holiday at the seaside. Nothing had been too much trouble. "Eh, Mrs Harker," they would say, "it's grand to be back." And Mum had laughed delightedly and said there'd be a cup of tea on the go when they'd finished unpacking. Lemonade for the kids. And there'd be a good high tea ready for them at half-past five; a bite of supper around nine, before the children's bedtime.

Looking back, Kate realised whence her housewifely instincts had sprung, her love of cooking, of homemaking: traits inherited from her mother, whose joy in life had lain in keeping other folk well fed and happy.

If only it were possible to turn back the hands of time, to hurry down the corridor of years to find her mother standing there, smiling, arms outstretched to embrace her.

Turning away, blinking back her tears, fighting hard to gain control of her emotion at seeing the old house again, Kate walked downhill to Aberdeen Walk, a busy shopping thoroughfare close to the heart of town, drawn by a desire to find out what had become of her school friend, Jenny Laird, the bubbly, fun-loving girl who had been bridesmaid at her wedding to Don Ford that cold winter morning twenty-odd years ago. Who had, indeed, been instrumental in arranging that blind date which had brought herself and Don together in the first place.

She couldn't remember the exact address, but she knew the house well enough: the street in close proximity to Gladstone Road Infants and Junior School, the Lairds' house above a corner shop where Jenny's dad had sold sweets, tobacco and groceries.

It was a longish walk from the town centre to Gladstone Road, a trip down "Memory Lane" as she recognised old, familiar landmarks – a clothing shop with a clock above the entrance, a triangular patch of grass, red-brick public lavatories, a butcher's shop, a post-box; half-forgotten street names, rows of prim Victorian villas with narrow front gardens and a preponderance of laurel bushes, iron railings removed during the war she scarcely remembered. She had been far too young at the time.

Hardly likely, she thought, nearing the corner shop, that Jenny's father would still be there behind the counter, bluff and smiling, serving schoolchildren aniseed balls, Spanish bootlaces and acid drops from cardboard boxes on display in the window. He'd have probably retired ages ago, but it was just possible that the Lairds were still living in the house above the shop.

Entering the shop, noting the inevitable changes wrought by modernisation – laminated shelving in place of wood, a counter display unit revealing piles of ready-cut ham and luncheon meat, pre-packed cheeses and bacon slices, plastic trays of coleslaw, Waldorf and beetroot salad, Scotch eggs and frankfurters – with the strong feeling that she was wasting her time, Kate asked the man in charge of the counter if he knew the present whereabouts of the Laird family.

"*Who?*" he asked, frowning. "Sorry, love, never heard of 'em!"

"They used to own this shop," Kate explained patiently, "a long time ago, but I thought they might still be living in the area."

"Naw. Like I said, I've never heard of 'em! Why don't you try next door? The old lady there's been here since 'Dick's Days'. Going on ninety, I reckon, an' a right old busybody. If anyone'll know, *she* will!"

"Do you happen to know her name?" Kate asked.

The man laughed. "Mrs Parker! Mrs 'Nosy' Parker, we call her!"

"Thank you." Kate beat a hasty retreat from the delicatessen counter with its piles of pale spotted luncheon meat and sweating ham slices, as fast as possible without causing offence to the new owner of the premises.

Not exactly looking forward to her possible encounter with a ninety-year-old tittle-tattle, nevertheless Kate rang Mrs Parker's doorbell and waited, in a state of nervous tension, until, after much fiddling with bolts and locks by the old lady inside, the door finally opened to reveal, not a wizened crone, but a spry looking lady, white-haired, with sharp, intelligent eyes and the complexion of a schoolgirl, who said mildly, "If you're one of those 'do-gooders' from the Town Hall wanting to move me into an old folk's home, the answer's *No*! The only way I'll leave my home is feet first, in a wooden box! So there!"

Kate smiled, liking the old woman at first sight. "I'm not from the Town Hall, Mrs Parker. I'm just trying to discover the whereabouts of the Laird family – friends of mine from way back."

"You *are?*" Mrs Parker beamed like a sunburst. "Then you'd best come in, my dear. I'll put the kettle on for a cup of tea!"

"No, please don't bother," Kate protested weakly, not wanting to intrude on the old woman's privacy, at the same time following her into a neat little kitchen with an old-fashioned stone sink, wooden draining-boards and gleaming brass taps; a pre-war gas cooker; ceiling clothes' airer draped with celanese knickers, woollen camisoles and stout hook-sided corsets, two brushed-wool nightgowns and several pairs of lisle stockings.

"As you can see, I still manage to keep myself clean and decent," Mrs

Parker said chirpily, filling the kettle and applying a match to a ring on the cooker, "despite my years! Eighty-five next month, would you believe it? And still going strong! Except, I have to say that my eyesight isn't quite what it used to be, so I can't quite make out . . . Have I seen you before? What's your name, by the way?"

"Kate. Kate Ford, née Harker," Kate supplied. "Jenny Laird and I were at school together, and her parents were very good to me when – that is after the death of my parents." She paused painfully. "In fact, I was married from the house next door, and Jenny was my bridesmaid."

"Oh yes, of course, now I remember. Not very clearly, I'm afraid, but vaguely. The Lairds were such nice folk, and Jenny was as pretty as a picture, as I recall, in her pink bridesmaid's dress," Mrs Parker reminisced, warming the teapot and measuring into it two spoonfuls of tea from a tea-caddy commemorating the Coronation of King George the Sixth. Closing the lid of the caddy with gnarled fingers, she continued, "I was sorry when the Duke of York had to take on the job of King when his brother renounced his throne to marry that dreadful American divorcée, Wallis Warfield Simpson. And what a fluttering in the royal dovecote that caused!" Mrs Parker said disapprovingly, pouring boiling water on to the tea-leaves in a brown earthenware pot with a chipped spout and a cracked lid, indicative of its many years' usage as an eighty-five-year-old lady's dearest companion of the past four decades.

Sipping her tea, very delicately Kate asked the burning question: "Have you any idea, Mrs Parker, what became of the Laird family after their retirement?"

Handing Kate a plate of digestive biscuits, the old lady said confusedly, "They moved away to Warminster, as I recall, or could it have been Ilminster? I forget which, but Jenny stayed on in Scarborough, of that I'm sure – at least I think I am!" She wrinkled her forehead. "The last I heard of her, she'd started a second-hand dress shop somewhere in the Old Town, near the Market Hall, though whether or not she's still there, I can't say for certain."

Thanking her hostess, Kate got up to leave. Mrs Parker followed her to the door. Smiling sadly, she said, "I miss the old days. That's why I want to stay where I am, to keep things the way they were. Do-gooders tell me I'd be better off in a home. But I've got a home, and here's where I'm staying."

Kate said gently, "I envy you your home, Mrs Parker. I had one once. Foolishly, I let go of it. I often wish now that I'd clung on to it, the way you have done."

"You'll have a home of your own again one day," the old lady said perceptively. "Believe me, I *know!*"

Kate looked puzzled. "But how? I mean, how can you be so sure?" Mrs Parker's cheeks flushed slightly. "I daresay you won't remember a fortune-teller's shop in Eastborough. A – Madame Zara?" She chuckled softly. "*I* was Madame Zara!"

Curiously, Kate did vaguely remember the shop, which she and Greg had often passed on their way to the sands. She certainly remembered her mother having consulted Madame Zara once or twice at times of emotional stress and indecision; the comfort she'd derived from her visits; the good advice she'd received from the bizarrely named clair-voyant, whom she had described as "a nice, ordinary little woman, not in the least bit frightening."

On an impulse, bending down, Kate kissed the old woman's soft pink cheek. "I'm so glad to have met you," she said warmly, "and I do believe what you told me about having a home of my own again, one day."

"You were wise to part with your cottage," Mrs Parker said. "It had served its purpose. Staying on there, you wouldn't have been happy. Too many unhappy memories; too many – ghosts. My advice is, forget about the past. Look to the future. Many people, some close to you, others not so close, are in need of your help right now. You'll need to be strong for their sake. And you will be, of that I'm sure!" She smiled happily. "And this will not be your last visit to my home. So, goodbye now, my dear, until we meet again."

Walking back the way she had come, Kate felt strangely comforted and uplifted, as if a strong link had been forged between the past, present and future. Incredibly, Mrs Parker had mentioned parting with her cottage, which she had not referred to directly as such. Kate had merely mentioned her home. An educated guess on the old lady's part? Kate thought not. After all, for all Mrs Parker knew, she might have lived in a flat, a maisonette, a modern house or a bungalow. Yet she *had* known, not just about the cottage but Kate's reasons for leaving it – too many unhappy memories, too many ghosts.

Deep in thought, Kate remembered Alex once asking her if she believed in reincarnation, and she had said no. Now she wondered what she *did* believe in? A life hereafter? Fate? Destiny? Ghosts? Almost certainly that the presence of those who had gone before possessed the power to live on, unseen, in places close to them in their earthly lives – as the spirit of John Fairgray Sharpin may well still live on in his beloved Crown Hotel; as the shades of Albert, Mavis, John and Lucy Kiddy lived on in her imagination, awaiting their rebirth, at her hands, on the keys of Alex Arden's typewriter.

Thirteen

Having "mulled things over", Dot Paulson presented Kate with a list of what she termed "times of availability": Mondays, Thursdays and Fridays.

She had, apparently, persuaded her husband to attend a day centre three times a week, and a neighbour to keep an eye on her mother. Not that her hubby had needed much persuading to get shot of his frenetic mother-in-law thrice weekly, Dot confided to Kate, and vice-versa. Her mother had expressed satisfaction that her son-in-law would be "out from under her feet" three days a week.

"All this has blown up quite recently," Dot explained ruefully, "since Mum started losing her memory. Asking the same questions over and over again. Forgetting where she'd put things and blaming my hubby for hiding them from her. That's when the rows started. And there was I – pig-in-the-middle – trying to keep the peace between them. Not that I succeeded. Things went from bad to worse. That's when I decided to hand in my notice. I honestly didn't know whether I was coming or going between the pair of them!"

Kate understood completely. "Mondays, Thursdays and Fridays will suit me fine," she said. "And not to worry if you have to change days occasionally. I'll give you all the help and support I can."

Dot fiddled up her sleeve for a hanky, saying emotionally, "I'm sure I don't know what I'd have done without your help. You've been a tower of strength to me, you really have!"

Suddenly Kate thought back to her meeting with Mrs Parker. The old lady's words: "Many people, some close to you, others not so close, are in need of your help right now. You'll need to be strong for their sake."

Many people? Kate puzzled. So, apart from Dot Paulson, who else?

Why the strange feeling that Dot Paulson's problems were merely the tip of a very large iceberg indeed?

Only time would tell.

Raking the streets of the Old Town for a second-hand dress shop in the vicinity of the Market Hall, Kate reached the conclusion that it no longer existed – if, indeed, it ever had.

Evidently, "Madame Zara's" clairvoyancy had certain limitations in the area connected with Jenny Laird's present whereabouts. A pity, really, Kate had looked forward to a possible reunion with her old schoolfriend, the bright, bubbly blonde whose enjoyment of life had somehow rubbed off on to other people, teachers and pupils alike, all of whom had liked Jenny enormously because, quite simply, she was one of those rare human beings who radiated happiness and goodwill to all of her fellow human beings. Mankind in general. Men in particular, perhaps, Kate realised. And why not? With her looks, her personality, Jenny had only to smile, to throw back her mane of naturally blonde, curly hair, to glance teasingly at any member of the male sex with those innocent blue eyes of hers, to have them at her beck and call.

No one Kate asked remembered a dress shop in that part of town, even the shopkeepers she approached when buying chocolate, postcards or newspapers she didn't really want. "No, sorry love," they said, shaking their heads.

In the Market Hall, Kate asked various stallholders, buying meat and vegetables which she did want, if they recalled a second-hand dress shop, and met with the same response, until one woman, weighing apples, said, "If it's second-hand stuff you're wanting, you could try that stall down yonder, near the exit. She often has a few bargains mixed in with the tat. But don't let her con you into buying summat you don't want. She could sell ice-cubes to an eskimo, that 'un!"

"Thanks. Might as well take a look." Paying for the apples, Kate walked between the stalls towards the rear exit.

The woman, powerfully built, with a mass of dyed blonde hair, serving a customer, had her back to Kate. The stall was crowded with what could only be described as junk oddments of china, gimcrack ornaments, items of brassware and cheap jewellery; knitted toilet-roll covers and tea-cosies; off-cuts of dress material, a few electrical appliances; piles of dog-eared magazines and paperback books. Suspended on hangers above the stall, a variety of out-of-date dresses, suits, skirts and jackets. In boxes on the floor space fronting the stall, a jumbled mass of shoes, sandals and slippers.

When the woman turned towards her, "Hello, Jenny," Kate said mistily. "Remember me?"

Jenny's reaction startled Kate. Her cheeks flushed to the colour of beetroot, she held on to the stall to steady herself, then the colour drained away suddenly, leaving her cheeks deathly pale, and she burst into tears. Racking sobs shook her overweight body, rivulets of black mascara ran down her face. Staring at Kate with anguished eyes, she muttered hoarsely, "Well, go on, take a good look! No need to tell me what you're thinking! Why don't you go away and leave me alone!"

Deeply shocked by her friend's hostility, Kate said levelly, "I'm not going anywhere until you tell me what all this is about. I've been searching high and low for you. Now I've found you, you'll not get rid of me that easily. Here –" handing her a hanky – "dry your eyes. Your mascara's running. Now, give me a smile and tell me you're as pleased to see me again as I am you!"

"*What*? The state I'm in?" Jenny dabbed her eyes. "A fat, blowsy old tart like me? Well, go on, admit it!"

"Very well, then, if it will make you feel less sorry for yourself. So you've put on weight, dyed your hair. But not so much of the 'old', if you don't mind. We're the same age, remember? More importantly, I'm still your friend. Or have you forgotten how much we once meant to each other?"

"No, of course not," Jenny admitted reluctantly. "But oh, what's the use? Look at you, still slim and attractive; well off too, I daresay, not like me, a fat bloody failure, up to my ears in debt, eking out an existence at a – junk stall!"

"We need to talk," Kate said compassionately, "but not here. Could we meet later, perhaps, at your place or mine?"

"Sure. Why not?" Jenny said recklessly. "I'll give you my address. I'd really like you to see where I live: the depths I've sunk to. Just be prepared for a shock, that's all. You see, Kate, the Jenny Laird you knew and cared for no longer exists!"

A memory stirred in Kate. Seemingly she had a strange penchant for forming friendships with people whose former personalities no longer existed. First Alex, now Jenny.

She experienced some difficulty in finding Jenny's address that evening. Possibly that also was non-existent? She came upon it at last up a narrow alleyway off Queen Street, a small house in a state of decay with a sash window on the ground floor, two more on the first floor, and with two dormers above a length of sagging guttering, leaking water on to the doorstep close to where Kate was standing, looking in dismay at the peeling paintwork and grimy windows, wondering if she had come to the right place after all? Surely not? The place looked ready for demolition, if it didn't fall down of its own volition.

The door opened suddenly to reveal Jenny, bizarrely dressed in a voluminous ankle-length Indian cotton skirt, a black jumper strained tightly across her ample breasts, several strings of brightly-coloured beads about her neck, dangling gilt earrings, scuffed red slippers on her feet, and with her mane of bleached hair spread about her shoulders.

"Well don't stand there, come in," she said aggressively. "Welcome to my 'palace of delight'. What you'll see will amaze you! In fact, I've a good mind to charge you admittance!"

"Stop it, Jenny," Kate uttered hoarsely, unbelievably angry. "Make a damn fool of yourself if you like, but don't try making a fool of me! It just won't wash, that's all!"

"I don't know what the hell you're on about," Jenny retorted. "You said you wanted to talk. What about? The good old days? Now you're getting up on your high horse; telling me I'm making a damn fool of myself, if it's any of your bloody business!"

Kate's anger faded. Remembering a joyous schoolgirl of long ago, opening her arms, smiling, she said gently, "Come here, you daft ha'porth. I came here because I love you. I always have and I always will."

Next thing she knew, their arms were about one another, and Jenny was crying on her shoulder, saying, "I'm sorry, Kate. I really am sorry. Please forgive me."

"What is there to forgive? You've done me no harm," Kate murmured soothingly, drawing the weeping woman indoors, an arm about her waist. "Quite the opposite, in fact. Remember how you came to me after my parents died? None of our other classmates even bothered. But *you* did, and I'll never forget that." She paused to find the right words. "You gave me a – reason for living."

"You mean Don? Don Ford?" Jenny asked wistfully, her tears, pretence and aggression forgotten in memories of the past. "You know, Kate, I was a bit jealous of you and Don. The way he looked at you, especially on your wedding day. And there was I stuck with his flatmate, John Spivey. Oh, a nice enough bloke, but not half as handsome and clever as Don." She paused briefly. "So where is he now? Don, I mean."

Kate drew in a deep breath. "He's in New York," she said calmly, "with his new wife and their son. Don and I went our separate ways some time ago. The reason why I'm here now, trying hard to create a new life, a new future for myself."

"Oh, Kate, I'm so sorry. I had no idea," Jenny said sadly, leading the way to the kitchen, an untidy, cluttered apartment, to make coffee for her guest. "And there was I thinking you had everything in life you'd ever wanted. All that any woman could possibly want – a nice home, a handsome husband, children! The kind of things I've longed for all my life!"

Sitting down at the kitchen table, head in hands, close to tears once more, Jenny said dully, "The trouble with me, I was so vain, so sure of my power of attraction over men that, when John Spivey asked me to marry him, I turned him down flat.

"I thought he wasn't quite good enough for me, you see? I wanted excitement, admiration, a good time."

Raising her head suddenly, choking back her tears, Jenny said defiantly, "Well, now you see before you a woman who hasn't the sense she was born with! What price my attraction now? I'm fat, ugly, disillusioned, disappointed, and it's all my own fault! So for God's sake, Kate, face facts! I'm a whore at heart. I've had more men than you've had hot dinners! I don't deserve your love or your friendship. So why don't you leave now?"

"Because," Kate replied simply, "you are still – Jenny Laird."

The state of the house was appalling. There was junk, which Jenny referred to as "stock", everywhere. "I could just open the rooms to the punters and save myself the cost of renting a stall," she said ruefully, with a flash of her old sense of humour, "except that the landlord wants me out of here at the end of the month. I'm in arrears, you see?"

Jenny's stock derived from jumble sales. "First through the doors picks up the best bargains," she explained. "That's when my size comes in handy. 'Fat Jen, the human bulldozer', they call me. I try not to mind, but I do."

She paused to kick aside a box of hats in the middle of the sitting room floor. "My own fault for letting the weight pile on. Comfort eating, I suppose. Too many sandwiches, cakes and fish and chips. And the booze didn't help any! Whisky, beer, rum, gin. You name it!

"I'd get my men friends to bring a bottle with them when they came to call. A few drinks and they couldn't have cared less what I looked like!"

Kate remained silent, realising that Jenny needed to spill out her anger, hurt and disappointment at her own folly in spoiling her life the way she had done. If confession was good for the soul, chances were she'd feel a lot better in revealing the extent of that folly to someone who cared about her.

Even so, Kate could scarcely bear to listen to the sordid details of her friend's fall from grace: the men she had known who had used and abused her for their own ends, resorting to physical violence more often than not, enjoying her humiliation at their hands. A fat woman in need of not sex, but love, they had given her nothing but sex. Certainly not love.

"I told them, over and over again, that I wanted nothing more to do with them," Jenny said wearily, "but they just laughed at me; told me I should be grateful for the booze – and bed! The shameful thing is, I knew deep down that I couldn't do without either. Especially the booze! You see, Kate, downing a half bottle of whisky, gin or whatever to ease the pain of living, I couldn't have cared less about what would happen later, upstairs in my bedroom. And – well – having sex made me feel 'special' somehow. Like a real woman, not just a – whore!"

Swallowing hard, she continued, "I'm off the booze now, thank God, and those men friends of mine are a thing of the past. Don't ask me how or why it happened. I just woke up one morning to the realisation that what I was doing to myself was all wrong somehow. A bit too late though. Far too late to make up for the mess I've made of my life so far!"

Speaking at last, Kate said quietly, "That's where you're wrong, love. It's never too late to make a new beginning. If you really want to, that is."

"*Want* to?" Jenny's eyes filled with tears. "Of course I do. If I only knew how!"

"We'll think of something," Kate promised.

"*We?*"

"Remember, Jenny, you're not on your own now. You have someone on your side. First thing, how much rent do you owe?"

"A hundred quid."

"Right. We'll settle up with the landlord. But you'll be leaving here at the end of the month anyway. That will give you time to clear out your – stock." Kate smiled.

"But what shall I do with it?" Jenny asked, aghast at the thought of getting rid of so much junk.

"How about a jumble sale? Several jumble sales, if necessary. We'll hire a van, put the stuff inside and send it on its merry way. I'm sure the local vicars will be delighted at not having to beg for jumble, to find bags of it on their doorsteps."

Jenny giggled helplessly. "Like sending coals to Newcastle?" she suggested mischievously. "Oh, how I'd love to see their faces when they see what's in the bags!" She paused uncertainly. "And when I've got shot of the jumble, then what? What about my stall? How shall I earn a living when I've nothing left to sell? And if I leave here, I shan't have a roof over my head."

"Not *if* you leave here, *when* you leave here," Kate said briskly. "And having nothing to sell will present no problems since you'll be giving up your stall as soon as the house has been cleared, and coming to stay with me for a while until we decide what to do next. All right?"

Jenny looked puzzled. "I honestly wouldn't have believed it," she said.

"Believed what?"

"Time was when you couldn't say boo to a goose! Now look at you! Talk about taking the initiative! Telling me what to do!"

"High time someone did. So what do you think of my plan of action? Are you for it or against it?"

"You mean I have a choice?" Jenny felt suddenly trapped, resentful of Kate's well-meant interference in her life. But what alternative was left to her?

"Of course you do. I'm sorry, I had no right to assume you'd want to leave your home or give up your livelihood at my say so. But I would like you to accept payment of your arrears. Otherwise, you wouldn't have any choice about leaving here, would you?"

"I suppose not," Jenny admitted gloomily, "as long as the money is in the nature of a loan. I'm not looking for charity. I'll pay back every penny once I'm back on my feet."

"Fair enough," Kate conceded, "a loan it is then. Let's make it two hundred pounds, shall we? That way you won't need to worry about next month's rent." Opening her shoulder-bag, she produced her chequebook and pen.

Signing the cheque, she handed it to Jenny, then got up to leave, realising there was nothing more to be said for the time being, fully understanding Jenny's reluctance to accept charity, as she herself had been when Alex offered her the job as his housekeeper.

On the doorstep, dodging drips from the leaky guttering, she said, "If you should change your mind about staying with me, you'll find me at Gull House in King Street. I'll write it down for you."

Smiling brightly, she added, "Well goodbye for now, love, and good luck."

Afterwards, Kate thought how badly she had handled a delicate situation. Jenny had put it in a nutshell when she'd said, "Talk about taking the initiative. Telling me what to do." The "girl" had been resentful of her well-meant interference, and rightly so. (Strange, she still thought of Jenny as a girl, not a middle-aged woman.)

More to the point, how did Jenny see *her*? As a rich meddler, most likely, with her readily available chequebook and pen. Worst of all, a patronising rich bitch. Nothing could be further from the truth. All she had really wanted was to get her friend well away from her present environment, to offer her a ray of hope for the future. Apparently she had failed utterly to do so. And this was her own fault. Marching in where angels might fear to tread!

As she made ready for bed, an old adage of her mother's sprang to mind. "One may lead a horse to water. Twenty cannot make it drink!"

Next morning, in the kitchen making toast and coffee, she heard the rattle of the letterbox. Hurrying downstairs in her dressing gown, her heart skipped a beat. There, at last, was a letter from Alex.

Fourteen

T he letter gave no clue as to Alex's present whereabouts. It was post-marked Turkey and had been written in Ankara over a week ago.

Dear Kate,

To let you know that I am staying here for a few days to catch up with overdue correspondence and make the necessary arrangements for the next stage of my journey. Where to, I haven't yet decided.

Have been away from so-called civilisation these past few months and I'm finding an overcrowded city difficult to come to terms with after the solitude of the Arabian Desert. My hotel suite, though quite large and air-conditioned, feels as claustrophobic as a shoebox.

But needs must, as the saying goes, and there are certain compensations – the benison of hot running water in my marble-tiled bathroom, a balcony from which it is possible to catch a breath of air and to look up at the stars at nightfall.

I think of you often, and hope that you are enjoying Gull House and coping well with the responsibilities which I, perhaps selfishly, heaped upon you.

Knowing you as well as I think I do, I could not have chosen a more reliable person to take care of my home during my absence.

Yours ever sincerely,

Alex

Bitterly disappointed by the contents of the letter she had awaited so long – "Yours ever sincerely", indeed – stuffing it into her shoulder-bag, Kate marched down the fire-escape to the yard to apply a second coat of whitewash to the brickwork, slapping it on with abandon, her disappointment laced with anger that Alex had not begun the letter, "My dear Kate", had not ended it "With love from Alex".

Except, of course, that he did not love her, and she was not and never would be anything more to him than "Dear Kate"; certainly not "My dear Kate".

Deriving a grim satisfaction from the task in hand, Kate thought angrily that Alex might have saved himself the trouble of buying a stamp, might just as well have not bothered to write to her at all to say – virtually nothing of importance. He might at least have told her where he was heading. He must have had some idea, some destination in mind. Presumably he would not simply drive to the nearest airport and toss a coin on the tarmac? Heads the North Pole, tails Timbuktu!

Deep in thought, slap-dashing away with her paint brush, she looked up sharply when someone called her name: "Mrs Ford? Mrs Kate Ford?"

Two young police constables were standing outside the back gate, looking into the yard at her. Startled, she dropped the brush she was holding, splattering the paving stones with wet paint. "Yes, I'm Mrs Ford," she said hoarsely. "Why do you ask? What do you want? Is anything the matter?"

"Just a word please, if you'll unbolt the gate for us."

"Yes, of course, if you'll hang on just a sec till I wipe my hands." She did so hastily on a paint-rag she had placed on the fire-escape next to a bottle of turpentine for that purpose, her mind racing, stunned by the appearance of the Law on her doorstep, wondering what she had done wrong.

She withdrew the bolts, facing them squarely. "Please, come in," she said as calmly as she could, "and tell me what all this is about."

"I'm PC Newton, and this is PC Warburton," the spokesman of the pair informed her, speaking quietly. "There's been an accident, I'm afraid, and your name and address was found in the woman's possession in the Casualty Ward of the hospital, where she was taken in the early hours of this morning, before being admitted to the Intensive Care Unit."

"*Woman?* What – woman?" Kate asked perplexedly, her mind a blank momentarily. "You don't mean Mrs Paulson, do you?"

Police Constable Newton consulted his notebook. "No, not Mrs Paulson, a Miss Jenny Laird, who suffered a fractured skull and other

119

injuries after, apparently, falling down a steep flight of stairs at her home sometime between two and three a.m."

"*Jenny?*" Kate looked at the man in horror. "Oh my God! I must go to her at once. They will let me see her, won't they?"

"Are you related to her, Mrs Ford?"

"No, just a friend of long standing. We were at school together."

"Has she any next of kin?"

"I don't know. Her parents may still be alive but they left Scarborough some time ago. We, that is Jenny and I, had lost touch with one another till yesterday. She invited me to her home last evening."

"At what time?"

"Seven thirty." Impatiently, "Why do you ask? Is it important?"

"And what time did you leave?"

"I can't remember exactly. Around nine o'clock, I imagine."

"Did she mention expecting another visitor later on that night?"

"No." A dreadful thought occurred to Kate. "Are you telling me that what happened to her wasn't an – accident?"

"That's not up to me to say, ma'am. We are simply making further enquiries into the cause of the incident, based on the possibility of an intruder entering the house in the early hours of the morning."

"I see," Kate said bleakly, wondering if Jenny had been speaking the truth about ending her relationships with the men in her life? Probably not. The fact remained that she was lying, seriously injured, in hospital, in need of all the help and support that she, Kate, could provide.

"May I go to her now?" she said. Tears filled her eyes. Poor Jenny, she thought. Poor, dear, foolish Jenny. Her own worst enemy.

And, "Yes, of course, ma'am," PC Newton assured her. "Our car's parked just round the corner. We'll drive you to the hospital right away, if that's OK with you?"

"Thank you," Kate murmured gratefully, at the same time dreading what might confront her at the journey's end.

It was far worse than she had imagined. Never till her dying day would she forget seeing Jenny lying, still and pale, in a hospital bed, her head swathed in bandages following an emergency operation to remove a blood clot from her fractured skull.

Sitting beside her bed, holding her hand, Kate thought how young and innocent she looked with her face devoid of make-up, her eyes tightly closed against the pain of consciousness of a world which had treated her so badly.

There were hospital sounds all about her – the swish of curtains on metal rods, quiet yet purposeful footsteps, the movement of trolleys, voices; overlaid with smells peculiar to hospitals – of antiseptics and food, of cut flowers and sickness, recalling memories of her mother's final illness when every room in the house had smelt of . . . death.

What really had happened in the early hours of this morning to cause Jenny's headlong fall down a steep flight of stairs? And what were her chances of recovery from her injuries?

Please God, don't let Jenny die, Kate prayed inwardly. Give her a second chance to make something of her life.

The ward sister entered the cubicle at that moment. "I think you should leave now, Mrs Ford," she said kindly. "Leave your phone number at the reception desk on your way out. We'll contact you in case of an emergency."

Rising to her feet, relinquishing Jenny's hand, Kate said tautly, "Please be honest with me. What are her chances?"

"I'm sorry, Mrs Ford, it's too early to say right now. At a rough guess, about fifty-fifty. She's a very poorly lady indeed."

"May I come back this evening?" Kate asked wistfully.

"Yes, of course you may." Drawn towards Kate, realising the depths of her distress, the ward sister said sympathetically, "Come as often as you wish. You are the only one who has come forward so far to show even the slightest interest in her welfare. Apparently she has no next of kin, but surely she must have friends, apart from yourself?"

"I really don't know," Kate admitted despondently. "I just wish I knew what happened to her in the early hours of this morning."

The ward sister said, sotto-voce, "As far as I know, a neighbour rang up the police station around two a.m. to complain of a so called 'domestic' row going on next door, followed by a scream, then silence. Then, to the best of my knowledge, failing to alert Miss Laird, policemen broke into the house to discover her lying unconscious at the foot of the stairs."

"I see, and thank you for telling me," Kate said quietly, with a backward glance at Jenny as she left the cubicle, made her way to the reception desk to leave her telephone number, and phoned for a taxi to take her back to Gull House.

In restless mood, Kate returned to the yard to clean up the paint from the paving stones. She worked automatically to wipe up the mess before it hardened, her mind centred not on the job in hand but on Jenny in her hospital bed with a fifty-fifty chance of survival.

The thought of her slipping away from life without regaining consciousness was impossible to come to terms with. Kate thanked God for the nosy neighbour who had called the police, otherwise Jenny would have stood no chance of survival whatsoever.

But who had been in the house with her in the early hours of the morning? It was almost certainly a man with whom she had quarrelled violently. Presumably one of her many men "friends", so called, whose presence had been unwelcome.

The only crumb of comfort, there would be a full-scale police enquiry into the matter to discover the identity of the man involved in the tragedy. Small comfort indeed if Jenny lost her battle for life. And if she did? Facing that terrible possibility, Kate, as her proxy next-of-kin, would do all in her power to ensure that her girlhood friend was accorded a fitting farewell, with a church service and lots of flowers. Jenny had always loved flowers, especially long-stemmed red roses.

And if she miraculously survived, what then? Impossible to cross that bridge till she came to it, Kate realised. "One may lead a horse to water, twenty cannot make it drink." Jenny alone would have the right to decide about her future, if she survived. *If?* Pray God that she would.

Having cleared up the spilt paint, Kate went to a florist's in town to buy flowers to take with her to the hospital that evening: a dozen long-stemmed red roses . . .

There had been no change in her patient's condition, a nurse advised Kate as she entered the cubicle to sit by her friend's bedside, clasping her hand until visiting hours were over and she had to return to Gull House, where, in a state of mental turmoil, she went up to the attic studio to attempt a return to normality, a sorting out of her muddled emotions in this, her favourite room of the house, where she felt closest to – Alex, no matter how far away from her he appeared to be right now. Or was she doing him a grave injustice in not having read his letter more carefully?

Seated at his desk, she took the letter from its envelope. Re-reading it, her eyes fell on the words "I think of you often", which she had scarcely noticed before, as if, reading the lines, she had failed to read between them.

A sudden feeling of warmth invaded her being, as though a small part of her had been with him even in the desert and that marble-tiled bathroom in Ankara, his balcony beneath the stars, if only as a recurring memory trapped within the recesses of his mind. And this, possibly, had been his reason for writing the letter, to let her know that she occupied at least a small corner of his life, if not his heart.

Darkness had long since fallen. The room was very still, very quiet; lamp-lit. Instinctively, Kate placed her hands on the typewriter keys, a kind of reaching out for – something. She scarcely knew what. Release from pain, perhaps; her mental anguish over Jenny? Forgetfulness of her present problems? An escape route into the past; make believe instead of reality?

Whatever the motivation, feeding a sheet of A4 bond, a carbon and a backing sheet of copy-paper into the machine, in that quiet, lamp-lit room, Kate began writing her novel: Chapter One. Page One.

Then suddenly, miraculously, the present day world ceased to exist, and she was one of a joyous crowd of folk trooping down Plantation Hill to witness the opening ceremony of John Fairgray Sharpin's "People's Park". She described the event in almost graphic detail: the heady scent of may blossom threaded with the tang of the sea washing in on the shore; the glimmer of gaslight from the arched, overhead brackets; the Kiddy family: the gentle giant, Albert, his pretty, shy wife, Mavis, their seriously minded son, John, and their problem daughter, Lucy, in search of enjoyment, fun and laughter, not knowing what the future held in store for them.

Totally immersed in the story, Kate's thoughts and imaginings simply flowed from her mind on to the paper by way of her quickly tapping fingers on the typewriter keyboard, until, at last, having completed the first chapter, totally exhausted, without bothering to undress, she lay down on the divan in a far corner of the room, and fell fast asleep.

In time to come, the long days and restless nights that followed would seem dreamlike to Kate, as they had done during her mother's illness when, alert to every sound and movement from the sick-room next to hers, she would get up to plump up the dear invalid's pillows, to gently sponge her forehead with lavender-water, to slake her thirst with sips of barley water from a feeding-cup, more often than not in the darkest hours before the dawn. A privilege, not a penance.

In time to come, Kate would also remember the pattern of her days during Jenny's fight for life. Morning and evening visits to the hospital, taking with her bunches of fresh flowers which Jenny could neither see nor scent – roses, carnations, freesias – plus fresh, clean cotton night-gowns, bottles of spray-on eau-de-Cologne to kill the hospital smells of antiseptics, boiled cabbage and decay.

Afterwards, her return to Gull House to get on with the next chapter of her book, forgetful of time, of the present, as she conjured up the arrival of rich folk, gentry families from London, at the Crown Hotel, in their horse-drawn carriages, to spend the summer months in pursuit of pleasure in those balcony suites overlooking the panorama of Scarborough's South Bay spread before them from Castle Hill to the Flamborough Head cliffs in the distance, as far as the eye could see.

Immersed in the opening chapters of her novel, possessed of an overwhelming fondness for the attic studio, Kate decided to sleep there from henceforth, in close proximity to Alex's divan, desk, typewriter and bookshelves. After all, the house was hers alone during his absence, and she needed no one's permission to sleep where she chose. And she had chosen to sleep here, as close as possible to the man she loved, wherever he happened to be right now, halfway up Mount Ararat in search of Noah's Ark, in a Tibetan monastery, in Mongolia, or down a salt-mine in Siberia!

Frankly, she couldn't care less where, just as long as he came home again one day, all in one piece, as large as life – and twice as difficult. A more than likely possibility. After all, Alex without bite would be like a boiled egg without salt and pepper; toast without butter and marmalade; rainy days without an umbrella!

Advertisements in the evening paper had yielded a crop of applicants from whom she and Dot Paulson had chosen one Cora Clegg, a smart twenty-five-year-old brunette, as the likeliest candidate for the job of sales assistant: the only interviewee with experience of selling what Dot referred to as "fancy goods". Not that Kate had cottoned on to Cora entirely, though she couldn't for the life of her have said why. She was a shade too smart in Kate's opinion, the type unlikely to risk breaking a polished fingernail opening boxes in the stockroom, or dirtying her hands dusting shelves.

On the other hand, she had worked in a Leed's jeweller's shop prior to coming to Scarborough to "be with her boyfriend" – in the biblical sense, one imagined. Hardly likely, Kate thought, that a smart cookie like Cora Clegg would have remained inviolate in the rat-race of life, especially not in Leeds.

Sensibly, Kate had left the final decision-making up to Mrs Paulson as the one responsible for showing Miss Clegg the ropes and in deference to Dot's role as the manageress of the shop below. Just as long as Dot was happy with her under-strapper, as she appeared to be, and as long as the shop remained open to cater to the requirements of customers during the busy summer season ahead of them, Kate saw no valid reason to interfere with Dot's decision to hire Miss Clegg as her assistant.

Later, Kate wrote to Alex's firm of solicitors in London, advising them of them of the changed situation regarding Mrs Paulson and the addition of Miss Cora Clegg's name to the payroll. She reminded them, at the same time, that she, Kate Ford, acting as their client's agent, had handled a tricky dilemma to the best of her ability on his behalf.

There would be no repercussions and no questions asked, due to her forethought in getting the legal aspects of her guardianship of his home and business affairs neatly sewn up before his departure for faraway places with strange sounding names.

She remembered his words at the time: "My God, Kate. I have to hand it to you. You've certainly got a wise head on your shoulders!"

"Well, at least I've got something going for me," she'd replied sarcastically. "Far better a wise head than a foolish heart, don't you agree?"

He'd laughed and said," You're right as usual, of course!"

If only she'd kept the sarcasm out of her voice. Why had she always felt the need to fence with him? A matter of pride, of self-preservation, she imagined, to keep her feelings towards him well under control. Now she wondered if, thinking of her often, he remembered her as a snappy, defensive individual, bossy and interfering? Her own stupid fault if he did.

Fifteen

A month passed, during which Jenny showed signs of physical improvement. Out of intensive care, she was moved into a side unit away from the bustle of the main women's ward, where she would receive the specialised nursing required after her close brush with death.

Now her mental state was causing concern, the ward sister told Kate. Not that she needed telling. Jenny's state of mind was apparent in her cavalier attitude towards herself and the nursing staff in general, fed on her deeply-rooted belief that there was nothing left to live for.

Making allowances, Kate understood why. Jenny's hair, her crowning glory, had been cut off – her head shaved prior to removal of the blood clot from her brain. A hard cross for any woman to bear, more so Jenny, who had taken a pride in that flowing mane of hers even as a schoolgirl, long before she had resorted to peroxide to "enhance" its fairness.

And it couldn't have been easy or pleasant for her when, regaining consciousness after the operation, police detectives, awaiting their opportunity, had begun asking questions about her so-called "accident". The name of the man with whom she had quarrelled so violently before her fall downstairs.

"I don't know! I can't remember!" had been her initial response to their questioning, the ward sister who had been present at the time, told Kate. "So I gave them their marching orders! Told them to clear off and give the poor lady a bit of peace. Asked 'em how *they'd* feel having questions fired at them after a brain operation!"

"Good for you! Then what happened?" Kate asked, liking the sister enormously for her gutsiness and courage in flying in the face of the Law.

The ward sister shrugged wearily. "Back they came next day. Well, I couldn't very well have stopped them, could I? Then Jenny admitted that her landlord had called on her the night in question, to collect the rent owing him – and more besides, if you get my meaning! Now I think she's scared of the repercussions, being forced to go to court to give evidence when his case comes up. The trouble is, she won't talk about it, she's bottling everything up inside. Even the counsellor who came to see her couldn't get through to her."

The sister paused. "We hoped that you, perhaps . . . ? After all, you are the one closest to her. In fact, the poor thing has no one else in the world – except you."

Kate shook her head. "Believe me, I've tried. She won't look at me half the time; just pretends to be asleep, or stares past me as if I were invisible. I don't know what to do about it. Frankly, I often wonder why I bother to come at all."

Sister Sheridan frowned. "That could be the answer! Stay away for a while. See how she reacts."

"Oh, I don't know," Kate demurred. "Wouldn't that be rather cruel?"

"Sometimes you have to be cruel to be kind," Sister Sheridan reminded her. "Another problem arises. What will become of her when she leaves hospital? She has nowhere to go that I'm aware of. Presumably she wouldn't want to go back to the – scene of the crime! It's a poor outlook all round. Apparently she had a stall in the market, but our welfare people discovered that it's been let to someone else. In any case, she'll be in no fit state to work for some time to come. So I guess she'll end up in sheltered accommodation: one of those state-registered homes for 'drop-outs', to put it bluntly."

"Not if I can help it," Kate said grimly. "The fact is, when I saw her on the eve of the accident, I invited her to live with me; offered to take care of her financially until she was back on her feet. She turned me down flat, I'm afraid. Her pride stood in the way of accepting what she thought of as – charity from a 'do-gooder'! My own fault entirely! I should have handled the situation more carefully, not charged in like a bull in a china shop! I've been kicking myself ever since!"

Sister Sheridan, christened Wendy, nick-named Dinah, a deeply caring person, said quietly, "We all make mistakes from time to time: say and do things we regret later." She paused momentarily. "The thing is, if, by chance, Jenny could be persuaded to change her mind about accepting your offer, would you still be willing to take care of her?"

Kate said hoarsely, close to tears, "Need you ask? Jenny was my childhood friend. I'd do anything – anything at all – to help her."

Sister Sheridan said understandingly, "Then take my advice, Mrs Ford, stay away from the hospital for a while. Give Jenny time to miss your daily visits, to switch her mind into other channels, to begin thinking in terms of the future ahead of her without your help and support. Above all, your – love."

"Very well, then, Sister, let's give it a whirl, shall we?" Clasping the ward sister's hand tightly in hers, choking back her tears, she said "My name is Kate, by the way. And yours is . . . ?"

"Dinah," Sheridan said wryly.

The shop appeared to be running smoothly, with Dot Paulson doing the ordering and keeping a watchful eye on Miss Clegg, who appeared not to need "showing the ropes", having a full complement of reef knots, bowlines and sheepshanks at her polished fingertips, Dot remarked, somewhat tartly, when Kate asked her how Cora was coping, to which complaint Kate turned a deaf ear. She had more than enough on her plate to contend with right then, without adding the shop to her list of worries.

All else had paled to insignificance compared with her anxiety concerning Jenny's future. Staying away from the hospital – being cruel to be kind – had left her weary from lack of sleep, guilt-ridden that she had, seemingly, deserted her friend at a time when she stood in dire need of her love and support.

And yet, weighing up the pros and cons, Kate realised how little her daily visits, her gifts of fruit and flowers, had meant to Jenny, who had seemed to despise, rather than welcome, her presence at her bedside. Even so, staying away from Jenny for a day, let alone a week, had proved a burden almost impossible to bear, until . . .

When Kate revisited the hospital on the seventh day of their separation, miraculously, propped up with pillows, with tears streaming down her sunken cheeks, hands outspread in greeting, Jenny uttered weakly, "Oh, Kate, I'm so pleased to see you again! I've missed you so much! I thought you'd forgotten all about me!"

Kate cradled the weeping woman in her arms. "Forgotten about you, Jenny? Never in this world, my love," Kate said mistily. "So let us make this a new beginning, shall we? Taking care of one another as we used to in the old days?"

"Yes," Jenny murmured drowsily against Kate's shoulder, "I'd like that. Taking care of *you*, I mean! Helping you in the house, anything at all. I'll find myself a job; pay back the money you lent me."

"All in good time. As soon as you're back on your feet," Kate said gently. "Try to rest now, and stop worrying. Everything will work out fine, you'll see."

Plumping up the pillows, smoothing the counterpane, kissing Jenny goodnight, Kate turned to smile at her as she left the ward, but she was already fast asleep; looking for all the world like a little girl.

Dinah was in the corridor, anxiously awaiting news of the encounter. "Well?" she asked, in a low voice. "How did it go?"

When Kate told her, "Oh, thank God," Dinah said fervently. "That's the best news I've had in ages. How wonderful to know she'll soon be going home!"

"How soon? At a rough guess?"

"A month or so," Dinah reckoned. "Of course, she'll still need nursing, but we'll give you all the help we can. We have a great team of district nurses. Best of all, she'll have *you!*" She paused, "Now, take my advice, go home and get a good night's sleep. You look all in!"

Up early next morning, like a giant refreshed, Kate walked briskly up Newborough to the town centre, a shopping list a mile long tucked into her shoulder-bag, feeling more alert, far happier than she had done for many a long day, as if a whole new future had suddenly opened up before her on this glorious, sunshiny June morning, with loneliness dispelled, and with so many plans in mind to give Jenny the welcome home she deserved.

Kate would continue to sleep in the attic studio, close to Alex's desk and typewriter. Meanwhile, she intended to make over her old bedroom as Jenny's special and private retreat from the world, if that's what she wanted, complete with brand new furniture – a deeply sprung single bed, rosy-shaded bedside lamps with matching bed-linen, and a triple-mirrored dressing table skirted with rose-embellished cretonne, its surface arrayed with crystal flagons of French perfume.

This, Kate realised, along with her plans to refurbish the double bedroom in readiness for Greg and Cynthia, whom she intended to invite for a visit sometime in July, during her brother's summer vacation, quite apart from the cost of the Provençal pots and the plants she had ordered to enhance the back yard of Gull House, would bite into her building society "nest-egg". So what if it did? What, exactly, was she saving up for anyway? A lonely old age?

Jenny came home on the second day of July, accompanied by two stalwart ambulancemen who helped her up the stairs to her room on the first floor, on the threshold of which, taking in the decor, the vase of red roses on the dressing table, alongside the elegant flagons of French perfume, she burst into tears, stumbling blindly towards Kate's arms, opened wide to receive, to comfort and caress her.

"It's lovely," Jenny sobbed. "I don't deserve it."

One of the men had gone downstairs to bring up a wheelchair. "Here you are, my duck," he said cheerily, "in case you feel like a spin!"

"If you think I'm going out in that thing," Jenny sniffed, "you think wrong!"

The man laughed. "No skin off my nose, my duck, but it'll come in useful about the house, if nowt else!"

Sensing an awkward situation, Kate asked the men if they had time for a cuppa, but felt relieved when they turned down the offer, saying they were running late as it was, and clattered downstairs, leaving her alone with Jenny, seated forlornly on the edge of the bed, tears streaming down her cheeks, staring at the wheelchair as if it were an instrument of torture. "Why did they have to bring that bloody thing?" she uttered hoarsely. "I can manage perfectly well without it!"

Kate's heart sank momentarily, faced with the realisation that coping with an invalid, no matter how dear to her, would not be easy: entailing both tact and determination on her part to strike an acceptable level of give and take. Not to allow her fondness for Jenny to stand in the way of doing whatever was necessary in her own best interests.

She said quietly yet firmly, "The bathroom's at the end of the landing. The wheelchair, I imagine, will come in useful should you wish to get there in a hurry!"

"Without bothering you, you mean?" Jenny asked sharply.

"No, not exactly that," Kate said levelly, "more as a means of retaining your spirit of independence! Now, love, it's almost lunchtime. Come through to the kitchen when you're ready. That's the door opposite yours. All right?"

Shock tactics had worked once before, hopefully they would do so again, Kate thought, peeling mushrooms and beating eggs in preparation for the simple omelette lunch she had planned, but what if she was wrong? She had been wrong so often in her life before,

What if, despite her good intentions, she proved inadequate to cope with Jenny as she now was, a tetchy, demanding, insecure invalid, no longer even faintly resembling her laughing girlhood companion of long ago?

Suddenly, Kate remembered her visit to "Madame Zara", and the old woman's words: "Many people, some close to you, others not so close, are in need of your help right now. You'll need to be strong for their sake. And you will be, of that I'm sure."

Strong? Kate had never felt weaker than she did right now, more uncertain of herself or her motivation in living – a far cry from the day she had walked into town so confidently to buy the new furniture and fittings for Jenny's room and the one intended for Greg and Cindy if they accepted her invitation to spend their summer vacation at Gull House.

If only she knew for certain that she was not "wasting her sweetness on the desert air". That the garden she had created in the back yard of Gull House would not bloom in vain; that Alex Arden was alive and well somewhere in the world; that the omelette she was about to cook wouldn't stick to the bottom of the frying pan! If only she could receive a sign, a signal, a message of some kind, to restore her flagging self-confidence, her faith in the future.

Suddenly, Jenny entered the kitchen, in her wheelchair.

"All right, Kate, you win," she said quietly, close to tears. "I'll behave myself from now on, and that's a promise!"

Hiding her emotion as best she could, Kate said, tongue-in-cheek, "Well, don't just sit there doing nothing! Set the table! The cutlery's in that drawer over yonder!"

The old rapport between them developed slowly at first. This Kate accepted patiently, knowing they both needed time and space to adjust to their altered circumstances. She had no intention of forcing Jenny to talk about the night of the accident or anything else for that matter, until she felt like it. On the other hand, she had her own life to live, her book to get on with.

One day, bursting with curiosity, sounding somewhat piqued, Jenny said tartly, "What I can't figure out is what you get up to in your bedroom for hours on end! Have you a secret admirer by any chance?"

Kate laughed. "Who, me? Hardly likely! No, something far more interesting. I'm trying my hand at writing a novel."

"You are? What's it about?"

When Kate explained, Jenny advised, "You'll need to spice it up a

bit, I reckon, otherwise it won't stand a chance of getting published."
Speaking as one who knew, she said, "People want sex nowadays, lots
of steamy bedroom scenes, naked bodies, flashing eyes and heaving
breasts!"

"You may be right," Kate conceded cannily, sensing Jenny's need to
talk, not about the novel, but herself, and what had really happened on
the night of the "accident". The kind of breakthrough she had hoped
for ever since Jenny came to live with her.

A long silence ensued, then Jenny said hoarsely, "I was upstairs,
getting ready for bed, when I sensed that I was not alone in the house. I
called out, 'Who's there?', but I knew it was *him*. It had to be him, the
only person who had a key to the front door!

"Oh, God, Kate, it was awful, hearing his footsteps on the stairs,
knowing he was bound to find me sooner or later. There was no place
to hide, you see? I was scared stiff of him, too scared to move, so I just
stood there, petrified, near the bed, knowing he'd be the worse for
drink, dreading what he might do to me when he found me!

"Then, when he opened the door of my room, swaying on his feet, I
ran past him on to the landing and started shouting for help. Next thing
I knew, he caught up with me, calling me names, threatening to kill me
if I didn't keep quiet, if I didn't give him what he wanted.

"But I didn't keep quiet. I couldn't. I just kept on screaming at him to
go away and leave me alone. Then he hit me in the stomach and I fell
back against the banister, gasping for breath, clawing at the rail for
support, only I couldn't get hold of it properly, and I fell backwards
down the stairs, with him on the landing above, watching me, doing
nothing to help me.

"I remember the pain when my head hit the floor, then everything
blacked out. The next thing I knew, I was in hospital and . . . " Jenny
stopped speaking abruptly.

"And?" Kate prompted her gently.

"When I opened my eyes, you were there, and there were red roses on
the locker."

"So you did notice them?" Kate smiled.

"Yes, but I was too upset about my hair to bother about flowers, and
then those detectives came to fire questions at me. It was awful, just
awful, lying there with all those wires attached to me and knowing I was
bald! I felt like a criminal – one of those women collaborators who had
their heads shaved for sleeping with German soldiers during the war!"

"I know, love, and I'm sorry. But your hair's beginning to grow now, and it looks quite charming, a bit like Ingrid Bergman's in *For Whom The Bell Tolls*. I saw the film on television a while back, and I read somewhere that her short curly haircut started a craze for a style named after her screen character, Maria. Apparently hairdressers were swamped with clients wanting short, 'Maria' hair-dos!"

"Oh, I know what you're driving at," Jenny uttered sarcastically, "You're just trying to make me feel better about my inch-long stubble! But you're wasting your breath!"

Kate sighed deeply. "In which case I'd better stop talking and start typing," she said lightly, determined not to let Jenny get the better of her; fast becoming inured to those rapid mood swings of hers – sweetly compliant one minute, irritatingly hostile the next.

Refusing to engage in a battle of wills and words, to succumb to emotional blackmail, Kate went upstairs to her studio to get on with the next chapter of her book. The chapter in which Lucy Kiddy had run away to Brighton with her cellarman lover, so madly in love with him that she couldn't have cared less that he was twice her age, married to someone else, and the father of four children, the oldest of which was a mere two years younger than herself.

And this, Kate recognised, immersed in her novel, was her means of escape from the exigencies of the present into the less stressful, shadowy world of the past, at her fingertips on the keys of Alex Arden's typewriter.

She loved Jenny with all her heart. Of course she did, but not to the extent of becoming her "whipping boy", spoiling her rotten, when what the girl most needed was the incentive to stand up, tall and proud, on her own two feet. She'd need to face the future ahead of her with all flags flying when it came to appearing in a court of law to give evidence against her former landlord.

Mulling over Jenny's advice to add steamy sex scenes to her novel, Kate decided not to. For one thing, she knew next to nothing about torrid bedroom encounters, flashing eyes and heaving breasts. All she really knew about was love – the finer feelings of a wife for her husband. In the early days of her marriage, there had been intense pleasure and delight in the act of physical intimacy with the man she loved. It was love, not sex, she wished to portray, to capture within the the pages of her book. Albert Kiddy's deep, unselfish love for his wife and family, for instance.

Above all, she had no intention of casting Lucy Kiddy in the role of a wanton, a whore, a home-wrecker. Rather as a romantically minded young woman desperate for the good things in life, glimpsed at the Crown Hotel, where girls not half as pretty as herself wallowed in the lap of luxury.

How easily Lucy must have succumbed to the blandishments of a handsome older man, earning good wages, who had promised her the earth if only she would go with him to Brighton to an even better paid job he'd applied for and accepted.

How could she have possibly refused that offer? Blinkered by love, seeing before her an escape route from her humdrum life in Scarborough, feeling herself to be the heroine of a romantic novelette, she had rushed headlong into an affair of the heart destined to end in failure: the humiliation of being hauled back to the bosom of her family by her caring father; the appearance also on the scene, in that Brighton hotel, of her lover's plain, middle-aged wife, the mother of his four children, of whom she had known nothing until the day of reckoning had arrived.

So what if her book received the thumbs down sign from potential publishers? Kate considered carefully. Frankly, she couldn't care less about publication. She was writing this book to please herself. "This, above all, to thine own self be true. Thou cans't not then be false to any man," she remembered.

Sixteen

The garden was looking quite lovely, Kate thought: worth all the effort she'd put into it. Apart from the flower-filled Provençal pots, she'd also splashed out on hanging baskets of trailing ivies and lobelia to enhance the colour-washed walls, and a wrought iron table and chairs, with Jenny in mind, thinking it would do her good to sit outdoors in the sunshine and fresh air, now that she was regaining the use of her legs and was able to negotiate the fire-escape, albeit slowly and clinging to the handrail for support.

In reply to Kate's invitation to her brother and his wife to spend their summer vacation in Scarborough, Greg had responded eagerly that they would look forward enormously to a holiday at the seaside. Above all, to seeing her again, which Kate took with a grain of salt, doubtful that Cindy shared her husband's enthusiasm for her sister-in-law's company. Somehow, she and Cindy could never quite see eye-to-eye, for the usual reason: that Cindy was jealous of Greg's close sibling relationship with his sister, resentful of their shared memories of growing up together.

Curiously, Jenny remembered Greg quite well from Kate's wedding day. "Is he as handsome as ever?" she asked eagerly.

"Handsome? Greg?" Kate laughed. "I doubt he ever saw himself as such. Certainly not as the dashing hero type."

"Well, nice-looking then," Jenny insisted. "Kind of warm and cuddly, with a lovely smile and charming manners."

"I'm sure his wife would agree with you," Kate said warily, "if you were daft enough to voice that opinion in her presence."

"Oh, I get the message! The jealous type, is she?" Jenny wrinkled her nose disdainfully. "But all's fair in love and war, and I should know!"

"If you mean what I think you mean, forget it," Kate retorted, irritated by Jenny's stupid remarks. "Remember that you are a guest here beneath my roof. Greg is my brother, and blood is thicker than

135

water! I'm warning you, Jenny, any of your fancy tricks and you'll be out of here faster than you can say knife!"

"All right, keep your shirt on," Jenny replied huffily. "The trouble with you is, you can't take a joke. I've had enough trouble with men to last me a lifetime."

"All right. Let's leave it at that, shall we?" They were in the garden at the time, Jenny holding a mug of coffee, leaning back in her chair, eyes narrowed against the sun. Glancing sideways at Kate, looking worried, she said, "That stuff about giving me the elbow. You didn't really mean it, did you?"

"Look at it this way," Kate, said levelly. "Hopefully, that's a decision I shall not be called upon to make."

The conversation had left a sour taste in Kate's mouth. For the first time she faced squarely the realisation that Jenny, as she was now, bore no resemblance to the girl she used to be. Some essential sweetness in her nature was gone beyond recall.

Scarcely surprising, Kate reflected, after all she had been through in her adult years. She had felt so certain that, given time, she might rekindle the embers of her friend's former kindness of heart, and there had been times when, in Jenny's gentler moments, she had glimpsed something of the tender young girl of long ago.

Now she wondered if she had ever really known Jenny at all? Or had she, along with teachers and classmates alike, simply fallen under the spell of the most popular girl in school? Blinded by her beauty, her bewitching personality, had she failed to recognise her underlying selfishness and shallowness of mind?

That day, for instance, when turning up on her doorstep, insistent on making up a foursome for a trip to the cinema with Don as her blind date, had she been concerned about Kate's welfare, or her own frustration at being lumbered with her current boyfriend's flatmate when she wished to be alone with – what was his name? – John Spivey! Ah yes, John Spivey, the man who had asked Jenny to marry him – who, in the long run, she had turned down flat because he wasn't good enough for her.

The truth struck Kate forcibly amidships! Lying sleepless in bed that night, she reflected that if it hadn't been for Jenny's interference, she might never have met Don Ford! There would have been no hastily arranged winter wedding, no April Cottage, no dead babies to mourn – no Lucia Keane, no divorce. And more than likely, no Alex Arden, no

Gull House, no Jenny Laird beneath her roof to pose even the slightest threat to her own peace of mind and, more importantly, that of her brother, Greg.

Peace of mind? Kate thought wearily, longing for the benison of sleep. Peace of mind had been at a premium since she had invited Jenny to live with her, since when she had been strung on a high-wire of emotional tension occasioned by her guest's rapid mood swings, from elation one minute to despair the next. Calculated? More than likely, Kate pondered, coming to grips with the realisation that the Jenny Laird she had so loved and admired in the days of her youth and girlhood, no longer existed. If, indeed, she ever had done so, beyond the realms of her own imagination. Well, Jenny had warned her that this was so.

And yes, blood was far thicker than water! Greg needed a holiday, freedom and relaxation away from the exigencies of his job. Teaching was no easy option. She had seen for herself the faint network of worry lines on his face at their last meeting, noticed the tenseness about him, the weary droop of his shoulders, the signs of a man growing old before his time, and her heart had gone out to him: wanting to ease his burden in some way. That was when the holiday idea had taken root and she had thought how much he'd enjoy a month by the sea, revisiting all the old familiar places he had known and loved as a boy.

Common sense told Kate that Cindy would have tried to talk him out of spending his summer vacation in England, much less a common-or-garden seaside resort like Scarborough. Knowing her sister-in-law, she would have plumped for Spain or Italy, Rimini or the Costa del Sol: one of those package holidays with sight-seeing tours included in the deal, hotels serving English food, rather than all that "foreign muck" – pasta and paella, pizzas, olives and anchovies, with not a decent cup of tea to be had. In which case, why bother to go abroad in the first place, Kate thought irritably. But this was typical of Cindy, in search not of culture but kudos.

Kate's assumption was correct. Cindy's resentment showed the minute she crossed the threshold. Obviously she regarded her holiday home for the coming month as below par, faced with flights of creaking stairs, narrow landings and passages, a far cry from her spacious, labour-saving bungalow on the outskirts of Manchester.

Greg, on the other hand, was over the moon with Gull House, and especially the bedroom, smelling of fresh paint and wallpaper, soap and water and sea air, with spotlessly clean linen and summer flowers from the vase of stocks and long-stemmed roses on the dressing table.

"You've gone to an awful lot of trouble," he said quietly. "I just hope you haven't worn yourself out, that's all."

Kate laughed. "I didn't do the decorating myself, if that's what you mean, and a dear friend of mine comes in twice a week to help with the housework." She meant Fanny Kiddy who came in on Tuesdays and Fridays to give the place what she termed "a good bottoming".

Cindy simply stared round the room with lack-lustre eyes, at logger-heads with her husband because he had refused, point blank, to spend his summer vacation on the Costa Brava along with a coach-load of British tourists wearing sun-glasses, shorts and colourful shirts, armed with cameras, and wanting bacon, sausages, fried eggs and baked beans for breakfast.

At the height of their quarrel, Greg had uttered wearily, "Very well, then, Cindy, make your own arrangements. Go to the Costa Brava if that will make you happy! But my mind is made up. I'm going to Scarborough!"

Changing her tune in a matter of seconds, she'd retorted sharply, "Not on your own, you're not. The very idea! To suck up to that precious sister of yours, I suppose? Well, I'm your *wife*, and don't you forget it!"

As if he could, Greg had thought despairingly. Chance would be a fine thing, wondering why he had married Cynthia in the first place. But of course, deep down, he knew why. Because she had been very pretty in her younger days and lionised him, a university student with a promising career ahead of him. Desperately lonely and unhappy following the death of his parents and his sister's departure to the West Country, in dire need of comfort, of release from his loneliness of spirit, he had seen a solution to his problems in the shape of a comely young woman more than willing to offer him the benison of a shoulder to cry on, with certain reservations, of course. Marriage, above all. A wedding ring placed firmly on the third finger of her left hand.

And so Greg had placed, unthinkingly, that band of gold on his bride's left hand, realising too late that, like Esau in the Old Testament, he had sold his birthright of freedom for a "mess of pottage".

Aware of Cindy's hostility, Kate pointed out the bathroom and the whereabouts of the kitchen, remarking that she had a friend staying with her at the moment, and that tea would be ready in the kitchen when they had finished unpacking.

Catching Cindy's look of disapproval, she said brightly, "We have all our meals in the kitchen. The old dining room was swallowed up some years ago when the property was altered to make room for a shop. Fortunately the kitchen is quite spacious, and remarkably handy for the person doing the cooking." She added, "My room is upstairs – a bedroom-cum-studio, with a view of the sea from the dormer window. I'll show it to you later. But first things first. I daresay you're ready for a cuppa."

Jenny had been into town yesterday, by taxi, to do some shopping, refusing Kate's offer to go with her, saying she could manage perfectly well on her own. She needed some new clothes, which was true enough. Since her dramatic weight loss, she had taken to wearing a dressing gown about the house, hardly suitable attire to wear in the presence of what she termed "company". And Kate agreed with her for once, dreading Cindy's reaction to a woman in a satin robe and slippers putting in an appearance at meal times.

Kate simply hoped and prayed that Jenny had not wasted the money she'd given her on anything too outlandish or bizarre. She'd have to wait and see, since Jenny had stubbornly refused to reveal the contents of the various carrier bags she'd brought back with her.

Setting the tea-table with cups, saucers, plates and cutlery, thinly cut egg and cress sandwiches, homemade scones and cakes, Kate had nervously awaited the arrival of her guests. Not Greg, but Cindy and Jenny, knowing that her sister-in-law would not take kindly to eating in the kitchen. As for Jenny, heaven alone knew how she would react to meeting the impeccably dressed Cindy. Not to mention Greg. Pray God she wouldn't fling her arms about him, smother him with kisses and chatter on inanely about having met him before on his sister's wedding day. But she wouldn't bet on it! Discretion was a word unknown in Jenny's vocabulary.

Preceding her husband into the room, Cindy glanced coldly at the well set table. Greg positively glowed. "What a lovely spread," he remarked, "and what a charming kitchen!" taking in the prettily curtained windows, gleaming paintwork, red geraniums blooming on the windowsills, and the fire-escape door, standing wide open to let in sunshine and fresh air. "Where does that lead to?" he asked eagerly.

"The garden," Kate said proudly, putting on the kettle to boil. "Mind if I take a look?"

"Feel free!" Kate smiled at his boyishness, his enthusiasm as he stepped on to the fire-escape, his obvious pleasure in the small oasis she had created from a once dreary back yard. She could have wept when he said quietly, " 'And yet the fool contends that God is not.' " A quotation from a half-forgotten poem of long ago. How did it go? Making the tea, suddenly she remembered. "Not God in gardens when the eve is cool? Nay, but I have a sign. 'Tis very sure God walks in mine".

"Oh, for heaven's sake, Greg, come in and have your tea," Cindy said irritably, destroying his moment of pleasure in a fraction of a second, wiping away his enthusiasm in less time than it would take to shatter a mirror with a well-aimed clod of earth.

"Sorry," was all he said, sitting down at the table.

Kate was pouring the tea when the door opened and Jenny appeared on the threshold, a slender figure wearing a pencil-slim grey skirt, a pink, lightweight, short-sleeved cashmere sweater, her face devoid of make-up, and with her newly washed, inch-long hair, curling gently on to her forehead, about her ears and on to the nape of her neck.

"I'm sorry if I've kept you waiting," she said breathlessly, "but I fell fast asleep. You see, I've been ill recently, and I haven't yet quite recovered my full health and strength. My name's Jenny Laird, by the way. Kate and I have been friends since our childhood days. As a matter of fact, I was her bridesmaid on her wedding day, all of twenty-three years ago. But we were friends long before that, at school, weren't we, Kate?"

Jenny Laird, a bridesmaid at Kate's wedding? Greg thought, casting his mind back to that day almost a quarter of a century ago, vaguely recalling a curvaceous blonde with waist-long hair, who had given him the "glad-eye" over a glass of champagne. But surely this could not possibly be the same woman?

"I gave my sister away, on her wedding day," he said hesitantly. "Don't you remember?"

Glancing at him coolly, Jenny said, "No, I'm afraid not," lying through her teeth, to Kate's infinite relief, "but it was a long, long time ago."

"Yes, I suppose so," Greg conceded. He added, feeling foolish, "Well, since you have so obviously forgotten all about me, my name is Greg, and this is my wife, Cindy."

"Oh, how do you do, Mrs Harker?" Jenny uttered solemnly.

"Quite nicely, thank you," Cindy replied frostily, suspecting some kind of liaison, however long ago, between this woman and her husband, which she would ferret out in due course, to her own satisfaction.

Oh God, Kate thought, pouring out the tea, handing round the cups and passing the plates of food, better by far a bizarrely clad Jenny complete with over-the-top make-up and long dangling earrings, or even wearing a dressing gown and slippers, than her understated alter-ego, all prunes and prisms, as if butter wouldn't melt in her mouth. So what, precisely, was she up to? Only time would tell. Or had she really turned over a new page in her life, at last?

After tea, Greg persuaded Cindy to take a walk to St Nicholas Cliff to look at the sea. Jenny had excused herself prettily, in the manner of "La Dame aux Camellias" about to suffer a relapse, and gone to her room for "a bit of a lie down", while Kate had elected to stay behind to make preparations for their evening meal: roast chicken with all the trimmings, followed by a substantial steamed pudding and custard such as their mother used to make in the old days, knowing Greg's fondness for custard, and jam sponge pudding in particular.

No doubt Cindy would jib at anything so fattening. But then, Cindy jibbed at most things nowadays, apart from holidays abroad, smart new clothes, tightly permed hair, and garden gnomes – with or without fishing-rods! In which case, she would be offered the alternative of fresh fruit salad or ice-cream.

Stuffing the chicken, preparing the vegetables, rubbing fat into flour, Kate realised that her brother had married the wrong woman, and he was paying the full price of his mistake, just as she had paid the full price in marrying the wrong man. But who could tell, at the beginning of things, lacking experience of life, what the end result would be?

Supper, or "dinner" as Cindy preferred to call it, was a fraught occasion. Jenny appeared, bright eyed and bushy-tailed after her nap, wearing a blue cotton dress which gave her the appearance of Alice in Wonderland.

Serving the food, Kate sensed Cindy's hostility towards Jenny, and vice-versa, and knew that Greg sensed it too, sitting there like a rose between thorns. At least he and Jenny did justice to the meal; Cindy merely picked at her portion of roast chicken, and pointedly pushed aside the runner beans and potatoes to the edge of her plate, declaring peevishly that she wasn't hungry, and felt like an early night.

"You *do* look a bit washed out," Jenny remarked, biting into a chipolata sausage. "Must be all the excitement and fresh air!"

Kate could have strangled her with her bare hands! Telling Cindy she looked "washed out" was akin to playing Russian Roulette with a fully loaded revolver. Oh God, she thought nervously, how would Cindy react to jam sponge pudding and custard? But, deep down, she knew exactly what her reaction would be.

Rising quickly to her feet at the appearance of the pudding, and despite Kate's offer of ice-cream or fresh fruit salad as an alternative, she stalked out of the kitchen in high dudgeon, closely followed by Greg, who, murmuring an apology, went after his wife, presumably in an attempt to pour oil on troubled water.

Jenny said virtuously, "I feel really sorry for a nice bloke like Greg married to a spoilt cow of a woman like that, don't you?"

"All right, Jenny," Kate said levelly, "you've made your point, had your idea of fun, plus a darned good supper. Now, it's high time you had an 'early night' too, before I wipe the floor with you!"

Greg reappeared in the kitchen an hour later, looking drained, by which time Kate had cleared the table and done the washing up. Cutting short his apology on his wife's behalf, she said lightheartedly, "I have a present for you, upstairs in my room. A belated birthday present. Something rather special!"

Greg smiled, grateful for her understanding. He'd spent a miserable half hour listening to his wife's accusations of not caring tuppence about her welfare, flirting with "that woman" – she meant Jenny – and sucking up to his sister, making such a damned fuss of her cooking, as if he never got a decent meal at home.

Eventually, tight-lipped, he had walked out of the room. And, "Where do you think you're going?" she'd called after him, infuriated by his lack of response.

Now, on the threshold of Kate's eyrie, he said, "What a marvellous room," taking in the desk and bookshelves, the neat divan bed, dormer window, pictures and paintings on the walls; shaded lamps, the piles of neatly stacked folders and reams of paper near the typewriter, thinking how happy he would be if only he had a bolt-hole like this where he could work and sleep undisturbed, far removed from Cindy's constant, grating presence in his life.

Recently, he had begun to wonder how much more of her he could take without telling her exactly what he thought of her. But old habits died hard. He had learned to bite his tongue rather than precipitate a full-scale row, knowing her propensity for tears bordering on hysteria at the least sign of resistance to her iron-clad will.

Knowing exactly what was going on in his mind, Kate said, handing him a box wrapped in coloured paper and tied with matching scarlet ribbon, "This is for you. Happy Birthday, Greg. A bit late, but better late than never."

"What on earth?" He laughed, his trauma of the past half hour forgotten in the pleasureable anticipation of opening his present.

"Why not open it and find out?" Kate suggested, thinking how eager, boyish and carefree he looked all of a sudden, just as he used to when building sandcastles in the days of their youth and childhood long ago.

Placing the parcel on the floor, he knelt beside it to remove its wrapping carefully, not wanting to crease the paper unduly. So like Greg, she thought, a careful, considerate human being in every respect. The reason why she loved him so much.

And now the moment of discovery had arrived! Never till her dying day would Kate forget the expression of joy on his face when, delving into the box, he held in his hands the books written by his hero, Sandy Alexis. First editions, signed by the author.

Greg said bemusedly, "These must have cost a small fortune. Where on earth did you find them?"

"In a house in London. The author was about to burn them. I persuaded him not to."

"You mean you actually met – Sandy Alexis?"

Kate smiled mysteriously. "Would it surprise you to know that this is his room? His house?"

Light dawned. Standing up, facing his sister, Greg said, "Alex Arden? The man you're in love with?"

"Yes," Kate said softly, knowing she spoke the absolute truth, "the man I'm in love with!"

The stairs creaked suddenly. Cindy appeared in the doorway. "I've been looking for you everywhere," she said angrily. "I might have known I'd find the pair of you together, as usual! Talking about me, behind my back, I daresay!"

"Not at all," Greg said restrainedly, "we were discussing the birthday present Kate has given me. Books by Sandy Alexis, no less. First editions, signed by the author."

"What? *More* books? As if you hadn't got enough of the damn things already! Well, do you intend staying up here all night?"

Stepping into the arena, Kate said pleasantly, "Of course not. I was about to suggest having coffee in the garden. It's such a lovely evening. You will join us, won't you, Cindy?"

"No! I have a splitting headache! Coffee's the last thing I need! Greg, I asked you specifically to pack that bottle of asprin in the bathroom cabinet. Apparently you neglected to do so!"

Kate said lightly, "Oh, if that's all. I've plenty of – pain-killers! Come with me Cindy, I'll have your headache cured in no time at all!"

Seventeen

C indy had not responded kindly to her sister-in-law's ministrations when, turning a deaf ear to her complaints about Greg and the missing asprin tablets, Kate had persuaded her to get into bed, handed her a glass of water and a couple of mild sleeping pills, wished her goodnight, and gone to the kitchen to make a pot of coffee.

The evening was silken soft, threaded with birdsong and starlight. The garden was heady with the fragrance of lavender and night-scented stocks. Greg was seated at the wrought-iron table, looking tired, Kate thought, and with good reason. Coping with Cindy was no easy option, as she well knew. Upstairs in the bedroom, listening to the woman's diatribe, she'd longed to tell her exactly what she thought of her constant whining and complaining, that she should think herself damn lucky to have a husband at all, a lesser man than Greg would have left her years ago to stew in her own juice. Of course she had not done so, for Greg's sake.

"It's so peaceful here," he said. "Like a different world. The kind of world we lived in a long time ago. Or that's how it seems to me. But how about you, Kate? Are you happy living here beneath someone else's roof?

"Forgive me for asking, but what will happen when Alex Arden comes home again? Shall you be prepared to stay on as his housekeeper? And where does Jenny fit into the picture? I don't understand the set-up! Is she here on holiday, or what?"

"It's a long story," Kate said, unmindful of the coffee pot and mugs she'd carried down from the kitchen, "and I'm not sure where to begin."

"No need to begin anywhere in particular," Greg said gently. "Just sit down and talk to me. I was always good at jig-saw puzzles, remember?" He poured the coffee; handed her a mug.

And so Kate talked, and Greg listened intently until, imperceptibly, twilight deepened into the darkness of night. The birdsong was silent, and the sky was filled with an amazement of stars: the Great Bear, the Pleiades; the Milky Way.

Talking to Greg helped Kate to come to terms with the problem of Jenny. Until that evening in the garden, she hadn't even realised the full extent of her frustration at Jenny's erratic behaviour, thinking one minute they were drawing closer together, having her hopes dashed the next, linked to a sense of failure that she had begun to lose patience with her, to doubt the validity of their girlhood friendship.

Loyalty forbade her revealing details of Jenny's sordid past. She simply told Greg about the incident leading to Jenny's brush with death, the arrest of her assailant, the forthcoming trial, the reasons why she had offered Jenny a home, a resting place at least, a kind of caravanserai until she was well enough to make decisions about her own future.

She added with a trace of bitterness, "I can't see her wanting to stay here with me when the court case is over and she's back on her feet again."

"In which case, problem solved," Greg said reasonably.

"I guess so," Kate admitted, "but I'll still feel that I somehow mishandled the situation."

"There are situations which are impossible to 'handle'," Greg reminded her, and Kate had known by the look on his face, that he was speaking from experience of his life with Cindy.

When Cindy had discovered the sitting room, which she referred to as the "lounge", she took to spending much of her time there, watching television. She was sulking, to put it mildly, muttering darkly that she couldn't see the point of eating in the kitchen when the lounge was big enough to contain a dining table and chairs, at which point Kate had begun taking "madam's" meals through to her to eat from a tray placed on the low table in front of the fireplace. A thankless task, as she had quickly discovered. A source of embarrassment for Greg; of some amusement to Jenny.

"I won't have you dancing attendance on Cindy," Greg said harshly. "If she prefers to eat in the sitting room, she should carry her own trays!" He paused. "Sorry. Here, let me take it!"

"I honestly don't mind," Kate said brightly, inwardly relieved at being spared her sister-in-law's company in the kitchen – as a kind of skeleton at the feast.

Overhearing the conversation, Jenny supplied innocently, tongue-in-cheek, "Perhaps I could help?"

"Thanks, Jenny, but that's not necessary," Kate assured her, imagining Cindy's reaction to her arch enemy's appearance in the sitting room, knowing full well that her sister-in-law had not forgotten or forgiven Jenny's "You *do* look a bit washed out" remark.

A fraught situation all round, Kate considered, especially since Jenny and Greg appeared to be hitting it off rather well together; talking over old times, drinking their after supper coffee in the garden, whilst Cindy sulked in the sitting room and she cleared away the supper things and did the washing-up prior to going upstairs to her room to get on with the next chapter.

One valuable lesson she had learned so far – that fate had a way of spinning its own complicated designs without the aid of human intervention.

Absorbed in her novel, she had now reached the stage of Lucy Kiddy's involvement and subsequent marriage to a rich man, twice her age; giving full reign to her imagination when poor Lucy, trapped within a loveless union, had begun seeking means of escape from her elderly, lecherous husband; curiously drawing a modicum of comfort from the trials and tribulations of a girl, long dead and gone, whose life, akin to Kate's own, had not been a bed of roses. A girl who had suffered the pain and misery of rejection, the hopelessness of unrequited love, as she herself had done.

The difference between herself and Lucy Kiddy was that Lucy's days were over and done with. Her own were not. The strong link between them was that the passage of time, the difference in dress, the social shibboleths of a century ago, had no bearing whatsoever on the emotional responses of women in love, either now or then.

She had told Greg about the book, and he had been up to her studio twice to read the opening chapters, until at Cindy's call, "Greg, where are you? What are you doing?" he'd hurried off to placate her. "Anything for a quiet life," he'd murmured wryly.

Later, helping Kate with the washing-up when Cindy was in the lounge watching television, referring to her brainchild, he said, "For what it's worth, Sis, and if the opening chapters are anything to go by, I think you're on to a winner! Well on your way to fame and fortune as a best-selling author!"

Kate laughed. "Pull the other one," she said dismissively. "Writing is simply a hobby of mine. Something I enjoy doing to fill in time." She paused momentarily, then continued, "When Alex went away, I knew I needed to do something positive to add a sense of purpose to my life, so I took a course in touch-typing. I might just have easily taken piano lessons, except that I hadn't a piano, only a typewriter! So what are you saying? That had I taken piano lessons, I might well be on my way now to giving Chopin recitals at the Wigmore Hall?"

"Knowing you, Kate, I shouldn't be at all surprised," Greg chuckled, entirely at ease and relaxed in his sister's company, as he had been all the days of their lives since he had first espied her as a small bundle in their mother's arms, whose tiny fingers, holding his, had placed a kind of hammerlock of love on the heart of a two-year-old toddler.

Fanny had taken a liking to Greg. Not so Cindy or Jenny. Kate detected a hint of jealousy in her attitude towards Jenny, whom she regarded as an interloper. Cindy she regarded as a stuck-up snob, undeserving of such a lovely husband. Not that she had ever voiced her opinions all that clearly. But Kate could read her like a book, and she sympathised with her to a great extent. "I know I *am* a servant," Fanny had blurted one day, "but I don't like being treated as such."

"When have I treated you as a servant?" Kate asked mildly. "So far as I'm concerned, you're doing me a favour helping me the way you do."

"I weren't meaning you or that nice brother of yours," Fanny muttered darkly, "but I can't say the same of others I could mention."

"I shouldn't worry about that, if I were you," Kate said placatingly. "It won't be for very much longer."

How could she have known, at the time, how prophetic her remark would turn out to be?

In retrospect, the unfortunate train of events to come had started with Dot Paulson's appearance at Gull House to lodge a series of complaints against Cora Clegg, whose behaviour was fast becoming intolerable.

Asked, "In what way, exactly?" Dot, obviously upset and bridling like a turkey cock, went into a long diatribe about Cora thinking she owned the shop. Several times recently, she'd found her entertaining her boyfriend in the stock-room and the office behind the shop.

"There he was, as large as life and twice as ugly," Dot spluttered indignantly, "his feet on the desk, drinking coffee and smoking cigarettes. The air was fairly blue with smoke. He didn't bother to get up neither, and what they'd been up to in the stock-room . . . Well, I ask you? I mean, it's just not on, is it?"

"No, it certainly isn't," Kate agreed. "In which case, the sooner we dispense with Miss Clegg's services, the better. Will you break the bad news to her, or shall I?"

"I'd rather you, if you don't mind?" Dot said tremulously. "I really couldn't face her or that beastly boyfriend of hers again. To tell the truth, I was scared stiff of him just sitting there, the cheeky young devil, as bold as you please, grinning at me: almost daring me to give him his marching orders! As for *her*! There she was, as bold as brass, standing behind him, her hands resting on his shoulders. And do you know what she said? 'Why, if it isn't old Dotty herself come to poke her nose in where it isn't wanted!' I ask you? That's why I'm here! What I mean is, you can't blame me, can you, for feeling so upset?"

And so it devolved upon Kate to give Miss Clegg the brush off – a month's wages in lieu of notice, to face the abuse showered on her as Cora marched defiantly out of the shop that self and same evening, towards the powerfully built young brute awaiting her on the street corner. A nasty experience, all told, Kate thought, turning the "Closed" notice on the shop door in the full realisation that the shop must necessarily remain closed for the time being, until a new manageress had been appointed to fill Cora's inadequate high-heeled shoes. Hopefully, not a sex-symbol next time, but a plain, intelligent ordinary woman in need of a job. Not necessarily a young woman with long fingernails, inimical to dusting and polishing. Someone like Fanny Kiddy, for instance.

Fanny Kiddy! Of *course*! Why not? Leaning back against the door, weighing up the pros and cons, she could at least ask Fanny if she would take care of the shop, even on a part-time basis, until the end of the season.

Fanny was over the moon. "Well, if you think I could do it," she said modestly, "I'll give it a go! Eh, I shall have to hev my hair permed and treat meself to a new jumper and skirt!"

One problem solved, Kate thought. Others were to follow in rapid succession.

Waking up suddenly in the early hours of next morning to the feeling that something was wrong, a light sleeper, Kate could have sworn she'd heard footsteps on the fire-escape.

Getting up, quickly shrugging into her dressing gown, not switching on her bedside lamp, she ventured on to the landing and stood there, listening intently, knowing that what she suspected was true. Someone *was* in the house! A burglar presumably.

Heart pounding, she tiptoed downstairs. The intruder was in the kitchen! Regardless of her own safety, sick at heart, angry beyond belief at this invasion of her home, switching on the landing light, she called out, "Who's there?" flinging open the kitchen door.

At the sound of her voice, the intruder ran full tilt down the fire-escape, a powerfully built young man whom she identified vaguely, in a split second of partial recognition, as Cora Clegg's boyfriend. No burglar but an arsonist! The air was smoke-filled; curtains and furnishings well alight from a pile of petrol-soaked rags planted in the centre of the room. The fire was spreading rapidly.

Miraculously, Greg appeared at that moment, alerted to a sense of danger by his sister's voice calling out, "Who's there?" Taking in the situation at a glance, he said calmly, "Ring the Fire Brigade, Kate! Tell them to hurry!"

"But what about Cindy and Jenny?" Kate asked anxiously, wondering how on earth he would cope with a hysterical woman and a semi-invalid at dagger's drawn with one another. The main priority, to get them out of the building as quickly as possible.

"Leave me to worry about that," he advised her, speaking more urgently. "Just do as I say, for God's sake, before the entire house goes up in flames!"

Kate fled to the sitting room to dial 999. Greg hurried to alert his wife and Jenny. The call made, Kate raced back to help Greg, by which time Cindy was on the landing in her dressing gown and slippers, complaining bitterly that she had known all along that something awful would happen, and what about her belongings?

"Where's Jenny?" Kate asked in alarm.

"In her room. I knocked on the door. There was no answer," Greg said, hustling Cindy towards the front staircase.

"She must have taken sleeping pills! I'd better find out," Kate said shortly, praying to God that Jenny hadn't also locked her bedroom door. "She's probably out for the count."

"I'll go to her," Greg said. "You take care of Cindy!"

"I'm warning you, Greg!" Cindy called after him as he hurried towards Jenny's room, at the same time shaking off Kate's hand on her arm. "Your place is with *me*, not *her*!"

Kate's patience snapped suddenly. "Tell me, Cindy, do you ever think of anyone but yourself? Well, don't just stand there like Lady Macbeth! *Move*, woman! There's a fire behind you, a staircase in front of you. So which is the better option? Since you don't want my help, make your own way for once in your miserable life! I'm going to help Greg!"

The fire brigade had arrived. Someone was hammering urgently for admission. Brushing past Cindy, Kate hurried down to let them in. Overwhelmed by the sheer physical presence of so many strapping men on the doorstep, she flattened herself against the wall as they crowded in, wearing breathing apparatus, to tackle the blaze on the upper landing where Greg was standing, holding Jenny in his arms.

"You'd best get out of here, mate," the fire chief advised him, "whilst the going's good! The blaze started in the kitchen, you say? Everyone accounted for?" Greg nodded.

Meanwhile, uttering a hoarse cry, Cindy had stumbled downstairs as if the devil were after her, her face a mask of fury as, looking up, she saw her husband carrying Jenny in his arms towards the safety of the street beyond.

Oh God, Kate thought, dreading the reckoning to come. Hell hath no fury like a woman scorned. No doubt about it, a full scale confrontation between Cindy and Greg was about to erupt once the fire had been brought under control.

It was far worse than Kate had imagined it would be. Greg listened to his wife's tirade in complete silence, saying nothing in his own defence, face haggard, trembling slightly as her cruel, whip-lashing tongue gave vent to her feelings of bitterness, scorn and disgust – the unjust accusations levelled against him.

The scene took place in the sitting room at five o'clock in the morning, after the fire brigade had left the premises and Jenny had gone back to bed, still woozy from the effect of the sleeping pills she had taken the night before. Taking her cue from Greg, Kate also remained silent for the time being, realising, as he had done, the futility of attempting to stem the flow of vitriol from Cindy's lips, resisting the strong temptation to throttle her sister-in-law with her bare hands.

"Call yourself a man?" Cindy screeched hysterically. "Take a good look at yourself, why don't you? All these years I've put up with you, and what have I to show for it? *Nothing*! The trouble with you, you have no drive, no ambition! You should have been a headmaster by now, earning a decent salary! But oh no, not you! And not a thought in the world for *me*! How do you think I've felt stuck away in that damned bungalow in Manchester as the wife of a bloody failure? And that's what you are, Greg Harker, a rotten bloody failure!

"I blame your precious sister for that, if you really must know! The truth is, you've always cared for her far more than you ever have done for me! Well, deny it if you can! The pair of you as thick as thieves – talking behind my back, kissing and fondling each other I daresay! I'm not blind, you know? A pretty peculiar relationship between brother and sister, I'd say! Bloody unhealthy, to put it mildly!

"Now, obviously you're having a hole and corner affair with that Jenny woman, aren't you? My God, the way you carried her downstairs made me feel physically sick! Not giving a damn about *me*. Only *her*! Well, admit it, if you are man enough to do so, which I doubt, knowing you, a poor excuse for a man!"

She paused dramatically before launching her final bombshell: "Well, I've had enough of you, Greg Harper, to last me a lifetime! I'm leaving here on the first available train to Manchester, and you'd better come with me if you know what's good for you! I'm warning you, I mean what I say! Otherwise I'll leave without you. Is that perfectly clear? Moreover, I shall institute divorce proceedings against you on the grounds of your adultery with Jenny Laird. Well, what have you to say to *that*?"

Breaking his silence at last, Greg said quietly, "I'll drive you to the station, if you like. Unless you'd prefer to take a taxi!"

Eighteen

F or the first time, Kate felt sorry for Cindy, whose stupidity had cost her her marriage.

Sick at heart for Greg's sake, watching his face as his wife poured forth her venom, she knew that his strong sense of loyalty towards her, his belief in the sanctity of the marriage vows, had been damaged beyond pair, destroyed by her diatribe against him, shredding every vestige of his dignity and self respect.

"Look, Greg," she said quietly, "why not go for a walk; a breath of fresh air? I'll stay here with Cindy, help her to pack: make certain she's at the station in time to catch the eight o'clock train."

"Thanks, Sis." He nodded briefly and hurried downstairs.

Incensed, Cindy turned on Kate in a fury. "How dare you interfere in a matter between husband and wife? But if you think for one moment he won't be coming home with me, you have another thing coming! Greg knows which side his bread is buttered right enough!"

She sneered unpleasantly, "Oh, I know what's going on in your mind. You think you've got him back, don't you? Given the choice, that he'll stay here with you and that fancy woman of his?"

Kate said wearily, "Tell me, Cynthia, were you born a fool or, in your case, has practice made perfect? Hasn't it entered your head that your marriage is virtually over and done with, bar the shouting?

"Think about it, Cynthia, if you are capable of thought, that is. Ask yourself how any self-respecting, decent man on the face of the earth, would react to his wife's denunciation of him as a 'rotten bloody failure'; allied to his propensities to commit incest and adultery into the bargain. None of which allegations are remotely true, and you know it!"

"Now you listen to me, Kate Ford—" Cindy interrupted rudely.

"No, Cynthia," Kate riposted angrily, "*you* listen to *me* for a change. The fact is, and you'd better believe it, this is the end of the line so far as your marriage to Greg is concerned. Oh, he may well decide to return to Manchester with you. Knowing my brother as well as I do, and not in the biblical sense, I assure you, he will see it as his duty to make certain that you are well provided for, after the divorce."

"Pah! There won't be a divorce! Greg can't afford to leave me. He has financial commitments – mortgage repayments to meet, bills to pay. He couldn't afford to leave home. Where would he go? What would he do? In any case, he has no reason to leave me. *I'm* not the guilty party! *I* haven't done anything wrong!"

"Neither has Greg," Kate reminded her, "but this much is certain, you'll never live together again as man and wife."

Again came Cindy's sneering laugh. "Ha! If that's meant to frighten me, forget it! Greg and I haven't lived together as man and wife for years now! Not since he started harping on about wanting a family. Well, I soon put paid to that nonsense, I can tell you! The very idea! We'd only just nicely got back from our honeymoon when he started on about my getting pregnant! *Ugh*! The last thing I wanted was a baby messing up my life!"

"*Your* life? What about Greg's life?"

"Oh, *that*?" Cindy shrugged her shoulders dismissively. "He soon got the message when I told him I'd share a bed with him, but he'd best keep to his own side of it in future."

"I see," Kate said thoughtfully. "Now, isn't it about time you started packing? Meanwhile, I'll ring for a taxi."

"I shouldn't bother, if I were you," Cindy replied airily. "Greg will be back soon, his tail between his legs, as usual, to drive me back to Manchester where he belongs. With *me*, not *you*!"

Greg had walked slowly towards St Nicholas Cliff, where he stood for a while, looking out to sea.

Deeply shaken by the events of the past few hours, he could scarcely believe that they had all really happened – the fire, that moment of panic when he had failed to rouse Jenny; his fear that the fire might spread out of control and she might be trapped in her room.

Then, having got to her in time and realising that in her state of confusion from the sleeping pills she had taken at bedtime, she was incapable of walking downstairs, what else could be have done but carry her to safety?

And that had been the cause of Cindy's jealous outburst. Deeply shocked, he had experienced a sudden revulsion towards her, as if his life had swung out of focus, as though everything he had hitherto believed in, his marriage vows, his home, his responsibilities, no longer mattered a damn.

Cindy had always been jealous of Kate. This he had learned to live with and accept, as he had accepted her laziness and inate snobbery, her constant complaints at his lack of ambition, her refusal to bear his children.

A gentle man at heart, he had turned to books and music and pride in his work as a teacher as alternatives in a loveless marriage. But that she had imagined for one moment his relationship with his sister was in some way unhealthy beggared belief, as did her wild assumption that he had committed adultery with Jenny Laird.

He liked Jenny enormously, and why not? He was, after all, a full-blooded male, but not some blasted pervert engaged in a sexual relationship with his own sister. And Jenny was still pretty in a forced kind of way. Not as wildly pretty as she had been at Kate's wedding twenty-odd years ago, but exuding the same sexual aura as she had done then. Possibly the reason why Kate held certain misgivings about her and Jenny's present day friendship. Essentially, Kate had grown stronger throughout the passing years. Jenny had not.

In retrospect, there had been something faintly repulsive about Jenny's deviously worded invitation to take advantage of her room, her bed, her body, if he – how had she put it? – "If he felt the urge to release his physical tension once in a while." No such thought had entered his mind. He had simply enjoyed her company; talking over old times out there in the garden.

He loved this place, this town with its memories of happier times before the deaths of his parents had turned his own and Kate's lives topsy-turvy. As much as he longed to remain here, he knew this was impossible, a pipe dream until he had settled his marital affairs. He had his job to consider. Quitting the teaching profession without due notice would jeopardise his chances of future employment at, say, a private school, as a housemaster or a part-time tutor. Teaching was all he knew, and he was not prepared to throw away years of experience in his chosen profession without due care and consideration.

Leaving Cindy would be no easy option. Knowing her, she would fight tooth and claw to hang on to the bungalow, and him too, if he allowed himself to be bullied into submission, as he had so often done before. Divorce was an ugly business, he imagined, a possibility he had not even considered until, sick at heart, he had realised for the first time the depth of her bitterness towards him as she muck-raked their marriage in front of Kate. He had known then that it was over and done with at last – that sham edifice of his marriage to a woman devoid of humour, understanding or compassion. An edifice akin to a sandcastle built within reach of the incoming tide.

Returning to Gull House, finding Kate alone in the sitting room, he said wearily, "I'm sorry, Sis, but I have to go back to Manchester. To settle things once and for all. You do see that, don't you?"

"Yes, of course I do. And you are right. Just promise me you'll see a good solicitor as soon as possible. Tell him the whole story from beginning to end. And I do mean the *whole* story. Need I say more?"

"I guess not." He smiled awkwardly. "Then you don't blame me for wanting my freedom?"

"I'd be surprised if you didn't. And remember, if I can help in any way, all you have to do is ask!"

"It could be a long drawn out business," he said, dreading what lay ahead of him. "I have no valid grounds for divorce."

"I'm not so sure about that. The reason why you must choose the best possible solicitor." No use beating about the bush. "Cindy told me the reason why she has been your wife in name only for the past eighteen years."

Kate paused, understanding her brother's distress that his wife had taken her marital muck-raking far beyond the limits of acceptable human behaviour – his utter disgust that she had chosen to reveal, to Kate, of all people, intimate details of their non-existent sexual relationship since the days of their short-lived honeymoon period in a small hotel in the Lake District.

She said quietly, compassionately, "Don't you see, Greg, that you have valid grounds for divorce. But only you can decide if you want your freedom enough to fight for it fairly and squarely, just as I had to fight for mine and financial independence into the bargain, when I divorced Don on the grounds of his adultery with Lucia Keane.

"And Don's handing over the deeds of April Cottage to me was due not to his largesse, as I led you to believe, but to my persistence in refusing to divorce him, point blank, until he'd secured my own future to some extent. So now you know!"

Feeling suddenly much stronger and light-hearted, as he always had done in Kate's presence, Greg said, "So what if Cindy persists in retaining the deeds to the bungalow as a condition of my divorce proceedings against her?"

Kate laughed. "Then hand them over to her, by all means. With one proviso, that she also retains full custody of those blasted garden gnomes."

Cindy was in the front seat of the Volkswagen, staring straight ahead, when Greg, having stowed away their cases and Alex Arden's books in the luggage compartment, kissed Kate goodbye. Cindy had simply stalked past her without a word.

On the doorstep, clasping Kate's hands firmly in his, Greg murmured, "Please say goodbye to Jenny for me. Wish her well for the future; a happy outcome of that court case of hers."

When the Volkswagen had driven away from the side door, Kate went upstairs to face the ruination of the kitchen: smoke-blackened and virtually unusable for the time being, thanks to Cora Clegg's boyfriend, whose arson attack on the premises, she realised, had been in the nature of a wilful act of revenge levelled against herself for having given Cora her marching orders from the shop.

Bone-tired and weary from the exigencies of the night before, all Kate really wanted was to crawl into bed and sleep till the cows came home. An impossibility in the present circumstances.

First of all, she would have to inform Alex's solicitors of the arson attack and the fire damage to their client's property; also to report the break-in to the local police, and decide what to do about meals for herself and Jenny whilst the kitchen was out of commission. Moving into a hotel, for the time being, seemed the obvious solution to that problem.

Jenny appeared put out when she heard that Greg had gone without saying goodbye to her: "Huh, and there was I thinking I'd made a hit with him!"

"Unfortunately, so did Cindy. She accused him of having an affair with you," Kate said.

"*What*? Some fat chance! It wasn't for the want of trying, believe me." Jenny laughed. "If ever I saw a man in need of a roll in the hay! I'll bet he doesn't do much of that with the miserable cow he's married to!"

Common sense warned Kate not to mention the divorce threat hanging over Greg. Instead, she passed on his message and asked Jenny how she felt about moving into a hotel for the time being.

"Great," she enthused. "I could do with a change of scene, a bit of fun for a change now I'm getting back to normal."

"Just as long as your idea of fun doesn't include making a fool of my brother," Kate warned her, afraid that Jenny might take it into her head to further complicate Greg's life if she felt like it. She wouldn't put it past her.

"If that's what's worrying you, forget it," Jenny said carelessly. "Greg's a nice bloke, but as dull as ditchwater. And, well, to be honest, I bumped into an old friend of mine again, last week. John Spivey! You remember John? The best man at your wedding?"

"Yes, I remember. The man you turned down because you felt he wasn't quite good enough for you?" Kate reminded her.

Ignoring the remark, Jenny continued, "We had quite a long talk. As a matter of fact, I'm having dinner with him at the Royal Hotel next Wednesday. And why not?"

Why not indeed? Kate knew that she had not misread Jenny after all. She was just as selfish and manipulatative now as she had been all along.

She said quietly, "Your life is your own to live as you see fit from now on, and I'll not stand in the way of your independence. I'm glad that you feel able to tackle life on your own terms again. So what will you do when we have parted company? I am right in thinking that we have reached the end of the road? That you will not be returning to Gull House, even when the workmen have finished the redecorating?"

"No, I guess not," Jenny admitted reluctantly. "You see, John has suggested my moving in with him, to live, in a fortnight or so, when he has the keys to a penthouse apartment on the South Cliff."

"A – penthouse?"

"Well, a top floor flat," Jenny said, catching Kate's look of surprise. "I gather you disapprove?"

"What gave you that idea?"

"Because you have always disapproved of me, at rock bottom. That's true, isn't it? You've never accepted that I need men in my life; excitement; having a good time."

"And have you always had a good time so far as men are concerned?"

"No, but I can't stay cooped up forever, and John Spivey's doing really well now. I know he'll take care of me just fine."

"In which case there's nothing more to be said, except to wish you well." Kate added perceptively, "I take it that you won't object to being 'cooped up' with me in a hotel for the time being?"

"You really couldn't resist saying that, could you?" Jenny flung back at her. "So what do you want me to do? Fall down on my knees and thank you for picking me up out of the gutter? Or would you prefer a framed testimonial to hang on your wall?"

"Blessed are they who expecteth nothing, or words to that effect," Kate said quietly. "I helped you because I wanted to; because I valued your friendship at a time when I needed a friend to turn to. You, Jenny, were that friend! And so, perhaps, it is I who should provide a testimonial to hang on your wall? 'To Jenny. Friend of my formative years. With love and thanks for all the sweetness and happiness she brought into my life once, long ago.'"

Her eyes filled suddenly with tears. She said mistily, "I'll be lonely without you, Jenny."

But then, loneliness was something she had learned how to live with since Alex had disappeared from her life so abruptly. Yet never a day passed by without wondering where he was. And, whether or not he loved her in return, she knew that she would forever remain in love with him.

And so, Kate had booked rooms for herself and Jenny in a small hotel in West Square, near the town centre, but went daily to Gull House to find out how the repairs were progressing, and to pick up the mail, if any. She had not had word of Greg so far; had thought it best not to try to contact him, afraid of worsening the situation if Cindy answered the phone.

At a low ebb, physically and emotionally drained, beset by problems, worried sick about Greg, Alex and Jenny, her inability to get on with her writing, she felt that her life had suddenly ground to a halt, leaving her as stranded as a starfish in a rockpool, with no one to turn to for help or advice unless . . . It was then she thought of Madame Zara.

One morning at Gull House, having discussed with the foreman the paint and paper she wanted for the kitchen now that the fire-damaged units, furniture, floor covering and electrical equipment had been replaced, hearing the rattle of the letterbox, she hurried downstairs to find two letters on the mat. One from Greg, addressed to herself, the other addressed to Jenny.

Greg had written:

159

Dear Kate,

To let you know that I have found a solicitor willing to act on my behalf. Taking your advice, I told him the story of my marriage from start to finish. A bit daunting from my viewpoint, as you can imagine, but nothing compared to Cindy's reaction when I told her that I'd set the divorce wheels in motion.

Not to put too fine a point on it, she ordered me out of the house. When I refused to leave, she packed her bags and went off to Bradford to stay with her sister. The relief was enormous.

Sorry I can't write more fully at the moment, but I'll phone you as soon as possible. Truth to tell, I'm dog-tired. I know that you must be, too. But not to worry unduly, I see a ray of light on the horizon.

Ever yours affectionately,
Greg

Thank God. Thank God, Kate thought, for that ray of light on the horizon.

Jenny's letter contained news of her court appearance to give evidence against her former landlord, which she threw aside carelessly, saying that John would go with her to the York Crown Court when the time came. Kate made no comment. There was virtually nothing left to say. Jenny's eyes were firmly fixed on the future with her latest lover. Kate accepted the fact that she had no further role to play in her friend's life. She had, at least, played a small part in helping her over a rough patch, as Jenny had once helped her. Now, seemingly, those debts had been paid in full. No regrets.

Kate had been home for over a week when Fanny called to see her one evening after work. Thinking how tired she looked, Kate put the kettle on for a cup of tea and asked if she would like something to eat.

Fanny shook her head, "No," she said, "I just came to see how you were. I expect it's given you a bit of a shock, like. I know it did me. Not that I know the man. But, well, I couldn't help wondering what will become of all this, if the worst comes to the worst."

Kate frowned. "I'm sorry, I haven't a clue what you're on about. What man are you talking about? And what do you mean by what will become of all this? All what?"

Fanny looked stricken. "Oh lord, then you ain't read the evening paper?"

"No. It hasn't been delivered yet." Kate's bewilderment turned suddenly to fear, a cold feeling inside. "Why? What's in it? What's wrong?" But deep down, she knew the name of the man Fanny was talking about. She said hoarsely, "It's Alex, isn't it? Something has happened to him! He's dead, isn't he?" She sat down abruptly, trembling like a leaf, her face ashen.

"Eh, love, I'm sorry," Fanny placed a comforting arm about her shoulders, "I shouldn't have sprung it on you like that. But it ain't as bad as you think. He ain't dead, just missing. An' it mightn't be him at all. They're not sure yet – them Foreign Office folk, I mean."

"For God's sake, Fanny, *tell* me!"

"Here, you'd best see for yourself." Fanny fiddled in her shopping bag for her copy of the *Evening News*, and laid it on the kitchen table.

Kate read, with a kind of horrid fascination:

BRITISH CITIZEN BELIEVED KIDNAPPED. The Foreign Office today confirmed rumours of the capture by tribesmen in a remote area of Turkestan of a British citizen. The man, travelling alone and on foot, named as Alex Arden, better known as the author Sandy Alexis, is reported as being held to ransom somewhere in that area, for an undisclosed sum of money.

Foreign Office sources have also confirmed that a team of negotiators is being flown to the area immediately, hopefully to secure the release of the hostage as quickly as possible.

Kate buried her head in her hands. Oh God, she prayed inwardly, keep him safe. Let no harm come to him.

The distance between them seemed limitless, unimaginable. And yet she hoped and believed that wherever he was in the world, he would know that she was thinking about him; praying for him. Loving him.

Next day, she went to Gladstone Street to visit "Madame Zara", remembering the old lady's words: "And this will not be your last visit to my home. So goodbye now, my dear, until we meet again."

This time, the door was opened by a young pleasant-faced woman wearing a district nurse's uniform, who invited her into the hall. Kate's heart sank abruptly. Her fingers tightened suddenly on the bouquet of flowers she had brought with her.

The nurse said kindly, "It's bad news, I'm afraid. Mrs Parker suffered a stroke in the early hours of this morning. I'm awaiting the arrival of an ambulance to take her to hospital."

"May I see her?" Kate asked quietly.

The nurse smiled sympathetically, "Yes, of course, if you want to, though I must warn you, she is barely conscious, unable to speak properly, the poor old soul, and I doubt she'll recognise you."

"Even so, I'd like to see her," Kate said heavily, her eyes dim with tears as she followed the nurse upstairs to the old lady's bedroom.

Laying the flowers on the bedside table, looking down at Mrs Parker's twisted face on the soft feather pillow cradling her head, and gently stroking the withered hands lying uselessly on the counterpane, Kate whispered, "I'm so sorry, my love, but you were right in saying we'd meet again, remember? That I'd come here again, one day. Your prediction has come true."

Slowly, painfully, the old woman opened her eyes, the twisted mouth lifted in the semblance of a smile, the withered hands clinging to Kate's momentarily.

Bending closer to her, Kate caught her last, scarcely audible words: "Zara. Thirsty." And then she was gone from the world as easily and painlessly as a candle-flame puffed out by a breath of wind from an open window.

Part Three

Nineteen

Since Alex's disappearance, Kate's life had seemed frozen in a time-warp of memories, longing and regret.

Now November was here, and there was still no news of him. Foreign Office negotiators had failed to contact his captors. Efforts were being made to discover his whereabouts in a wild, remote region largely uninhabited apart from nomads – small bands of itinerant tribesmen lacking communication with the world beyond their own inhospitable territory.

At night, Kate had lain awake remembering the words of the poem "He Fell Among Thieves", the final terrifying stanza: "A sword swept. Over the pass the voices, one by one faded, and the hill slept". This was a poem she had hated even as a schoolgirl, conveying as it did the thoughts of a captive Englishman awaiting his dawn execution by a band of bloodthirsty brigands.

Possibly Alex had already paid the price of his bid for mental freedom. And if he had not, how could she bear to think of him denied the liberty he loved? Shackled hand and foot most likely, cold, hungry and dirty, faced with the realisation that each day that dawned may be his last.

Meanwhile, she must face each new day as best she could, gathering up the threads of her life as she had tried to do ever since leaving April Cottage.

More than a year had now passed since her return to Scarborough to make her brave new beginning. A year fraught with emotional problems: falling in love again; attempting to take care of Jenny, who, in the long run, had proved quite capable of taking care of herself, and with Greg in the throes of a prolonged divorce drama. Wife versus husband, with property, not love, at stake.

Love? A mockery more like. And yet . . .

* * *

165

On the day of "Madame Zara's" funeral in the old Dean Road Cemetery, according to the old lady's wish to be buried next to her parents, looking up through tear-dimmed eyes, Kate noticed a towering granite memorial erected to the memory of Jeanette, the beloved wife of John Fairgray Sharpin.

When Mrs Parker's coffin had been laid to rest, Kate walked along the path for a closer look at the granite obelisk in memory of Jeanette Sharpin, on which her face had been sculpted in bas-relief.

It was a strong face, striking rather than beautiful, and the lady had died young. Standing there in silent contemplation, the thought occurred that it was here, on this very spot, that John Sharpin had most probably stood on the day of his wife's funeral, head bowed, mourning the loss of a beloved person, just as she, as a young girl on the threshold of life, had mourned the loss of first her mother, then her father.

On the day of Madame Zara's funeral, the sun was shining and she placed on the old lady's coffin a bouquet of summer flowers: sweet-scented stocks, long-stemmed roses and carnations.

How could she possibly foresee then, that come November, the new life she was slowly rebuilding from the ruins of the old would suddenly crumble to dust beneath her feet?

Kate had lived with loneliness before, but never on this scale, with Alex dead, for all she knew, and Greg involved in a bitter divorce battle from which he might well emerge both penniless and homeless in the long run.

As for Jenny, she might as well be living on another planet. Kate had seen neither hide nor hair of her since the day she had announced her intention of moving into John Spivey's apartment to live with a man she had once turned down flat as being "not good enough" for her.

The final blow came when Dot Paulson, strung on the horns of her particular domestic dilemma, handed in her notice, closely followed by Fanny's.

"I thought serving in a shop would be a doddle," she explained tearfully. "Well, it ain't! Not at my age, anyway, with folk standing there firing questions at me, getting ratty at being kept waiting, an' me getting all confused; giving 'em the wrong change an' suchlike!

"Eh, I'm sorry to let you down, love, but I'd best stick to my caretaker's job in future. Summat I'm good at an' know like the back of my hand!"

And so Kate, having hung a "Closed" sign on the shop door, wrote to Alex's solicitors advising them that, in her present circumstances, she could no longer cope with the worry of keeping it open. But she missed Dot's appearances, regaling her with the latest news of her domestic troubles, and Fanny, she suspected, nursing a sense of guilt and hurt pride, would not be paying her usual frequent visits until she had come to terms with having "left her in the lurch".

All this at a time when Kate longed for someone to talk to, a reassuring smile, the comforting touch of a friendly hand to guide her through the dark days ahead.

Wandering the rooms of Gull House like a ghost, hearing the mournful sound of the fog-horn in the distance, she felt isolated, far distanced from her fellow human beings, her mind shredded with worry over Alex, wondering if he were alive or dead. And if he was dead, how could she face a future without him?

Slowly, painfully, she reached the conclusion that she must do something positive to fill the empty spaces of her life. But what?

Alex's typewriter beckoned, but she had lost the thread of her novel since the night of the fire, that cataclysmic event which had sparked off a chain reaction of disasters.

Feeding on memories, she recalled the morning she had come to Gull House to find Alex kneeling on the floor of his study surrounded by the material he had collected for his book on Scarborough's development as a seaside resort.

How angry he had been that day, frustrated because he had lost the ability to express his thoughts in the written word and he knew it.

She had not understood the depth of his humiliation at the time, that any sixth form schoolboy could have done better. How could she have done so, not knowing that here was a man whose former literary output had become classics of their kind?

If only she had taken the trouble to talk to him quietly on that occasion, to help him sort out the untidy piles of paper on the floor. Instead of which, nettled by his temperamental outburst directed against herself, she had told him, in no uncertain terms, that what he needed was not a housekeeper but a skivvy, prior to marching out of the room and downstairs to the side door.

What a fool she'd been! What a jumped-up, self-righteous idiot not to have realised that he stood in need of help, laced with sympathy and understanding, not condemnation.

The folders containing his notes and photographs were still on his desk, alongside his typewriter, just as he had left them when he'd reached the bitter conclusion that his glory days as a writer were over.

One night, unable to sleep, propped up with pillows in what had once been Alex's bed, reading the contents of the folders by the light of his bedside lamp, Kate derived comfort from the completeness of the past – laid away like love-letters, lavender-scented and tied neatly with the faded ribbons of a bygone age. All passion spent. A consummation devoutly to be wished: the pain and passion of living soothed by the long sleep of forgetfulness after death.

But what if Alex's belief in reincarnation was true? What if, having faced the traumatic events of one lifetime, heaven decreed a return to earth for countless rides on the merry-go-round of life? On the other hand, even as a child faced with her initial concept of a heaven somewhere in the sky, filled with haloes and harp music, she'd thought how boring it would be there without beaches to play on, donkey rides, and sandcastles to build: just being desperately good all the time, with nothing to eat except Ambrosia Creamed Rice!

A smile touched her lips as she recalled her first ever secret childhood companion, a figment of her imagination, though it – he, she – whichever – whom she had christened Reginald Missy (what would Sigmund Freud have made of that innocent slip-up? she wondered) – had always been with her, by day and night, to talk to whenever she felt lonely: especially in the middle of the night when the night-light in the saucer of water beside her bed had flickered and gone out.

Then he, she, it would tell her not to be afraid of the dark, that darkness was just a blue velvet curtain drawn down to separate dusk from dawn: a curtain pierced with holes to allow the stars and moon to shine through.

Often they had sung nursery rhymes together: "Baa-baa black sheep" and "Mary had a little lamb". Then suddenly, in the way of things, growing up, her strange hybrid guardian angel had flown away, never to return. How odd that she should think of it now, when what she most needed was a guardian angel to take care of her in her present darkness, loneliness and despair.

Up and dressed early next day, Kate walked along King Street to St Nicholas Cliff and stood there, near the Grand Hotel, looking out to sea. The air was cold and thin, like a whip's lash. The fog had lifted but no rays of light penetrated the greyness of the sky.

Chilled to the bone, she hurried down the zig-zagging paths to the seafront and turned in the direction of Valley Gardens; once the setting of John Sharpin's People's Park; of Lucy Kiddy's romance with a young lad from the fishing community based near the harbour whose dwelling places flanked the narrow, twisting streets and alleys of the Old Town in the lee of the ruined Norman fortress and the jutting headland separating the north and south bays of Scarborough.

The name of the lad Lucy had fallen in love with was lost in the mists of time, but Kate saw him clearly in her mind's eye as a strapping, broad-shouldered youngster, proud of his muscular physique, with a deeply tanned complexion from his days at sea in all weathers, wind, rain and sun; imagined him as blue-eyed and fair-haired in accordance with his Viking heritage – genes passed down the ages from father to son from the Danish invasion of Scarborough in the dim and distant past.

Scarcely likely that Lucy Kiddy, young, pretty and already sexually awakened from her abortive affair with that cellarman at the Crown Hotel, would have given so much as a second glance at any other than an equally sexually aware, handsome young male capable of satisfying her lust for love. Or – sex.

Poor Lucy. How difficult, at her age, and with her beauty, to differentiate between the two. Impossible to blame or condemn her for wanting to make the most of her youth and beauty for as long as they lasted.

Except, of course, Kate pondered, staring into the past, that in the flush of youth, the possibility of growing old never enters one's mind.

How strange to think that this place, these gardens now sadly neglected, had once rung to the sound of happy laughter, of music and stall vendors shouting their wares. Yet all those sounds must be trapped somewhere in the endless galaxies of time and space, if, as she had been led to believe, nothing in the world is ever lost beyond recall. Such were her mother's words, based on her unshakeable belief in the natural laws of life; witness the emergence of springtime after the long sleep of winter – frail snowdrops and crocuses pushing up through the frozen earth of January to proclaim their messages of rebirth, of renewed hope to the human race. And perhaps she was right.

But what about unrequited love? Neither flesh, fowl nor good red herring, Kate wondered, and the souls of unborn, or lost children, whose lives had ended before they had even begun?

Tears filled her eyes and flooded down her cheeks. If only she possessed the power to turn back the hands of time to that summer evening, long ago, when brilliantly coloured Chinese lanterns, strung between the trees of The People's Park, had shone down on the faces of a multitude of Victorians, men, women and children, all dead and gone now, yet somehow more real, more important to her than those living people she had loved and lost along life's way – Don Ford and Jenny Laird, for instance, who had accepted and used her love to their own ends, then turned their backs on her deliberately without a word of regret for the heartbreak they had caused her. All over and done with now. She would far rather live in the past than a present devoid of love and understanding.

Returning home by way of Plantation Hill, passing the now stagnant duck pond, littered with discarded cigarette cartons and empty crisp packets, deeply regretting the loss of the aviary of singing birds remembered from her childhood days, now sadly demolished and forgotten, as if it had never existed, and the scummy pool beneath the iron stanchions of the Valley Bridge from which once, long ago, on the opening night of The People's Park, a sparkling central fountain had splashed on to an abundance of lily pads and white, cup-shaped blossoms, Kate thought about John Fairgray Sharpin, who had master-minded The People's Park well over a century ago, that young, charismatic first-ever tenant manager of the Crown Hotel, from whose influence, by means of cleverly worded advertisements in the London papers of that day and age, extolling the virtues of Scarborough as an up-and-coming fashionable seaside resort, the town had reaped rich rewards in luring the *crème de la crème* of London society away from the Continental spa's, such as Chamonix and Baden-Baden, to partake of the health-giving waters discovered by a Mrs Farrer on the beach at Scarborough in the 1600s.

John Sharpin's advertisements had included indications of the first-class cuisine available: freshly caught local fish, Scottish salmon and beef, Welsh lamb, English venison, grouse, woodcock and pheasant, in season; fine imported wines from France, plus details of the stabling available for horses and carriages to the rear of the hotel.

Yet, amazingly, catering to the snobbish elite of that day and age, he had remained a man of the people, the ordinary working-class folk of Scarborough – the reason for his success as politician, Kate thought. Glancing up at the high wall bordering the Sitwell estate on her right-hand side, she was rocked by a sudden, overwhelming feeling of *déjà vu*, as if the present day world had ceased, momentarily, to exist, and she was listening, not to the sounds of motorcars streaming across the Valley Bridge, but the steady clip-clop of horses' hooves – not crossing the bridge – there was no bridge for them to cross – it hadn't been built yet . . .

Pulling herself together, trembling from head to foot, gulping in deep breaths of air, Kate wondered, Was she losing her mind, her grasp on reality? Or had her momentary lapse of consciousness been to do with too many sleepless nights, her lack of interest in the food which she shopped for, prepared and cooked religiously, then consigned, untasted, to the kitchen pedal-bin?

Possibly, but how could she be sure? She longed, night after night, for the benison of deep, dreamless sleep, which never came, and the simple enjoyment of home-cooked meals, which, despite a deep down hunger inside her, a desperate longing for sustenance, she could not begin to swallow for the continual lump of misery in her throat.

Walking on up Plantation Hill towards the town centre, deeply shaken by her psychic experience, she wondered where to go, what to do next.

Then suddenly, miraculously, out of the blue there came to her the sound of a familiar voice: "Mrs Ford! Kate! Remember me? Dinah Sheridan. We met at the hospital when your friend, Jenny Laird, was so poorly."

Remember? Of course Kate remembered this charming woman who had been so kind to herself and Jenny in the springtime of the year.

Dinah frowned concernedly. "Are you all right?" She clasped Kate's arm. "You look as if you'd seen a ghost. And you're trembling."

"I'm all right," Kate said faintly.

"All right, my foot! Here, come with me," she said, taking command of the situation. "There's a coffee shop in York Place."

Kate allowed herself to be led, glad of Dinah's supporting hand beneath her elbow, her lack of small talk, which she could not have borne at that moment, glad of the woman's silent sympathy and concern for her welfare, expressed not in words but positive action.

"Mind the steps," was all she said when they reached the café. Then, "Now, sit down. I'll fetch the coffee. Do you take sugar?"

Returning to the table from the counter, setting down the cups and sitting opposite Kate, she said briskly, "I've ordered scrambled eggs on toast. Don't know about you, but I'm starving, and they do nice

171

scrambled eggs here, not all watery with hard knobs floating about in it. I often pop in for a bite to eat when I come off night duty, it helps me to unwind before going home to bed. Not that I sleep all that well during the day. Seems all wrong, sleeping during the day. A bit like living life in reverse. But one gets used to it in time I suppose, the way that one gets used to anything, in time."

"Do you really think so?" Kate said bleakly, staring into the past, "I wish I did." She paused to pick up her coffee cup, at least she tried to, and couldn't. Her hands were shaking too much. "I'm sorry," she whispered, "I've slopped it in the saucer."

Dinah thought how poorly she looked. She said, "So? It's cold out, and the cup was too full anyway!"

Kate said in a low voice, "No, it's more than that. I think I could be going out of my mind."

Twenty

S ister Sheridan's flat was in Bar Street, a narrow but busy thoroughfare linking St Nicholas Cliff and the town centre.

"It isn't very big, but it suits me fine," she said, leading the way upstairs. "The rent is reasonable and it doesn't take much heating."

Worried about Kate's state of mind, realising that she needed someone to talk to, she had persuaded her not to return to Gull House alone.

"But you've just come off night duty and need your rest," Kate demurred. "Not to worry," Dinah said briskly. "I never go to bed right away, just sit near the fire for a while to clear my mind, otherwise I'd never get to sleep at all."

The flat *was* small, but uncluttered and restful. The sitting room walls were pale green, hung with one or two gilt-framed watercolours and grouped-together etchings of nineteenth-century Scarborough by Turner.

Green velvet armchairs flanked the fireplace; the mantelpiece was decorated at either end, with trailing ivies in colourful Portuguese pottery containers. There were red-shaded lamps on the occasional tables near the armchairs. On the far side of the room, a dark oak china cabinet, cheek-by-jowl with a record-player. On the wall opposite the window, an elegant antique French escritoire, on top of which had been placed a cut-glass vase of dark red roses.

Glancing about her, Kate quoted softly, " 'To make one little room an everywhere,' " remembering her favourite poet, John Donne.

"Look, Kate," Dinah said quietly, "why not stay here with me for a little while? Talk to me if you feel you can trust me enough to confide in me. If not, there's a spare bedroom next to mine where you could sleep till the crack of dawn, if you feel so inclined."

She added, "And if you've got it into your head that you are going out of your mind, all I can say is – join the club!" She paused. "None of us is an island. We all need help occasionally. I know I do."

Switching on the electric fire, she continued quietly, "Tell me if I'm wrong, to mind my own business if you want to, but I'll hazard a guess that you haven't been eating or sleeping much lately, for whatever reason, and lack of food and sleep can play funny tricks on the nervous system, believe me."

"To the extent of losing one's grip on reality?" Kate asked fearfully. "When we met this morning, you said I looked as if I'd seen a ghost, and that came close to the truth. I can't begin to explain, but suddenly, walking up Plantation Hill, I had the strange feeling that I . . . that I had gone back in time to the days of horse-drawn vehicles. I heard the sounds of horses' hooves quite plainly, and I remember thinking they couldn't be crossing Valley Bridge for the simple reason that it didn't exist. Now, can you look at me and tell me truthfully that I'm not going crazy?"

"I'd say that depended entirely on your reason for walking up Plantation Hill in the first place, at that hour of the morning," Dinah said levelly, "whether or not you slept last night and if you'd had anything to eat before setting off on your early morning walk on a bloody freezing November day such as this. You hadn't, had you? I thought not! In that state, the wonder is you didn't see St Peter at the Pearly Gates with a 'Welcome Home' notice slung round his neck! You daft ha'porth! You're suffering from insomnia and malnutrition pure and simple, in my experience. In other words, lightheadedness from lack of food and sleep.

"Well, that settles it! The spare room bed's made up, and I keep it well aired just in case my kid brother turns up unexpectedly, in need of a place to kip whenever he feels like it, to eat me out of house and home and use up all my hot water. He's a student, you see? But I love him." She added, "Now just you snuggle down, and try to get some sleep. Promise?"

Too weary to argue, Kate nodded, and followed her hostess to the spare bedroom where, shedding her outer clothing, she lay down thankfully beneath crisply laundered cotton sheets and a puffy green-silk covered eiderdown, her head resting on lavender-scented pillows, against which she fell immediately into a deep, dreamless sleep.

Looking in on her, Dinah smiled, then went to her own room to sleep away the cares of her long, fraught hours of night duty, thankful of the muted sounds of humanity beneath her bedroom window: reminders that she was not alone in the world, either. Darkness had fallen when Kate emerged from her room. Dinah was in the kitchen preparing supper. "Well?" she asked in that forthright way of hers. "Feeling any better?"

"Much better, thanks." Kate smiled. "What are you cooking?"

"My *specialité de la maison*. Beef casserole, made yesterday before I went on duty. I think stew tastes better anyway the next day, don't you?"

"You are an amazing person," Kate said.

"Oh? In what way – amazing?"

"The way you cope with life, your job and your home. Managing both successfully. I wish I knew how. I just seem to muddle through. Especially now."

"Why – especially now?" Dinah asked, returning the stew to the oven. "Do you want to talk about it? If so, I'm listening."

"It's a long story."

"I'm in no hurry," Dinah said. "Sit down, I'll put the kettle on for a cuppa."

Slowly at first, the floodgates opened. With a sweet feeling of relief, trusting Dinah implicitly, Kate told her about Don's affair with Lucia, April Cottage, the breakdown of her marriage, her meeting with Alex Arden, the fire at Gull House; Jenny's defection, Greg's divorce proceedings; Alex's disappearance, her fear that she may never see him again; speaking softly, simply, unemotionally, her inner tension betrayed merely by the clenching of her hands on the kitchen table and the gathering of tears in her eyes now and then which she brushed away resolutely with the back of an unclenched hand before they spilled down her face.

A very lovely face, Dinah thought: heart-shaped, with a generous mouth, and eyes the colour of forget-me-nots. Grey-blue forget-me-nots, if such a species existed. More like love-in-a-mist perhaps? But then, botany had never been her favourite subject.

She simply found it hard to believe that anyone, especially Jenny Laird, could have treated Kate so badly after all she had done to help her after she'd left hospital. She said grimly, "At least that ex-landlord of hers got his come-uppance! Seven years in gaol, the brute, and serve him damn well right!"

Jumping up to rescue the casserole from the oven an hour later, Dinah said, "Look, Kate, I suggest that you spend the night here with me; go back to Gull House tomorrow morning, or whenever you feel up to it. No hurry!

"Meanwhile, am I right in thinking that the last thing on earth you need right now is a dollop of stew and mashed potatoes? So how about a couple of boiled eggs and bread and butter 'soldiers'?"

Kate's smile lit up her face. "Oh yes. How wonderful that would be! And thank you, Dinah. Thank you for – everything. Above all, for being my friend."

At breakfast next day, over porridge, toast and coffee, Dinah said, "I've been thinking, I have Christmas leave due to me, four whole days! Can you imagine? I'll be free on Christmas Eve, and I wondered if you'd care to – come with me?"

Pouring more coffee, she assured Kate, "You may not care for the idea, but I'd like you to think about it. What I have in mind is a Christmas weekend at the Crown Hotel. No, don't say anything just yet.

"We both need a break, to relax, have a bit of fun. No shopping or cooking beforehand; being with people in pleasant surroundings. Plenty of sea air if we feel like it. I've made enquiries; tentatively booked a twin-bedded room on the first floor. A balcony room.

"I'd thought of going alone. I wouldn't have minded in the least. Last night, it occurred to me how much nicer it would be to share the room with someone whose company I enjoy. You were the obvious choice. The reason why I'd like you to think about it."

She continued quietly, "I know the Crown has strong associations for you with – Alex. I'm not being insensitive, at least I hope not. Oh, it's difficult to put into words, and I'm not very good with words . . ."

"No need to explain," Kate said gently, "I think I know what you are trying to say, that I'll be thinking of Alex anyway, no matter where. And you are right in your belief that I might feel closer to him in spirit, at the Crown, than anywhere else on earth."

Dinah said bemusedly, "You mean you will come with me?"

Kate smiled. "Yes, and thank you for asking me."

Dinah asked, "How did you know what I was thinking?"

Kate replied, "I don't know. I just did, that's all."

The third week in December, Greg phoned to say that Cindy had gone to Bradford to spend Christmas with her family, leaving him alone in the bungalow. Not that he minded, he was glad of the peace and quiet, the "cessation of hostilities" as he put it, with a brave attempt at tongue-in-cheek humour.

Kate said decisively, "If you think you're spending Christmas in that blasted bungalow with garden gnomes for company, well you're not, that's all! You're coming home to Scarborough for a holiday at the Crown Hotel with me and my friend, Dinah Sheridan. I'm sure she'll be pleased to meet you. So just pack your bags and get over here right away. Tomorrow or the next day! Oh, Greg, I'm so longing to see you again after all this time. I've missed you more than you'll ever know! Please, *please* say you'll come!"

Greg breathed a deep sigh of relief. "OK, Sis," he said brightly, holding his weariness of spirit, his physical bone-tiredness and deeply etched mental suffering of the past few months in check for her sake. "I'll be there and, by the way, I've missed you too – more than *you'll* ever know!"

But Kate *did* know. And his pretended blitheness hadn't fooled her one iota. He was a man faced with the ruination of all his quiet hopes and dreams for the future if Cindy emerged triumphant from the divorce proceedings to establish her claims of non-consummation of her marriage, based on her husband's refusal to accept or assume the responsibilities of parenthood, which had, or so she had lied, been made abundantly clear to her on their honeymoon, when he had utterly refused to engage in the normal sexual intercourse – expected by every young bride on her wedding night. Her word against his! If only he could prove otherwise.

Now, Greg was coming home to her, and nothing else mattered a damn! Whatever the future may hold in store for them, they would make this a Christmas to remember – herself, Greg, Dinah, and someone else besides . . .

Hanging up the phone, Kate whispered into the silent air surrounding her, "Oh, Alex, my darling, if you are still alive in this world, *please* come back to me. Whether or not you love me as much as I love you doesn't matter at all. My life just seems so lonely and meaningless without you."

Waking suddenly in the early hours of next morning, as alert as she had been the night of the fire when she had heard footsteps on the fire-escape, getting out of bed, Kate crossed the room to the tallboy, in the bottom drawer of which she kept a few very private and personal belongings, including the dog-eared copy of *Wuthering Heights* Greg had given her on her fourteenth birthday, her mother's wedding ring, her father's silver pocket-watch, and a bundle of old letters, Christmas and birthday cards she had never felt able to part with.

Kneeling down, she opened the bundle of letters. She and Greg had been great correspondents during her "Don days", when she had written letters to Greg almost daily, in diary form, describing in detail her life at April Cottage, which he had kept beside him all these years, just as she had kept his less frequent, much shorter letters, revolving around his life in Manchester with Cindy. Letters which had deeply troubled her at the time. Certainly not those of a recently married man overjoyed by the prospect of future fatherhood of the family of children he longed for.

Re-reading Greg's letters, at last Kate came upon the most important one of all, in which he had written: "I have begged Cindy to seek medical help and advice, to no avail. Obviously, the poor girl has a deep-seated fear of childbirth, common to most women, I imagine. But enough of my troubles for the time being. Suffice to say that I live in hope of fatherhood one of these fine days . . ."

Going back to bed, tucking that all-important letter beneath her pillow, Kate thought, come Christmas Eve at the Crown Hotel, she would give her brother possibly the best Christmas present he'd ever received. Proof positive of his innocence in the forthcoming divorce case between himself and Cindy.

Dinah had been warmly welcoming of Greg's inclusion in the Christmas celebrations, and, thankfully, there had been a single room available due to a last-minute cancellation when Kate had rung up the reception desk to book Greg into the hotel.

Then suddenly, it was all happening: the beginning of the festive season, and Greg's arrival at Gull House, looking pale and strained – the rapturous reunion of brother and sister prior to their departure, by taxi, to the scene of the festivities.

Obviously Kate didn't know, and Greg hadn't the heart to tell her of a newspaper report concerning the discovery of a decapitated body, in Turkestan, believed to be that of Alex Arden, more famously known as the celebrated author, Sandy Alexis.

Twenty-One

K ate and Dinah had been shown to their room on the first floor, with long windows leading to the balcony beyond.

Dinah was over the moon. "I've always wanted to stay at the Crown," she said mistily, looking out at the lights of Scarborough springing into bloom as the evening shadows fell. "Oh, I daresay it's been modernised to a great extent, but there's still an aura of the past about it, a feeling of history, don't you agree? Kate, are you listening?"

"Yes. It's rather charming, isn't it? 'Bluebells of Scotland.' How odd! There must be a piano in the next room."

"Huh?" Dinah frowned, "What – piano? I can't hear a thing!"

"But surely," Kate began, then stopped speaking abruptly, knowing that her time-warp experience had happened again, that her mind was still playing tricks, as it had done that day on Plantation Hill.

Dinah said concernedly, "Kate, love, are you all right?" wondering if she had made a mistake in returning her friend to the scene of her first encounter with Alex Arden in her present precarious state of mind. Or was it possible that Kate was imbued with second sight? There were fancy medical terms for it nowadays, none of which she could re-member off-hand. The only term which sprang readily to mind was – clairvoyance.

Kate said quietly, "Yes, I'm fine. Just a bit tired and confused, that's all – trying to come to terms with what I imagine to be a legacy handed down to me by my friend, Madame Zara. A legacy I had rather have done without, I might add. Which begs the question, is it really possible for a dead person to enter the mind of the living?"

"But doesn't that happen all the time?" Dinah asked. "It's something more commonly referred to as – memory. In your case, I imagine, linked to your research into the Victorian era. How's that book of yours coming along, by the way?"

179

"It isn't. Not at the moment," Kate admitted. "I'm suffering a 'writer's block'."

"Hmmm, sounds painful," Dinah commented, hanging her clothes in the wardrobe, speaking lightly for her friend's sake. "Is it?"

"Yes, it is. Extremely painful, since you ask. You see, I can't make up my mind what happened to my heroine, Lucy Kiddy. Was she really drowned at sea, I wonder, or did she survive the shipwreck?"

"That depends on how you want the book to end," Dinah reflected, "happily or otherwise." She added, "I guess most people are in need of a happy ending in the long run. At least a glimmer of hope for the future." Finishing her unpacking, she said, "I like your brother, by the way. Strange, isn't it, that really nice people are often called on to endure the most suffering? That wife of his should have thanked her lucky stars to be married to a lovely man like Greg. Why she wants rid of him, I can't conceive. Oh, sorry! I didn't mean to imply . . ."

"That my sister-in-law refused to conceive? But that's the nub and kernel of the divorce proceedings. Cindy claims that Greg refused to consummate the marriage, but I know different. What's more, I can prove it. You see, I found this letter the other day . . ."

The hotel looked spectacular with its wealth of scarlet and gold decorations and jardinières of flowers in the public rooms. They had arranged to meet Greg, at the bar, for pre-dinner drinks. Kate's eyes misted over when she saw that he had bought a new suit for the occasion.

He had met Dinah briefly on their arrival at the hotel, and Kate had introduced them, before signing the visitors' book and being shown to their rooms; had known instinctively that they had "taken a shine" to one another. Come to think of it, Greg must have slung out his old clothes, crumpled shirts and threadbare jackets before leaving Manchester, and not before time.

On his arrival at Gull House, he'd been wearing a well-tailored tweed jacket and slacks, plus a brand new anorak, bless him. "My word, aren't you looking handsome?" had been her opening gambit, prior to giving him a bear-hug of delight at seeing him again.

"Well, I didn't want to let the side down," he'd responded cheerily, hugging his sister in return. And this was so typical of Greg, a rare human being incapable of letting anyone down. She had desperately wanted to show him the letter there and then. To have done so would have lessened the impact of a surprise packet on Christmas Day.

In his room on the top floor of the hotel, Greg wondered how he would break the news of that decapitated body discovered in a remote area of Turkestan when the time came to do so. Kate was bound to find out about it sooner or later. Hopefully later. It would be too cruel, too unkind to spoil the celebration of Christmas in such a way.

Approaching the bar, shrugging aside his misgivings, he pinned a smile to his lips for the benefit of his sister and her friend awaiting his arrival, warmed by an appreciation of this unexpected holiday far removed from the exigencies of his Manchester-existence, a life devoid of warmth, love and laughter – surely the birthright of every human being, especially at Christmas?

Slowly, he began to relax, to smile naturally once more, charmed by the hotel atmosphere, akin to stepping from the cold world beyond the windows into a cosily-padded red and gold brocaded jewel-case of Victorian vintage in which rich women, of that era, had kept their most precious belongings.

Curiously, even in this present day world of the 1970s, he had sensed the presence of long gone generations of men and women who had once celebrated Christmas here in the last century. He guessed that Kate was also aware of the ghosts in their midst, of laughter borne on other winds, the faint rustle of silken ballgowns on the curving staircase leading to the upper landings, the lingering scent of expensive French perfume in the air about them. Not Coty's "l'Aimant" or Bourjois' "Evening in Paris", but richly blended essences of jasmine, frangipani, musk and sandalwood, attar of roses, lavender water and eau-de-Cologne, belonging to a bygone age.

Memory drew Greg back to the days when he and Kate, as children, had often looked up at the balconied rooms of the Crown Hotel, and made up stories about all the rich folk who had once stayed there for months at a time, arriving by horse-drawn carriages, with retinues of servants in tow to do their slightest bidding. Then, eventually tired of the game of make-believe, they had raced down the Spa gardens to the seashore.

Entering the dining room, Greg placed a hand comfortingly beneath Kate's elbow, understanding her feelings at returning to the scene of her first meeting with Arden.

The room was packed, the food excellent, the waiters attentive. The two single tables near the window, Kate noticed, had been pushed together to accommodate a party of four. Thankfully, they were shown to a table for three at the far side of the room at which she elected to sit facing the wall, not the windows.

Dinah and Greg ordered roast duck and a bottle of Chablis. Kate settled for grilled plaice and Perrier. Keeping a watchful eye on her friend, Dinah noticed that Kate appeared to be enjoying her comparatively simple meal, and thought how attractive she looked in the midnight-blue chiffon dress and matching jacket she was wearing.

By the same token, glancing across the table at Dinah, Greg thought how nice, how wholesome she looked in her white silk blouse and black velvet bolero, with her long fair hair curling softly about her face. Not a young face, but animated, with clear blue eyes and a smile like a sunburst breaking through rain-clouds. A woman inured, by her profession, to the pain and suffering of others, who had nevertheless managed to retain her own identity, warmth and sense of humour despite the rigours of her work involving, as they did, matters of life and death.

Above all, he appreciated the loving care and attention that she had bestowed on his sister, which he had heard from Kate's own lips on his arrival at Gull House. He thought how different his life might have been had he met and married a woman of Dinah Sheridan's calibre in the springtime of his life. But too late now for either fantasies or regrets.

The meal ended, over coffee served in the reception area of the hotel Dinah mooted the idea of attending Midnight Mass at St Martin's Church, a mere cock-stride away from the Crown.

And so, at a quarter to midnight, the three of them, Greg, Dinah and Kate, ventured out into the cold night air, suitably clad in warm clothing, arms linked, Greg in the middle, savouring the quiet feeling of happiness which had suddenly touched his heart with a sense of springtime not winter, the possibility of better times to come when the spectre of the divorce hearing had ceased to overshadow his life as it had done these past months. Then he would be free, whatever the outcome, to reshape his future closer to his heart's desire: find himself a new job; shake the dust of Manchester from his feet once and for all. Cindy could have the bungalow, and she was welcome to it. He no longer cared a damn about that. All he wanted was his freedom.

Her hand tucked securely into the crook of Greg's right arm, Dinah thought how wonderful it would be to walk through life with someone like Greg beside her. Oh, who the hell was she kidding? Not someone *like* Greg, but Greg himself. Whoever said that love at first sight was an impossibility was utterly and entirely wrong, and she knew it. There was puppy love, of course, experienced in the blossoming days of one's youth and childhood, the object of one's desire some lanky, blazered schoolboy. In her case, a Sixth Form High School lad, whose desperately longed-for kiss, duly delivered, had resembled mouth to mouth recusitation hampered by the length of his tongue halfway down her throat, which she had spat out with difficulty and a great deal of disgust.

There had been other men in her life since then, some of whom she'd imagined herself to be in love with. But her feelings towards Greg were entirely different from any she had known before. This time she knew, beyond a shadow of doubt, that he was the one and only man in the world for her. Not because he was particularly handsome or prosperous. Simply because he was warm-hearted and kind, with a lived-in face, and he needed someone to love and take of him, just as she needed someone to love and take care of her.

Deeply aware of the rapport between Greg and Dinah, Kate rejoiced in her heart that this had happened between two people near and dear to her, so deserving of happiness. They were so right for one another. She had known that the minute she had introduced them, the moment she had seen the wondering expression on Dinah's face when she looked at Greg, the softening of Greg's features, and that uptight, worried look of his when he'd smiled at Dinah. Almost as if they had met before – long ago and far away.

Entering the church, gazing at the softly-lit crib, she wondered again about Alex's belief in reincarnation. Was it really possible that lovers could meet again in another lifetime, another existence, to an instant awareness that they had met before in the corridors of time? And if love ended in failure during one lifetime, given Alex's belief in reincarnation, might there not be a second chance of happiness in some future incarnation?

Deriving comfort from that possibility, Kate knelt in silent prayer until the congregation rose to the opening notes of "Once in Royal David's City".

After the service, in their bedroom, Dinah said quietly, "I'm so glad we went to church tonight. I felt it – set the seal on things, somehow.

The real meaning of Christmas. Not just eating and drinking and making merry. Something far deeper and more meaningful than just having a good time. Not that I'm knocking having a good time, believe me. It's great to let one's hair down once in a while." She smiled wistfully. "Well, I think you know what I'm trying to say?"

"It's Greg, isn't it?" Kate asked softly. "You've fallen in love with him?"

"Oh Lord, is it so obvious?" Dinah bit her lip. "Have I made a complete and utter fool of myself? Thrown myself at him? Well, they do say there's no fool like an old fool!" Her face clouded suddenly. "I couldn't bear it if he thought that! Not that I'd blame him if he did!" Her lips trembled. She was close to tears.

"I'm sure he thought nothing of the kind," Kate said. "Knowing Greg, he's probably upstairs in his room asking himself the same questions. Wondering, I daresay, what a man in his position has to offer you – a woman he fell in love with at first sight."

"Do you really think so?" Dinah, asked tremulously.

"I don't think so. I *know* so!" Kate assured her. "And I can't tell you how glad I am that this has happened. Greg means the world to me. I knew from the start that he and Cindy were never meant for each other. I don't want to go into all that, there's really no need." She smiled reflectively. "But you and Greg are – meant for each other. So no doubts or fears. Just have faith in your feelings for one another and lay hold of all the future happiness life has to offer the pair of you. Promise?"

"Yes, Kate. I promise. I just feel so selfish thinking of you and Alex. Knowing how you must be feeling now, without him."

Standing near the balcony window looking up at the stars, Kate said softly, "But you see, love, there's really no comparison. Alex went away not knowing how I felt about him. Pride got in the way. In any case, I knew that my feelings were not reciprocated, and I couldn't have borne being told so. Rejection is a bitter pill to swallow. It had happened to me once, I had no desire to go through it again."

"I'm so sorry," Dinah said compassionately. "So what will happen when he does come back?"

"*If* he comes back, I imagine he'll want me to stay on as his housekeeper, but I couldn't, I know that now."

"Then what would you do? Cut off your nose to spite your face? Wouldn't you rather be with him than without him?"

"I honestly don't know. Being with a man you love who doesn't love you is a no-win situation in the long run. I'd far rather make a clean break. I have a little money put aside for a rainy day. I could afford to buy a small property of my own somewhere in town, take in summer visitors for a living, the way my mother used to do." Kate shrugged her shoulders dismissively. "Only time will tell. Now, isn't it time for bed? So good-night and God bless. See you in the morning?"

"In case you hadn't noticed," Dinah chuckled, "morning's already here and has been for some time. Almost two o'clock! I wonder if Greg's asleep yet?"

Christmas Day dawned frosty and clear. Up bright and early, Kate and Dinah went downstairs to find Greg standing in the reception area – buttons and eyeballs polished – awaiting their arrival. How long he had been there was anyone's guess – most probably since seven o'clock when the chef had come on duty to start cooking the eggs and bacon, Kate reckoned, to cater to the needs of the residents wishing to attend the eight o'clock Mass at St Martin's. Not that communicants were supposed to partake of bread and wine on a full stomach, but what other people did was their own concern, not hers.

Aware of a slight hiatus between Dinah and Greg born of the knowledge, so far unexpressed, that they had fallen deeply in love with one another, Kate suggested that they went out for a walk together along the Esplanade, as far as the Holbeck Clock Tower and back, to work up an appetite for breakfast, saying she would wait in the reception area until their return.

Dinah went upstairs to fetch her coat. "Kate," Greg said, "there's something you should know."

She laughed. "I already do. Why do you think I want rid of you? I imagine you have things to say to Dinah that you wouldn't want anyone else to hear?"

Greg flushed slightly. "I haven't the right to say anything to her. Not yet at any rate, until I know what my future prospects are likely to be." He spoke wistfully. "Until this divorce case is settled one way or another. If it goes against me, I shan't have much to offer any woman."

"Perhaps this might help." Finding the letter in her shoulder bag, she gave it to him. "Merry Christmas, Greg. And remember, Dinah isn't 'any woman'. There are things she needs to hear from your own lips, and if you have the sense you were born with you'll tell her the way you feel about her and let the future take care of itself."

She added, as Dinah appeared on the stairs, "No, don't open the envelope now. Wait till you're alone together. It isn't a cheque, by the way. Something far more precious than money.

"Right, off you go now. Sure you'll be warm enough, Greg? Or should you nip up and get your anorak?"

"No, I'll be fine. This tweed jacket's quite thick, and I've a sweater on underneath, of the 'Polo-mint' variety, as you can see, not to mention my thermal underwear."

"All right, all right, no need to go into the gory details," Kate laughed as she saw them off from the front steps and watched them walking hand-in-hand along the Esplanade, deriving comfort and happiness from the thought that, God willing, they would walk together, hand-in-hand, for the rest of their lives.

It had been a wonderful holiday, Kate thought on her return to Gull House with Greg, who would be leaving for Manchester that afternoon.

He looked worried, she thought, putting the kettle on for a cup of tea: sad, vaguely withdrawn, as if he had something on his mind. Only natural, she supposed, having kissed Dinah goodbye, not quite knowing when they'd meet again. But no, it was more than that. She had the gut feeling that something was seriously wrong. Nothing to do with Dinah but – herself. She hadn't seen Greg look like this since that dreadful day at the hospital when their father had died and he had broken the news to her very gently, and held her in his arms to whisper soft words of comfort, to stroke her hair back from her tear-stained face and dry her eyes with his pocket handkerchief.

When he came into the kitchen prior to his departure for Manchester, switching off the kettle, turning to face him, she said, "It's Alex, isn't it? He's dead, isn't he? Please tell me! I need to know! Have they found his – body? Is that what you're trying to tell me?"

Carefully framing his words, Greg said quietly, "A body has been found, yes, but whose body has not yet been established. You see, love, difficulties of identification have arisen to cloud the issue." No way could he bring himself to utter the gruesome word "decapitation". Wild horses would not have dragged out of him that the body of the man had suffered the indignity of mutilation at the time of his death, or afterwards.

Curiously, Kate seemed to know instinctively what he meant. Her reaction puzzled him at first. Her softly uttered words: " 'Over the pass the voices, one by one, faded. And the hill slept'."

Much later he remembered the source of the quotation.

Twenty-Two

B eside herself with worry, Dinah telephoned Kate repeatedly; begging her to stay with her for a while, knowing what she must be going through – the horror of not knowing whether the body found in an icy wilderness far removed from civilisation, was that of the man she loved, or not – the grim reality of the lack of identification of the corpse.

All Kate would say in reply to the phone calls was: "Thank you, but I must stay here. I need to be alone. Besides, I have work to do." It was uttered in a cold, calm tone of voice, which Dinah recognised as that of a woman in a state of shock far beyond tears or hysteria, therefore all the more frightening to someone inured to various manifestations of grief. Some suddenly bereaved women became angry to the point of violence, swearing, screaming, shouting, others sobbed uncontrollably. The few, the very few, stared into space, saying nothing at all, frozen-faced, inarticulate with grief, shrugging aside offers of help, flinching at the touch of a comforting hand on the arm.

And this, above all, was the most dangerous manifestation of shock, in Dinah Sheridan's experience. The thought that this was happening to someone she cared for was unbearable. Even worse, the knowledge that she was powerless to help Kate in this present crisis of her life, by the simple expedient of giving her warmth, shelter and love beneath her own roof, close to but far removed from the ghost-ridden rooms of Gull House.

All she could possibly say, over and over again, on the telephone was: "Remember I'm here, Kate, if ever you should need me." And, "Yes, thanks, Dinah, I'll remember," came that cool, measured reply, "but I must stay here. I need to be alone. Besides, I have work to do."

Re-living the past, Kate discovered, provided the only solution to blotting out her present desolation of spirit; writing her only means of escape from the here and now, to that world of yesteryear that she envisaged as neatly packaged as a bundle of love-letters tied with the faded ribbons of a bygone age, all passion spent. It was a comforting premise that, with the passage of time, the present would be laid to rest as surely as the past had been. Then, there would be no more heartbreak or despair, no futile hopes for the future, only as yet unborn generations poking round old graveyards, reading the inscriptions on the headstones, not knowing or caring tuppence about the life stories of the long dead and forgotten buried there in the quiet earth, along with all their human faults and failures, shattered hopes and dreams and unfulfilled love affairs . . .

Every day, come hail, rain or shine, Kate went in search of not the Scarborough she had known in the days of her youth and childhood, but the town as it must have appeared to long gone generations of men and women of the Victorian era, rich and poor alike, who had witnessed, in the last century, the birth of the railway, the demise of the horse and carriage as a means of transport, along with the old coaching inns reminiscent of Charles Dicken's *Pickwick Papers.*

Absorbed in her research, she came across old buildings, seldom noticed before in the springtime of her life: The Talbot Hotel in Queen Street, for instance, a coaching inn of the seventeenth century, and The Bell, in Bland's Cliff – a steep hill linking the town centre to the seafront.

All these discoveries, and many more besides, were grist to her mill when she returned to Alex's typewriter to get on with the next chapter of her book in this very special place where she felt closest to him, as though he were still alive and watching over her now as he had done in the past. And wasn't that the simple truth of the matter? That love, however hopeless it may have seemed at the time, never dies?

Whether or not Alex had loved her during his lifetime scarcely mattered to her now that he was dead and gone. All that she really cared about, right now, was writing a book worth reading, in his honour, dedicated: "In Memory of Sandy Alexis. A Man For All Reasons".

Greg had wanted to stay on with her for a while longer after the Christmas holiday, but Kate wouldn't hear of it. "I'll be fine," she'd told him, "and I want you to keep your solicitor's appointment tomorrow. The sooner you show him that letter the sooner he'll know what to do about it."

"Kate, I'm truly sorry about – Alex. I wish now that I hadn't told you, but there's never a right time to break bad news, and I wanted you to hear it from me, so there was really no choice. I couldn't bring myself to tell you sooner, to spoil Christmas for you."

"I know, love. No need to explain. Now, isn't it time you were on your way? You have a long journey ahead of you."

"But I can't just go and leave you alone, like this."

"Of course you can, and you *must*! I'll be better off alone. It's what I want, Greg, believe me!"

Driving back to Manchester, Greg pondered Kate's cryptic response, "Over the pass the voices, one by one, faded, and the hill slept". Racking his brain, the source of the quotation suddenly dawned on him. Of course. It came from Sir Henry Newbolt's poem. "He Fell Among Thieves", the last lines of which began, "A sword swept!"

Sick at heart, he realised that Kate had known the reason why the body of the man discovered in an alien landscape had been unindentifiable, and yet she had not given way to tears or turned to him for comfort. She had simply stood there, as white as a ghost, her eyes a brilliant blue, wide open and staring in the colourless oval of her face.

Then, for the first time in his life, he had sensed an unbridgeable gulf between himself and his sister, as if her spirit had somehow left her body and all that remained was the remote shell of her, as brittle as glass, as if she could scarcely wait to be rid of him.

At home in the bungalow, dumping his luggage in the hall, he dialled Dinah's phone number, desperately in need of her support, help and advice.

"Sorry, darling," she replied, "I've rung Kate twice already this evening: invited her to stay with me for the time being, to no avail. She simply doesn't want to know."

Greg said hoarsely, "You don't think she'll do something – foolish, do you?"

"No, I don't think so. She spoke of having work to do. The fact is, I honestly don't know what she has in mind right now. All that I can possibly do is to keep on pestering her with phone calls in anticipation of a reply, no matter how dismissive that reply might be."

"And if she fails to answer? What then?" Greg asked wearily.

"Well, then, if necessary, I'll either alert the police, or batter my way into Gull House unaided! And you'd better believe it! You see, my love, I think the world of your sister, and I'd like her around as my matron of honour on our wedding day! So stop worrying unduly. Trust me to keep an eye on things this end."

John Sharpin had remarried in due course. His second wife, Mary, was much prettier than Jeanette, a graceful, petite woman with neatly braided brown hair arranged in a coronet above a sweetly smiling face.

Kate had scarcely believed her luck one day, in the library, when she had come across an exhibition of old photographs and memorabilia relevant to the lives and times of eminent local dignitaries of the Victorian era mounted, behind glass, in the library foyer.

Gazing intently at the exhibits, she saw the studio portrait of Mary Sharpin wearing a black velvet, bustled gown trimmed at the neckline and wrists with white lace, smiling not at the camera but into the middle distance. It was the face of a happy, contented woman in love.

Another, less formal photograph, apparently taken in the Sharpins' apartment at the Crown Hotel, revealed John Sharpin seated at a desk, Mary standing behind him, her hands resting lightly on his shoulders, as though, without those gently restraining hands of hers, he would have leapt up from his chair and rushed out of the room like a whirlwind.

That photograph spoke volumes about the man, young, dark-haired and vital. The way he was sitting, for instance, one leg clear of the desk, the other stretched out awkwardly, bent at the knee, reminiscent of an athlete awaiting the firing of a starting pistol. Somehow, the photograph had captured the magnetic vitality and enthusiasm of the man who had masterminded The People's Park and had left the imprint of his vivid, unorthodox personality on Scarborough for all time – whether or not future generations would even remember his name, as few, if any, would remember that of Alex Arden.

The thought occurred that she was, perhaps, beginning to imbue both men with similar characteristics, and she wondered if – writing about Sharpin – she had begun to imagine him as a living person whose strength and vitality seemed akin to a torch handed down to her to guide her through the darkness of her present existence.

Greg's phone call one evening a week later, came as a surprise when he told her that the court hearing was over and he was a free man at last.

"The date was brought forward unexpectedly," he explained, sounding apologetic. "I didn't tell you because I didn't want to worry you.

The great news is, that letter you gave me made all the difference. The judge believed me, not Cindy, when the letter was read out in court."

Kate's eyes filled with tears which ran down her face, unchecked. "Oh, Greg, my love, I'm so glad for you," she murmured, feeling as if a burden had been lifted from her shoulders. "I'm just so sorry that I wasn't there for you when you needed me. Can you ever forgive me?"

"There's nothing to forgive," he said gently, "nor ever will be, between us."

"But you wanted to stay with me, and I sent you away when I should have turned to you for comfort. The person closest and dearest to me in all the world!"

"I understood the reason why, Kate, believe me. You needed solitude, not comfort, at the time, and I respected that. All in the past now. Thanks to you, I have a future ahead of me, a roof over my head and a secure job. Not that I'm planning to stay on in Manchester once the decree absolute has been granted. I have no wish to stay on in the bungalow, for obvious reasons. Much depends on Dinah, what *she* wants me to do." He paused. "I really do love her, you see, and she promised to marry me whatever the outcome of the divorce, even if I ended up a pauper."

He added anxiously, "But how are *you*, Kate? I can't bear the thought of you alone in Gull House, not eating or sleeping properly. Not getting enough exercise or fresh air. Not always answering the telephone, and I should know."

"I'm sorry, but I've been busy writing: getting on with my book. Please don't worry about me. I'm coming to terms with what happened in the only way I know how."

"I understand, and so does Dinah. But please, Kate, don't shut her out of your life. Promise?"

"Very well, Greg, I promise, and I never meant to. I just couldn't bear the thought of seeing or talking to anyone a while back. I couldn't have borne sympathy – or being away from home. I needed to feel close to Alex, to remember everything about him, to face the probability that we will never meet again."

Twenty-Three

O n his retirement from the Crown Hotel, John Sharpin had built himself a villa in a cul-de-sac overlooking the railway, a splendid, turreted edifice with long, ground-floor windows leading on to a small lawn, with trees and flower-beds, which he master-minded in every architectural detail down to his J.F.S. "coat of arms" emblazoned in the landing casements and on the outer walls of his domain.

Staring up at those walls one chilly February afternoon, Kate imagined the ageing entrepreneur striding restlessly about his new home, regretful, perhaps, that his glory days at the Crown were over and done with forever.

Possibly, here was a man whose talents had blossomed too early and withered too soon? It seemed decidedly odd that he had chosen a site overlooking the railway, the coming of which had virtually put paid to the era of the horse and carriage.

Researching his background in detail, Kate had learned that as a young man he had begun his career as a grocer's assistant in his native town of Ripon, before transferring to London to set up, unsuccessfully, as a wine merchant.

Then, his spirits at a low ebb, he had seen in a London paper that the Crown Hotel, Scarborough, recently completed in the year 1844, stood in need of a young, energetic man of vision to become its first tenant manager. The rest was history . . .

In need of a hot cup of tea, walking down town towards home, suddenly Kate came face to face with Fanny Kiddy. The first time she had clapped eyes on her since she had left the gift shop, although they had exchanged Christmas cards, and Kate had sent her a small Christmas hamper comprising hand-made chocolates, tins of asparagus, red salmon, satsumas, a box of dates, and a watch-shaped bottle of eau-de-Cologne, for which she had so far received no thanks, nor even the faintest indication that Fanny had received her gift.

Perhaps leaving the shop had affected Fanny more than Kate had realised at the time. She should have taken the trouble to find out. Fanny had pride, and that pride had been stung. She said, "Hello, Fanny, it's good to see you. Have you time for a cuppa?"

"Well, if you're sure you want to see me."

"Of course I do. Why wouldn't I?"

"Oh, I don't know. You just seemed to change all of a sudden when that Jenny moved in with you, as if you couldn't be bothered with me any more."

So that was it. Kate said, unlocking the door, "Come upstairs, I'll put the kettle on."

Fanny, loosening her coat so she would feel the benefit of it when she went out, said, "You weren't exactly fat before, but now you're like two boards nailed together. Have you been fasting?" She mean dieting. "Or have you been poorly?"

"Something like that," Kate said, thinking that what she'd been through recently had been a kind of illness, both mental and physical. Then, for the first time in ages, she knew that she needed someone to talk to; to mend bridges, remembering how kind Fanny had been to her when she moved into that flat overlooking the Valley Bridge. And so she talked, and Fanny listened.

"Eh," she said eventually, "you've had a rough time of it an' no mistake. And there was I thinking – well, never mind what I thought. But you can't go on like this, living alone in this big house, not looking after yourself properly. That's why I'm coming in twice a week to give the place a good bottoming an' see you get some good grub inside you. And don't you try and stop me!"

"Fanny, I wouldn't dream of it," Kate said shakily, thinking she might as well try to stop a runaway train as Fanny in one of her decisive moods.

"That's settled then," Fanny nodded, re-buttoning her coat. "I'll come in Tuesdays and Fridays. It'll be like old times!"

Like old times, Kate thought wistfully, if only . . . At least she had taken a step in the right direction towards a more hopeful outlook on life. Meanwhile, there were other bridges to be mended.

Dinah welcomed her with open arms. "Come in and sit down," she said. "Isn't it wonderful news about Greg? We hope to meet again quite soon, to talk things over. Telephone calls are a bit inhibiting at times,

I've discovered. We're thinking of a long weekend in York, staying at the Station Hotel. Occupying separate rooms, incidentally." She chuckled softly. "We're old-fashioned enough not to want to spoil the thrill of our wedding night; daft enough to want to wander round the city hand-in-hand, and canoodle on the back row of the cinema like teenagers."

She added quickly, apologetically, "Oh, I'm sorry, Kate, I wasn't thinking . . ."

"About Alex, you mean?" Kate tilted her chin proudly, speaking his name without flinching. "You needn't be, not any longer. You see, I've accepted the fact that he won't be coming home again. I had to. My father used to say, 'Face the worst that could happen, the fact that it has happened, and take it from there.' And that's what I'm trying to do now."

"Yes, I can see that, up to a point," Dinah responded quietly, "but what about – hope? Surely you haven't given up hope that Alex may still be alive?"

"All I can say, it's easier for me not to build up false hopes, just to make the best of what I have left to me: tangible things I can touch, hear and see with my own two eyes."

"Like 'Bluebells of Scotland'?" Dinah suggested. "I'm sorry, love, I shouldn't have said that. But you were so certain of piano music in the next room that evening at the Crown. And I'm not doubting for one moment that you *did* hear it, just as I'm certain that you had heard the sound of horses' hooves that morning on Plantation Hill.

"What I'm trying to say is, the tangible things of life that most people take for granted, things they can touch, see, hear and scent – like flowers – are not everything for those gifted with second sight, as you are, and to deny that gift of yours is tantamount to tethering a race-horse to a muck-cart. Just as attempting to live without hope is tantamount to denying the spiritual messages of Christmas and Easter."

She stopped speaking abruptly. "Oh, God, me and my big mouth," she uttered despairingly. "I should have been a bloody Salvationist, not a Staff Nurse!"

Kate made no reply, but she knew, deep down, that Dinah was right, that she had not given up hope that, one day, Alex would come home again.

*   *   *

Reading through her manuscript, Kate felt hopeful that she had managed to capture something of the Victorian era: the careless ostentation and flamboyance of the very rich, the drudgery of the working class called upon to serve their lords and masters from dawn till dusk.

Weaving together the threads of the story had been difficult at times, and yet she had experienced little difficulty in breathing life into her characters, as if she knew them all as intimately as she knew herself, from the rich, vain women visitors to Scarborough, parading along the Spa promenade in their fine clothes, to poor Mavis Kiddy, Albert's wife, taking in washing and sewing to supplement the family income and to give her children, the studious John and the "fly-by-night" Lucy the best possible start in life.

Lucy, the complex heroine of the book with her many and varied love affairs, an endless troublemaker, a constant thorn in the flesh of her decent, ordinary hard-working parents, Kate had treated with compassion throughout the pages of her novel, understanding the girl's need of admiration, pretty clothes and sparkling jewels. Above all – love.

She was faced with the ending of Lucy's story. Strung on the horns of a dilemma, most likely, Kate thought, Lucy had never set out on a sea voyage at all, however dashing and handsome the captain of the vessel might have been. It was more than likely that poor Lucy had stood on the quayside watching the vessel go out of sight of land, and returned home to Scarborough to find the sailor lad she was really in love with. And this was how she intended to finish the novel.

Running throughout her book like a golden thread, was the life story of John Fairgray Sharpin – the catalyst linking the fortunes of both the rich and the poor people he had known so well during his lifetime.

So how had his story ended?

Writing about it, Kate could scarcely hold back her tears. She had, beside her on the desk, as she typed the penultimate chapter of her novel, a cutting borrowed from that exhibition in the public library, referring to the death of "The late Mr Sharpin, J.P.", on June 11th, 1895, aged seventy-five years.

The villa overlooking the railway lines had long ago been sold, and the Sharpins had moved closer to the town centre. Their new home in York Place, far less spectacular than the old, was perhaps better suited to an ageing couple in failing health.

No. 10 York Place was nevertheless a handsome residence, one of a terrace of similar houses, tall, with curved bay windows and steps leading to the front doors.

Looking at No. 10 one bright but cool and windy April day, Kate imagined the interior lay-out of the rooms. There would have been a long, spacious hall with an imposing staircase, red carpeted with mahogany banisters, a ground-floor drawing room, dining room, and kitchen quarters at the end of the passageway. On the upper landing, the master bedrooms; above these, the servants' rooms, one of which was occupied by a maid servant who, roused from sleep by the urgent ringing of a housebell at around ten thirty one night, had hurried down to the drawing room where she had found her master on the floor in a pool of blood.

Doctors had been sent for, to no avail. John Fairgray's seemingly indestructible life force had no longer existed in the body of a worn-out old man who, at the height of his manhood, had brought fame and fortune to Scarborough.

His widow, Mary Sharpin, had told the inquest jury that her husband had been in failing health for the past three years, but he had gone out daily as usual and refused to see a doctor, saying there was no point, that his time had come and he was worn out. She added that he was a man who quite understood his constitution, and had a great aversion to doctors.

A verdict of death from natural causes was recorded. The presiding coroner had paid tribute to a remarkable man whose vision and enterprise had earned him a well-deserved place in the annals of the town's history, and offered his sincere condolences to Mrs Sharpin and her daughter, Miss May Sharpin.

Kate wrote:

> The route to the Scarborough Cemetery was lined with silent onlookers, the men bareheaded, many women in tears, as they watched the passing of the cortège: the last journey of a man they had loved and admired, to his final resting place.
>
> The sound of the horses' hooves drawing the glass-sided hearse, and the jingling of their harnesses could be clearly heard in the warm air of that summer afternoon.
>
> The passing of the cortège reminded the older folk among the silent bystanders of the opening of The People's Park when their

hero, the young Mayor of Scarborough, dark-haired and hand-some, had bounded from an open landau and on to the flag-draped platform in the valley, like a jack-in-the-box, to declare the enterprise open.

How they had laughed, clapped and cheered him then, on that never-to-be-forgotten night, long ago, with brightly coloured lanterns strung between the branches of the trees in Valley Road; to the background music of the town's silver band, the quacking of ducks from the duckpond; the singing of birds from the aviary. And now . . .

But it was not just the older folk who remembered. A plump, middle-aged woman among the crowd of mourners, also remembered the night she had walked down Plantation Hill with her parents and her brother John, filled with an insatiable desire to show off the pretty new dress her mother had made for her, to attract the attention of the opposite sex in particular, knowing that she was beautiful because the swing-mirror on her bedroom chest-of-drawers had told her so.

Now, glimpsing John Sharpin's flower-decked coffin through tear-dimmed eyes, the plump middle-aged matron standing on the pavement, her husband and three children beside her, knew that even the rarest beauty is destined to wither and die in time, as hers, Lucy Kiddy's, had done. Then, the only thing that mattered in the world was – Love.

Her book finished at last, Kate lay down to sleep, emotionally drained, too tired to think any more for the time being. But sleep would not come. As she tossed and turned, eyes aching with fatigue, her brain still alert, writing about the death of John Sharpin, she realised, had been tanta-mount to writing about the death of someone close and dear to her, as if she had been present at the passing of his cortège on its way to the Dean Road Cemetery, leaving her alone in the world, with nothing left to cling to. So how to fill in the rest of her days? Tomorrow and the day after tomorrow, now that her manuscript had reached its fruition?

And she still hadn't thought of a title for it, a title that would capture precisely and convey her feeling of the past: neatly tied and laid lovingly aside like love letters, beyond change or alteration – out of reach of the tide. And there she had it. The title of her book. *Out of Reach of the Tide.*

Sleep came at last, albeit a troubled sleep threaded with dreams of a presence in her room, a ray of light from the landing beyond, the figure of a man beside her bed, looking down at her, speaking her name softly, over and over again: "Kate. Kate darling. Wake up. Please, wake up."

Opening her eyes, she discerned painfully the light from the landing, the tall figure of the man beside her bed. A ghost? A figment of her imagination? And yet there was no mistaking his voice. She would have known it anywhere.

"Alex?" she murmured disbelievingly.

Then suddenly the "ghost" had his arms about her, and he was holding her tightly, kissing her cheeks, her hair, finally her lips; telling her softly how much he loved her, had always loved her from the moment they had met; asking if there was the faintest hope that, some day, she would come to love him in return?

"Some day?" she whispered. "Oh, Alex! That 'some day' is here, is now!"

Twenty-Four

A lex's appearance had changed dramatically. His shoulder-length hair was liberally streaked with grey, he had grown a beard, and his body bore the marks of the savage beatings he had endured in his days of captivity, scars that would remain with him for the rest of his life.

Less obvious were the mental scars of his suffering, yet Kate knew they, too, existed, that it was up to her to ease that suffering in the only way she knew how, simply by expressing her love for him in little, ordinary ways – making certain that he had good, nourishing meals inside him, a decent haircut and shave, clean clothes to wear, plenty of rest, peace and quiet beneath the roof of Gull House. Not questioning him about his captivity, knowing he would speak of it if and when he felt able to do so, and not before; respecting his privacy; putting up with his moods and occasional outbursts of temper, reminiscent of the old days.

Frankly, she couldn't have cared less, knowing that he loved her as much as she loved him, expressed not merely in words but his gifts of flowers, expensive flagons of French perfume, silk scarves and, finally, one day, a small morocco case containing a flawless diamond engagement ring accompanied by a somewhat unorthodox proposal of marriage – as short and sweet as a donkey's gallop: "Well, do you want to marry me or not? If not, just say so and have done with it!"

Kate replied teasingly, "The thing I most admire about you, Alex, is your sublety and charm when it comes to romance. You might at least have asked me to marry you first and fished out the ring later."

Alex chuckled softly. "All right, Kate, you win," he conceded. "So how's this? I love you, Kate Ford, and I'm asking you most humbly to marry me as soon as possible, for the simple reason that my life would be meaningless without you. So please say that you will, and make me the happiest man alive."

Smiling up at him, Kate said, "Put that way, how could I possibly refuse?

"So how soon?" He was laughing now, excited as a boy. "Next week? The week after?"

"Next month would be nearer the mark. I have things to do."

"What – things?"

"Arrangements to make. Alex, I want my brother at our wedding."

"I should jolly well hope so. I'm looking forward to meeting him. Did you give him those books of mine, by the way?"

"Yes, and he was over the moon. He was staying here at the time with his wife – or should I say ex-wife? They were divorced recently. It was all a bit fraught. They had a blazing row over Jenny the night of the fire, and that was the beginning of the end . . ."

"Just a minute, you've lost me," Alex broke in. "What fire, for God's sake? And who is Jenny? Why haven't you told me this before?"

"There hasn't really been time. My mind's been on other things, in case you hadn't noticed. Waking up to find you standing beside me, and coming to terms with not only your reappearance in my life, but the fact that you loved me seemed like a dream come true after all the waiting and wondering, not knowing if you were alive or dead."

"Yes, of course," he said contritely. "I should have known. We have a lot to catch up on, haven't we?"

Kate nodded. "Yes, darling, we have, and I think it important that we should begin our future together with no secrets between us. The reason why I don't want to rush into marriage on an impulse, just because I happen to be head over heels in love with you, the way I did before. You too, I imagine?"

He said heavily, "That's all in the past now. Over and done with."

Kate disagreed with him. "You're wrong, Alex," she said quietly, "if that's what you think. We are both victims of our past lives to some extent: events which shaped our destinies and made us the people we are today. Our only hope for the future lies in not forgetting the past, but learning to live with it – not without regrets. That would be impossible. But relying on one another for sympathy and understanding when the bad times come uppermost. When you, for instance, remember the deaths of Leonora and the child you loved, and I remember the so-called birthdays of the three babies I miscarried during my marriage to Don."

Gathering her close in his arms, Alex murmured, "Oh Kate, my love, I had no idea. I'm so sorry, so very sorry."

Later, he told her haltingly of his captivity. They were sitting together in front of the fire as darkness fell, the rest of the room invaded with shadows.

Reliving the horror of those days, he said, "I was treated as an animal, beaten and starved. I thought at first it was money they wanted, but I was wrong. They wanted the pleasure of watching me suffer.

"Every day that dawned, I was threatened with execution. Their leader, who spoke a little English, would tell me, 'Tomorrow, maybe, we cut off the head so' – making a slicing movement with his right hand – 'You not be so proud then, eh?' "

Kate shuddered. Alex continued, "Then one day they brought another captive to the camp. A much younger man than myself, named Yuri. A Russian most likely, who quickly became their latest source of amusement. That's when I began to plan my escape, the Russian's also when the time came.

"I had devised a rough cutting tool from a jagged piece of rock, to free myself of the rope binding my hands behind me, taking advantage of the hours of darkness, the drunken stupor of our captors gathered round the camp-fire in the clearing beyond our tent.

"It was a simple plan, born of desperation, with little or no chance of success. I knew that, so did Yuri, with whom I communicated in sign language to indicate the slitting of the tent canvas when we were free of our bonds and, either sliding or rolling down the hillside away from the camp to make our escape."

Alex covered his face with his hands, reliving the horror of the moment when a couple of drunken tribesman had entered the tent, in the early hours of the morning, to drag the Russian from their prison to his place of execution in the clearing near the camp-fire. "It was so brutal, so unnecessary," Alex whispered hoarsely.

"No need to go on," Kate said compassionately, "I can guess what happened." Kneeling beside Alex, she held his trembling body close to hers, imagining that terrible downward sweep of an upraised sword.

Alex said urgently, "Promise that you'll stay with me forever, Kate? I love and need you so much. More than you'll ever know."

Kate promised. She had lost Alex once. She could never bear to be without him again.

*   *   *

She showed him her manuscript with some trepidation, explaining that writing the book had been a form of mental therapy to fill in what would otherwise have been time wasted in idleness.

"I'm impressed," he said. "I thought you said you couldn't type."

"I couldn't. I took lessons."

"What is it? A – romance?"

"In a way, yes. Why not read it and find out? Only don't be too critical. I'm no Emily Brontë." She couldn't decide if he was pleased or not by her literary aspirations. Knowing Alex, he might take exception to her having written her own version of Victorian Scarborough.

Alex's first meeting with Fanny was not an unqualified success. Startled by his presence, she said forthrightly, "So you've come back, have you? About time too. Well, now you are here, what are you going to do about that pesky gift shop below?"

"What do you suggest I do about it?" Alex asked coolly. Kate groaned inwardly. Trust Fanny to march in where angels might fear to tread.

"What any sensible body would do," Fanny went on. "Get rid of it. Have it put back to its original purpose. I used to come here as a child when there was a proper ground-floor sitting room, dining room an' kitchen, where they should be. Not a kitchen stuck upstairs like this 'un is.

"Another thing, that there fire would never have happened if it hadn't been for that there fakey shop an' that arse— arse— arsonite wanting to get back at Kate for sacking his girlfriend! Huh, fine goings on, I must say!"

Feeling that Fanny had said quite enough for the time being, Kate reminded her that Alex had bought the property as a going concern – the gift shop included – and that it was time, perhaps, to drop the subject. To her surprise, it was he who wished to explore the matter further.

"No, please, I'm interested in what – Fanny has to say," he said charmingly. "Do you mind if I call you Fanny, by the way? So you think that I should restore Gull House to its original state? So what should I do to set the wheels in motion?"

Flattered by his charm of manner and deference to her opinions, Fanny's initial hostility towards him melted away like mist on a summer morning. "Why, if I was you," she said confidingly, "I'd march right down to the Town Hall Planning Department for a reconstitutional order or some such!" She added girlishly, "An' yes, you can call me Fanny, if you like. Everyone else does."

Turning his attention to Kate, he asked, "What do you think? After all, as my wife to be, the future mistress of Gull House, the final decision rests with you."

Fanny's eyes fairly started out of her face with surprise at this nugget of information. "Eh," she burst forth excitedly, "you mean you've pledged your plight to one another?"

"Something like that," Kate laughed, showing Fanny the sparkling engagement ring on the third finger of her left hand. "We're planning to marry quite soon, at the registry office in Dean Road a week next Saturday, followed by a blessing of our marriage in St Martin's Church, and a small reception at the Crown Hotel. Nothing fancy, just a buffet luncheon; smoked salmon sandwiches, salmon and asparagus mousse, mushroom vol-au-vents and so on, you know the kind of thing I mean? Nothing too formal.

"And, of course, you are invited to join us, to help us to celebrate the happiest day of our lives. So please, dear Fanny, do say you'll be there to grace the occasion."

"*Be* there? Just you try an' stop me!"

Later, caught up in the romance, the excitement of it all, waiting ages for the electric kettle to boil for a mid-morning cuppa – her thoughts centred on a new hat for the wedding, something really smart with lots of veiling and an artificial rose on the brim, she realised, at long last, why the kettle was taking so long to boil. She'd plugged in the toaster by mistake.

One evening, after supper, drawing Kate into the circle of light shed by the dancing, simulated flames of the sitting room fire, Alex said intently, "I've read your manuscript, and—"

Hunching her shoulders against his expected harsh criticism of book, she interrupted, "And you're thinking up kind words to tell me how much you disliked it?"

"Well yes, in a way," he conceded, "because, reading it, I had to admit to myself that I could never have hoped to better it in a thousand years! And I don't accept defeat easily, as you well know.

"Frankly, I felt angry at first that you had plagiarised my idea for a book about Scarborough in the Victorian era. Then, reading on, I marvelled at your depth of understanding, not only of an era, but of the characters you so brilliantly portrayed in the cleverly woven strands of the novel. I was in tears by the last page. Sad and uplifted at the same time, if that makes sense? The way you felt, I imagine, when you first read *Wuthering Heights*."

"Then you are not too angry with me?" Kate asked wistfully. "For trespassing on your territory, I mean?"

"No, and to prove it, when we go to London I intend to take your masterpiece to my agent and rub it in that at least one member of the Arden family is capable of writing a potential bestseller."

"Oh!" Kate's head was spinning. Everything was happening so fast that she couldn't take it in all at once. He'd been to the town hall earlier in the day to see about the "reconstitution" of Gull House, and foresaw no problems on that score. Indeed, the planning official he'd spoken to seemed amazed that permission for the gift shop had been given in the first place. Now Alex was enthusiastic about her book, and they were, apparently, going to London. The first she'd heard of it.

"You mean we're spending our honeymoon in London?" she asked.

"Good God, no! It's just that I have business affairs to attend to, and I want to see my old batman before taking you to Paris, then on to Venice and the Italian lakes – if you'd like that, of course. Otherwise we could spend a month or so in Skegness, Bootle and Worksop. Entirely up to you, my darling."

"You *idiot!*" Kate laughed, throwing a cushion at his head, knowing that this was the Alex she loved most of all, a man capable of tenderness and humour, deep down kindness and sensitivity. The man she would be more than proud and happy to marry in ten days' time. Which reminded her – she hadn't yet bought her wedding outfit or trousseau. In which case, the sooner she got cracking, the better.

"Just one more thing," Alex said. "I thought it would be rather nice to spend our wedding night at the Crown Hotel; to invite Dinah and Greg to dine with us before calling it a day. Would you like that?"

"Oh yes, Alex. That would be wonderful. The perfect start to our honeymoon."

Twenty-Five

D inah accompanied Kate on her shopping spree, bearing in mind that she too would soon be needing a wedding outfit, when Greg's final decree had been granted.

"I can't believe all this is happening," she said. "It's so amazing, so wonderful, Alex coming home the way he did, and with Greg a free man once more. That happy ending in view at last, like a pot of gold at the rainbow's end!"

"I know. It takes some believing." Kate smiled, happier than she had ever been in her life before. In love, really in love for the first time, with a man who loved her.

She had asked Alex about that during one of their firelight trysts. "You said you loved me from the first moment we met," she reminded him. "So why did you go away and leave me?"

"Because I needed time and space to think about it," he explained, "to face the possibility of rejection. Remember, darling, I had no reason to believe that you were in love with me? You never gave me the faintest inkling of your feelings towards me. In fact, more often than not I had reason to suspect that you disliked me intensely."

"Well, what did you expect me to do? Throw myself at your feet? Beg you to stay? You were not the only one afraid of rejection. I'd been through that once before, when Don left me. I couldn't have borne going through it again." She smiled knowingly, "But there was more to it than that, wasn't there? Even if I had told you I loved you, begged you to stay, you'd have gone anyway, wouldn't you?"

"Yes," he admitted quietly. "You see, darling, I had a kind of restlessness inside me, a strange longing to recapture my – lost youth – if you like. To prove that I was still capable of repeating the exploits of Sandy Alexis. You must remember, Kate, that I'm older than you are. In retrospect, I wanted to prove, if and when I returned home to you, that I was worthy of your consideration as a husband."

He added, tongue-in-cheek, "It came as something of a shock to me, reading your manuscript, that you had not been entirely faithful to me during my absence."

Kate frowned, uncertain of his meaning. "I'm sorry," she said bemusedly, "I haven't a clue what you're on about!"

"Forgive me," Alex held her hands in his, "I was referring to your hero, John Fairgray Sharpin, whose life story you portrayed so lovingly in the pages of your novel, and whose death affected you so deeply. I had the feeling that you regarded him as a living person who had somehow taken my place during my absence. Am I right?"

Kate smiled wistfully. "Yes, I suppose so. You see, I needed someone to cling to to help me through the dark days when I believed that you were – dead and gone forever.

"Quite honestly, and I admit it, I drew strength and courage from a man, albeit a ghostly figure, conjured from my admiration of his vitality and down-to-earth humanity during his lifetime. But falling in love with a ghost is scarcely possible, wouldn't you say?"

Trying on one outfit after another, Kate finally decided on a slim fitting, cream-coloured jersey-silk dress and a matching jacket, which suited her to perfection.

Then, moving to other departments of the chain-store in Westborough, she chose pale-tan high-heeled shoes, a matching handbag and gloves, and a wide-brimmed hat in a deeper shade of caramel – the colour of brandy snaps, to complement the wedding ensemble and the simple bouquet of deep-orange tea-roses and lilies of the valley she intended to carry with her to the registry office on her wedding day.

Cream, pale-tan and orange, Dinah considered admiringly, and there she was thinking that the bride-to-be would have plumped for the blue outfit, white accessories, and a bouquet of pink roses, which went to show how little she really knew about her future sister-in-law. No longer a reclusive creature, repining the loss of the man she loved, but a strong personality in her own right, now that the man she loved had come back to her.

Meanwhile, Greg had been in touch with Kate to reassure her that he would be more than happy to participate in the wedding ceremony in any capacity whatsoever: to give the bride away, walk down the aisle with her at the blessing, even to make a speech at the reception if called upon to do so. "Greater love hath no man," he laughed.

Kate deserved her new-found happiness. He had never admired her more than he had done when she'd told him of her decision to return her nest-egg from the sale of April Cottage to Don Ford. Her way of laying her past to rest once and for all. And Greg knew she would have done the same had she been marrying a poor man.

Kate spent the night before the wedding at Dinah's flat. Greg had stayed at Gull House with Alex, getting to know his future brother-in-law, a man he had long admired and respected from a distance.

The four of them had enjoyed a quiet dinner in a York Place restaurant before going their separate ways – Alex's idea – as a preliminary to their wedding day, he'd explained to Kate, anxious to meet her brother and his fiancée beforehand. "Nothing too formal," he'd added. "Just a chance to chat to one another, to let our hair down, as the saying goes. The reason why I chose the Georgian Grill, so we needn't wear our best bib and tucker."

It had proved a highly successful occasion, with Alex at his most charming, Kate and Dinah starry-eyed, and Greg slightly in awe of the host initially, discovering to his relief that the man his sister was about to marry was much easier to get on with than Don Ford had been. Ford was a man he had never liked or trusted, from the moment they'd met – in his view, self-centred, far too ambitious, and utterly ruthless. Moreover, his judgement of Don Ford's character had proved to be entirely correct.

He held no such inhibitions concerning the character of Alex Arden. With the unmistakable air of a gentleman about him, not a shred of conceit or pretence in his warm-hearted, generous personality, he obviously adored Kate. And that said it all, so far as Greg was concerned.

At the same time, he could scarcely take in the fact that he was sitting opposite the celebrated author Sandy Alexis, his kid sister's future husband. That future a matter of a few hours away. Twelve hours, to be exact.

The wedding day dawned fair and clear, with a scent of springtime in the air. He and Alex would arrive at the registry office a few minutes ahead of Kate and Dinah, who would share a taxi to the somewhat grim-looking venue in Dean Road.

"How are you feeling?" Greg asked Alex as they entered the building.

"The way you'll be feeling when your turn comes, I imagine," the bridegroom chuckled, "when I shall ask you the same damn silly question."

Dot Paulson and Fanny were in the reception hall awaiting the arrival of the wedding party. Fanny's hat had to be seen to be believed. Carmen Miranda, eat your heart out! Mrs Paulson's navy blue titfer paled to insignificance beside it.

Dismounting first from the wedding car, Dinah thought how wonderfully serene and lovely Kate looked as the chauffeur of the sleek limousine helped her to dismount.

A small crowd of onlookers had gathered on the pavement, among them a thin, haggard looking woman whom Dinah recognised immediately as Jenny Laird. Oh lord, she thought, had Jenny come to make trouble? A so-called friend who had caused Kate so much misery in the past. It would be too cruel of her to upset Kate on her wedding day. But there was nothing she could do about it. Detaching herself from the crowd, Jenny was coming towards them.

"Hello, Kate," she said in a low voice, unsmiling, looking far from blooming, Dinah thought, as one might have expected a woman who had left her friend in the lurch to pursue a more glamorous lifestyle with her current male admirer.

Kate looked startled, then, "Hello, Jenny," she replied quietly, "you are the last person I expected to see."

"I know, but I *had* to come. I heard it through the grapevine that you were getting married today, and I just wanted to see you again, to wish you well, and to say how sorry I am that I caused you so much grief after all your kindness to me. Believe me, I've lived to regret it." Tears sprang to her eyes. "Please say that you'll forgive me. Not that I deserve your forgiveness."

"But there is nothing to forgive," Kate said warmly. "All I ever wanted was your happiness." She added perceptively, "But you are not happy, are you? Tell me, Jenny, what's wrong? I really need to know!"

Oh God, Dinah thought wildly, why all this? Why *now*? Time was ticking away. The registrar would not be best pleased by the delay. "Please, Kate," she said urgently, "it's high time we went inside. We're five minutes late already."

Jenny said, smiling through her tears, "Of course I'm happy. It's just that John and I will be leaving Scarborough soon to live abroad, in Canada as a matter of fact. He's been offered a fantastic job there. It's just that I haven't got used to the thought of leaving England. All the old familiar places, and *you*, Kate. Above all, you!"

Clasping Jenny's hand in hers, Kate said, "But we all have to move forward sooner or later, and memories never die. I shall always be here for you, loving you as much as I did when we were schoolgirls together. We'll still keep in touch. Now, I really must go. I have an important appointment to keep." Leaning forward, she kissed Jenny's cheek. "Thank you for coming, for being here on my wedding day," she murmured. Then, plucking a rose from her bouquet, handing it to Jenny, she whispered softly, "Goodbye, darling, and good luck!"

The civil ceremony was necessarily formal and uninspiring; the church blessing in St Martin's Church, quite simply breathtaking. The church itself was so beautiful to begin with, aglow with the coloured lights from the stained-glass windows dappling the aisle; the altar massed with white arum lilies and gardenias – the latter flown in from France, at the bridegroom's behest, to grace the occasion; the organ softly playing "Jesu, Joy of Man's Desiring" as the bride entered the church on her brother's arm, to walk the length of the red-carpeted aisle towards her newly-wed husband.

Never would Dinah forget the expression of sheer joy on Alex's face as he turned to welcome his bride, a radiant figure in her cream silk wedding dress, his wedding ring already placed firmly on the third finger of her left hand during that brief, formal ceremony at the registry office.

Now the pair of them were standing together on the steps of the altar, receiving a blessing on their union as man and wife, so utterly and obviously in love with one another that they seemed oblivious of their surroundings, the priest in charge of the ceremony, the organ music, the scent of flowers, or anything else for that matter, save their absolute joy in one another. The radiant bride and her handsome husband.

It had been a long, exciting day. Talking about it over dinner, they recalled the highlights, one of which was Fanny's hat and her enjoyment of the wedding reception, during which the hat had begun to tilt to one side a little.

"What a lovely idea of yours, Alex," Dinah said, "to invite the vicar and the church warden. I noticed that Fanny was making quite an impression on the latter. Is he married, by the way?"

Kate said, "I liked your speech, Greg. It was just right. Not too long, and delivered with a great deal of panache." She smiled teasingly. "How many sentences?"

"At least four, but who's counting? 'Always leave 'em wanting more,' is my maxim. Don't wait till they bring on the hook!"

"I shall have no such inhibitions at your wedding reception," Alex laughed. "My speech will make Lincoln's Gettysburg Address seem short by comparison."

"The church looked wonderful," Dinah said mistily. "All those flowers. There was a song once, wasn't there, something about gardenias?"

" 'For I bring a little white gardenia, as refreshing as a day in May. You may wear it if you care, or toss it away,' " Kate quoted softly. "It was Mum's favourite song, remember, Greg?" Her face saddened momentarily, thinking of the rose she had handed Jenny from her wedding bouquet, wishing she had not let go of her so easily, not really believing that all was well with her.

Now the conversation switched to talk of the future. Greg said, "The house in Manchester is already on the market, and I'll be leaving my school at the end of the summer term. I've already applied for teaching jobs in other places. Ideally, I'd like to settle closer to home, within striking distance of Scarborough."

"That shouldn't prove too difficult, a man with your qualifications." Alex suggested, "Have you thought of private tutoring? By correspondence course, if necessary? Working from home?"

"No, but it's certainly worth considering," Greg responded eagerly. "What do you think, Dinah?"

She smiled encouragingly. "Sounds great to me," she enthused. "By all means, give it a whirl. Not that I mind much where we end up, just as long as we're together."

Her voice faded as Kate stood up abruptly, eyes staring into the distance. "I'm sorry, I must go to Jenny at once," she uttered hoarsely. "Something's terribly wrong. I know it!"

There was a doctor's car, an ambulance and a police vehicle in the road outside the tall house where Jenny lived with John Spivey. Taking the initiative, Alex told the others to wait in the car until he found out what had happened.

He was gone some time, talking to the proprietress of the apartment building. It was a sad story. John Spivey had left for Canada some four or five weeks ago, leaving Jenny alone in the flat.

A sizeable amount of rent was owing, the proprietress, a Mrs Flynn, told him, which she had overlooked at first until it became apparent that "Mrs Spivey" had apparently no means of repaying the debt when, reluctantly, because she felt sorry for the woman, earlier that day, she had asked her vacate the premises as soon as possible.

"If I'd known what was in her mind," Mrs Flynn said shakily, "I wouldn't have been so hard on her. I knew how upset she was when her husband went away. Leastways I *thought* he was her husband. Mind you, they hadn't been getting on very well for some time: quarrelling and such-like. Not that I blame him entirely, far from. Not to put too fine a point on it, she'd been drinking a lot recently, staying out till all hours – seeing other men, I shouldn't wonder. But then, one shouldn't speak ill of the dead.

"I had the shock of my life, I can tell you, when I found her the way I did, the poor soul, lying there in the bedroom, as peaceful as a sleeping child, a rose clasped in her hands, a suicide note on the bedside table, propped up against an empty whisky bottle and the painkillers she'd taken."

"I see," Alex said grimly. "Thank you for talking to me."

Taking out his wallet, he asked, "Will this be enough to settle her rent arrears?" determined that poor Jenny's reputation should not suffer further harm at the inquest into her death.

"More than enough," Mrs Flynn replied, counting the wad of notes he'd handed her. She added nosily, "Were you a – friend of hers?"

"No. I never met the lady," Alex said briefly. "Now, if you'll excuse me."

He walked slowly towards the car. Kate got out of it and came to meet him. He put his arms round her and held her silently.

She said, "Jenny's dead, isn't she?"

"I'm afraid so, darling."

"Why? Why did she do it? If only she had told me. I might have been able to help her. I knew she was unhappy. I could tell by her face. She said she was sad at the thought of leaving Scarborough: going abroad to live."

"She told you that? When did she tell you?"

"This morning. She was outside the registry office. She came to beg forgiveness, to wish me well on my wedding day. I told her there was nothing to forgive. I kissed her, then I gave her a rose from my bouquet." Tears streamed down Kate's cheeks. "I told her I'd always be here for her. So where was I when she needed me?"

"Perhaps you were with her in a way," Alex said tenderly. "You see, she died holding the rose you gave her."

They walked back to the hotel very slowly. Dinah and Greg had gone back to her flat after a brief word with Alex who had outlined the situation and promised to phone them the following day. There was nothing they could do for the time being. Nothing anyone could do. His only concern lay in helping Kate come to terms with her grief, to cancel their honeymoon plans if necessary, just to be there if she needed him.

Walking back to the Crown had been her idea. "It's such a lovely night," she'd said, looking up at the stars. "So – peaceful."

After a while, she said, "You believe in life after death, don't you, Alex? Remember you once told me you believed in reincarnation. But I can't accept that. I'm not even sure that I believe in a hereafter any more."

"Because of Jenny?" he said simply, not a question but a statement of the truth as he saw it. "Perhaps she took her life as a means of escape from this world in the hope of something better to come?"

Perhaps, Kate thought wearily. If only she could bring herself to believe that this was true. Poor Jenny deserved a second chance of happiness in a world beyond the stars, if such a world even existed.

Reaching the hotel, she said wistfully, "Poor Alex. Not at all the kind of wedding night we'd planned. I'm so sorry, but I'd like to be alone for a while. Will you give me an hour or so?"

"Of course, my darling," he responded quietly, understanding her need of solitude to come to terms with the death of her friend. Not that he imagined, for one moment, that this would happen within the space of an hour. Possibly never, not knowing how much Kate had loved her, how deeply Jenny's death had affected her, as if she was somehow to blame for it.

Arden's deep-seated fear lay in the thought that he might prove inadequate, in the long run, to offer Kate the comfort she needed, to convince her that death was not the end. That life went on.

Very slowly, Kate went upstairs to their room. Opening the windows, she stepped on to the balcony and stood there for a while, breathing in the scent of wild flowers drifting up from the Spa gardens below; hearing the faint wash of the sea on the shore, remembering the first time she had stood there, a lonely woman facing an unknown future, unable to see the lights of home for the veil of fog obscuring her vision.

No fog tonight, and yet she couldn't see at all clearly the future ahead of her. Jenny's death had somehow put things out of perspective. A matter of a few hours ago, she had been part of the living world, now she was gone, and yet there was no sense that her life had been tidied away like an old, forgotten love letter – all passion spent.

Alex had told her of John Spivey's defection, that he had gone to Canada without her. Kate could only imagine Jenny's depth of suffering, which had led her to take her own life. If only she shared Alex's belief in life everlasting.

And yet, was there not clear evidence of that in the miracle of springtime? Her mother had told her, a long time ago, that nothing possessed of life ever died. Words of wisdom to comfort the sad heart of a child devastated by the loss of a kitten she had loved. She had been too young to understand at the time. All she knew was that some vital spark of life had been extinguished forever, beyond recall.

Now, deeply troubled, trying desperately to make sense of her confused thoughts and emotions, reaching out for *something*, she scarcely knew what – a shooting star, perhaps, or the passage of a lighted ship on the far distant horizon – suddenly there came the strange feeling that she was not alone.

Slowly turning her head, she saw at the far end of the balcony, the figure of a young man, dark-haired, not very tall but broad-shouldered, wearing a strangely-cut evening dress suit, a wing collar and a silk cravat, and heard somewhere in the background the music of a Chopin Nocturne played on a grand piano.

She would have known that man anywhere by the photographs she had seen of him, and something more important, an aura of restless energy about him, apparently directed towards herself, as if to prove to her the validity of life everlasting. The survival of the human spirit over which death held no dominion.

An amazing feeling of lightness and relief swept through Kate like a tide, as though a weight had been lifted from her shoulders; her vision miraculously restored so that her view from the balcony had broadened suddenly to encompass the past, present and future as one glorious whole. Indivisibly linked, not separated, by the passage of time.

Then suddenly the man on the balcony was gone, if he had ever existed beyond the realms of her imagination. But Kate knew that he *had* existed, and he would continue to exist in this place he had loved best on earth. His beloved Crown Hotel.

But what of Jenny? Resting her hands on the balcony, looking up at the stars, Kate knew that the death of her friend had, perhaps, been inevitable, and she had chosen to die, with dignity and grace, having come to terms with her destiny – beyond the stars.

And what of her own destiny? Kate wondered. This time, had she built her brave little sandcastle out of reach of the incoming tide?

Of one thing she was entirely certain, that she would love Alex Arden from here to eternity.

Looking up at the sky, suddenly she saw a brilliant shooting star; on the distant horizon, the passing lights of a ship at sea, and knew that she had not reached out for that unknown something, in vain.

It was then she heard the opening of the door as Alex entered the room, walking quietly so as not to disturb her, uncertain of his power to find the right words to comfort her.

Turning her head to smile at him, she held out her hand, and he stood beside her on the balcony, his arm about her, her head resting against his shoulder.

"Remember that letter you sent me from Ankara?" she said. "About your marble-tiled bathroom and the balcony from which you looked up at the stars."

"Shall I ever forget? I couldn't find the right words to say to you then, either." He paused. "Why do you ask?"

"Tell me, darling," she whispered, at peace with herself and the world, "could those stars have possibly been more brilliant, more beautiful than the ones we are looking at tonight?"